The Quickening

An Urban Fantasy

Ly de Angeles

Llewellyn Publications
St. Paul, Minnesota

First Edition
First Printing, 2005

Book design and editing by Connie Hill
Cover design by Lisa Novak
Cover painting © 2005 Jonathan Hunt

Llewellyn is a registered trademark of Llewellyn Worldwide Ltd.

Library of Congress Cataloging-in-Publication Data
de Angeles, Ly.
    The quickening : an urban fantasy / Ly de Angeles — 1st ed.
      p. cm.
    ISBN 0-7387-0664-7
    1. City and town life–Fiction. 2. Kidnapping–Fiction. 3. Terrorism–
Fiction. 4. Fairies–Fiction. I. Title.

PR9619.4.D39Q53   2005
813'.6–dc22   2005044239

Llewellyn Worldwide does not participate in, endorse, or have any authority or responsibility concerning private business transactions between our authors and the public.
    All mail addressed to the author is forwarded but the publisher cannot, unless specifically instructed by the author, give out an address or phone number.
    Any Internet references contained in this work are current at publication time, but the publisher cannot guarantee that a specific location will continue to be maintained. Please refer to the publisher's website for links to authors' websites and other sources.

Llewellyn Publications
A Division of Llewellyn Worldwide, Ltd.
P.O. Box 64383, Dept. 0-7387-0-664-7
St. Paul, MN 55164-0383, U.S.A.
www.llewellyn.com

Printed in the United States of America

The Quickening

An Urban Fantasy

About the Author

Ly de Angeles has been an initiated priestess for many years. She is High Priestess of an Australian coven known as Coven Crystalglade, and has been involved in the occult arts and sciences since her introduction to them when she was a young girl.

The author of several books, Ly is a worldwide Tarot consultant and has taught Tarot and similar subjects for years.

Acknowledgements

I would like to thank Martin McMahon (*I Cry for My People,* Australia, 1996) for his invaluable advice on the Irish history, Willie McElroy for his assistance in the correct pronunciations of my limited Gaeilge, m'bonny Scott Free, shield-arm and co-trouble maker, who traveled the wilds of Ireland with me in search of music and memories—he painted while I wrote, and listened to every unfolding chapter with just the kind of wide eyes one requires to spur one on with a story such as this, and Natalie Harter, Llewellyn, USA, for her encouragement, enthusiasm, and limitless patience. Look what I did with your suggestion!

Ly de Angeles

Other Books by Ly de Angeles

When I See the Wild God

Witchcraft: Theory and Practice

The Feast of Flesh and Spirit

Genesis: Legend of Future Past

Prologue

Hunter climbed the steep sides of the ancient hill fort, deserted now except for the ring of low standing stones and the barrow to which the king stone pointed. He sat down with his back against the tallest of the menhir as the twilight lengthened shadows into mysteries.

He'd said all this before, but it helped him get his grounding in the magic.

"Lady?" he called to the dusk. "You here yet?"

No answer. He would wait. She'd show up—she usually did when he reminded her of his travels and just how tired he was. In the meantime he'd just talk.

"It's me again," he said softly, "and I've wandered the great forests of oak and rowan and birch, oh yes, I have, knee deep in stone and bracken. And none have taken me down. And I was heedless of fear, because the forest was everywhere, and we were so much a part of it all. Do you remember, my Lady?"

The air became a listening thing—still and tense as he reminded it of smells it used to know.

"Now it all hides—what's left of it—and fear is very real amongst the survivors. You know? Proud? Silent? Desperate? Through their blood they can't forget; through our blood, Lady! Through the Mysteries?"

His boot slid out and rustled the loose stones.

"Sorry. Sometimes I get maudlin, yeah? Sorry about that. It's just that people seem so blind, you know? So blind to the repercussions of their needs for comfort and safety that they mostly don't realize the devastating effects that their not-knowing is having on the habitats of others who are not quite so voracious."

There was a shifting of the air as if a piece of night was manifesting from the twilight in just one part of the ring. Hunter pretended to ignore it, knowing what it was, but he talked to her anyway.

"Hey, you know? Willie and Matt and Jack and I have just come back from spending time with a couple hundred of the true people. You know what they do? They stay, day-in and day-out, defiant before the machine giants sent to take down 'a set percentage' of old-growth forest. The media were there, too, on and off, for the show, depicting the tale of the joke of the unwashed chaining themselves to the graders and each other as they attempted to stop the devastation—fair enough—who would be clean under the conditions they had to put up with?

"But of course, you and I both know how it works. Balanced journalism and all that.

"Are you there, Lady?"

"I'm here, Hunter." And the darkness gathered itself into form.

AUTUMN EQUINOX, THE PREVIOUS YEAR—
It's very late. The sky is huge and black and moonless and glittering with a million, billion stars accentuated in their brilliance by the late autumn frost.

We're all out around the remnants of the feast and the fire. Brighid lays the offering of food out over at the tree-line for the creatures of the forest as Hunter and Puck share out the last of the mead with the rest of us and pour some to the earth as a blessing to the land.

Everyone is quietly excited as Hunter raises the ancient horn to his lips . . .

The Quickening

Part One

Chapter One

Falconstowe—

Ark-aawl"—a hundred voices calling their territory from the tree-tops. Kathryn pulled the pillow over her head, not ready to get up yet.

"Ark-ark-aawl!"

She had the fleeting and shameful thought, *I know why farmers used to shoot them.* At least she knew the day was going to be fine.

"Ark-ark-ark-ark!"

She sat up and pulled the doona around herself against the dawn chill and looked out the window at the raven-tree. The ground outside was white with frost, the sun not yet breaching the horizon, but limning the air with fragile mauves and blues. The massive spreading branches of the old walnut tree were hosts to hundreds of ravens. The birds looked like kids on a playground—swooping, hanging upside down from branches, generally showing off and yelling as loudly as they could. Kathryn was sure they must do it just to get her out of bed.

Some days she could get away with sleeping through their raucous cacophony. Not often though. She was just thinking of lying back down and trying to get some more sleep when she remembered, *Oh no! Today's my birthday!*

She groaned. Instant downer. Kathryn hated birthdays. Pretense and fuss; anticipation that the coming year would be all new; different. Somebody always wanting her to appreciate their efforts—especially Martin—or their presents. *What a bitch!* she thought to herself.

Martin's side of the bed was already cold. It had been his idea to move this far out into the countryside, the trains being so laid-back compared to the bumper-to-bumper freeway charade that drove him crazy before he even got to work, and dish-ragged him for the evenings. That was her last birthday present: *Hey Kathryn! Let's get a place in the country—the trains are cool. It'll be quicker than being stuck in traffic.* She groaned again at the memory.

She was still not used to it. Sometimes her ears ached with the quiet. She remembered the birthday dinner with Martin's family when he made the announcement, and she'd simply smiled like she'd known he was going to suggest it and isn't Martin a wonderful husband?

"Ark-orl," from multiple sentries called.

It's like the suburbs out here, she'd realized after only a few days of living there. A polite graveyard. Nobody talked to her in the village except to ask how her husband was or to remark on the weather.

This is all about you, Kathryn, he'd said as she'd fumed herself out of her clothes after the party. *The quiet will help you get started with the book.* Yeah, yeah. Not a single inspired thought. A Bachelor of Arts major in English literature, and she couldn't even think about what was important anymore. All she ever seemed to want to read these days came off the science fiction/fantasy shelves at Dimity's.

"Arkarkarkark!" *Shit!* She dropped the doona and made a run for the bathroom, turning the hot tap on full until the steam obscured everything before adding just enough cold water so that she didn't cook herself. She stood under the blast until she was pink enough to trust herself to dress calmly. She threw on her jeans and one sweater after another until she was thick, pausing in the middle to pull on woolen socks and her new lace-up ugg boots.

The kitchen was still cozy. Martin had made sure the slow-combustion stove was banked up before he'd left, and there was a kettle slowly steaming on the back-burner. She put enough Lavazza Espresso into the plunger to get herself fully wired, popped some bread into the toaster, and wondered what on earth she was going to do with today.

It used to be, when Kathryn was a girl, that she could shut herself up in her bedroom for days with a good book and her imagination, traveling worlds and meeting princes and casting spells and pretending she was a changeling who was really a princess in her true realm who'd been spirited away into a human family by some goblin-girl who despised her because of her beauty. Her mother used to knock three times on the door and leave her food on the floor outside before she went to wherever. That was their agreement. Her mother never approved, but her life was much too busy for her to spend time bitching about Kathryn's antisocial behavior. She'd tell her friends that it wouldn't last; that boys would change things when the time was right. They did too. Peer pressure and the threat of a psychiatrist.

She figured she'd go into the city today anyway, only she was going to take the car because, she thought, *It's my birthday and I can do whatever I want.*

She was just about to turn on the radio for company while she drank her second cup of coffee, knowing that the background babble would save her from thinking about how her life seemed to yawn ahead of her, when the phone shrilled. *My god*, she thought, looking at her watch. *My god! It's only 6:45! Who on earth . . .*

"Hey, Cat! Happy birthday!" yelled Merrin on the other end.

"It's not even 7 o'clock, Merrin! What're you doing up this early?"

"What're you up to girl? What's the plan? What we doing, huh?"

"No plan. Thought I'd get in the car and drive into town."

"I'm out the door as we speak! How long before you get here?"

"'Bout an hour, depending on the traffic."

Merrin huffed on the other end, "Well, I figure I'll see you around nine then."

Kathryn knew she was probably right. She was going to end up driving straight into the peak hour. She sighed, "Will you be at Dimity's?"

"You betcha. You okay? You sound kinda flat."

"I hate birthdays, Merrin. They don't work for me, ever."

"No big deal, huh?"

"No, no big deal at all."

"Just come, okay?"

Kathryn hung up and smiled to herself. No one else called her Cat, and it gave her a sense of being two people, reminding her of her childhood fantasies all over again. She set about clearing the last of her breakfast things away, picked up her lambskin jacket and her wallet and keys, banged the front door behind her, and walked out into the crisp morning, hunching over with cold until she'd managed to get the car unlocked and turned up the heat.

KATHRYN HAD BEEN ADOPTED AT birth by a high-society couple whose only claim to failure was their inability to conceive. She'd been raised to fit their ideal of the perfect child but, while pampering her with material things, they had little time outside of their busy work and social lifestyles to devote to their daughter on any level or depth. She'd had a nanny for that—Mary Connolly—the person who inspired a love of books and stories and a world unseen. Mary was a staunch Roman Catholic with six kids of her own, but she was also steeped in the legends and folk-tales of her native land.

Kathryn had always been dressed in casual chic—beiges, creams, whites, and salmons to accent her pale red hair, cut short but stylish at the best salons. Minimalism was considered the height of class, so she wore only the slightest touch of makeup and only the slightest amount of jewelry; no outward display of eccentricity.

She'd been sent to a private school and had been given her first car (albeit a Toyota) for her seventeenth birthday. She'd majored in English literature at the university and had met Martin Shilton at the dinner party that her father's company—the company owned by Martin's father—always hosted. It was the Christmas after her graduation.

She liked him. She never loved him. She married him anyway because he was a very nice man and the pressure from her parents to do so was overwhelming.

She was lost.

They'd had a gala wedding, and Martin's parents had bought them their first apartment as close to his workplace as possible. Martin excelled as a market research consultant and joined his father's firm, the Schlesinger-Shilton Group of Investments and Technologies, on an annual salary in the six-figure bracket.

Kathryn had been determined to write quality contemporary literature, but was insidiously drowning in the entrenched mediocrity that society's idea of being "Martin's wife" involved. Her identity had become blurred into a mud of Martin-this and Martin-that, so much so that she had all but ceased to remember that she'd had her own ambition.

She'd taken to wandering the city during the days, on the pretext of shopping, to avoid the incessant calls from the wives of Martin's friends who sought to embrace her into the fold of corporate-widowdom and who had nothing better to do than pamper themselves, get drunk, or take cocaine, spend their husbands' money, and discuss secret lovers. She also wandered to avoid Martin's mother, with her endless desire for structuring social calendars that included her son and daughter-in-law.

On one such wander Kathryn had turned down streets and alleyways that she usually avoided. She knew she was headed in the direction of the docks, but that was all.

She passed through a series of streets dealing in duty-free goods, X-rated movie houses, take-away food joints, and shops selling everything that nobody really wanted, before turning into Copperhead Lane with its coffee houses and unrealized art boutiques, an English-style pub, heavily scented flower stalls, and vendors selling everything from fruit and vegetables to homemade pottery and clothing. The smells and sensations were overwhelming and exciting. Where was this place in relation to the concrete and steel of the rest of the city? Kathryn took her time wandering back and forth along the ragged pavements and cobbled roadway that hardly ever saw four wheels. Foreign voices hawked their produce, and the mouthwatering scents of barbecued lamb and garlic vied with the background smells of seaweed, barnacled wood, and maritime fuel.

Almost at the end of the lane, where the docks and Wharf Road met the railway, was Dimity's Books and Café (Books Bought and Sold): *City's Largest Collection of Second-hand Books/Scifi/Best Coffee* proclaimed in vivid colors on a sandwich board in the middle of the sidewalk.

Kathryn was unaware, as she walked through the front door, that Dimity's was her angel.

Inside were wall-to-wall shelves of old paperbacks, tables of damaged books even cheaper still, a section especially for collectible comics, and a smaller room, off the main shop, entirely devoted to science fiction, fantasy, folklore, poetry, and mythology.

Oh, my, God! thought Kathryn as she entered the room, her mouth gaping in awe. She couldn't do it. *Coffee first,* she told herself, knowing that the rest of the day didn't matter anymore because she wasn't going anywhere for quite a while.

She walked out into the main shop and asked a boy close to the door, browsing through the comic books, where the café was, and he pointed between two high shelves. His directions led to the rear of the building where a pair of chipped French doors led out onto a courtyard, partly covered by a wide awning, but otherwise dotted here and there with large yellow umbrellas over an odd collection of outdoor tables and assorted chairs.

The whole courtyard was cobbled, and the surrounding walls were of very old red brick, almost obscured by Virginia creeper, ivy, climbing tea-roses, and moss.

The classic Steeleye Span album *Hark! The Village Wake!* was playing "Blackleg Miner" in the background as Kathryn looked around to determine if there was table service—there wasn't. She found her way to the service counter and ordered a strong latté and a turkey-breast sandwich. The dark-haired girl taking orders handed her a plastic number 11 and attended to the next customer before turning to the old coffee machine. Kathryn found herself a small table beside the wall and sat down to wait for her number to be called.

She had kept her new passion a secret. Most days Kathryn walked or jogged the same route and had her morning coffee, rain or shine, in the courtyard of Dimity's.

She had set herself the ritual of never buying more than one book at a time, and recycling the ones she'd read back into the shop's system. She watched people when she wasn't reading—lots of people—some downright weirdoes, some plain, many she wished she knew and would have struck up conversations with had she remembered how.

She hated her life. Except for this. She spent many hours just sitting and seeing how far down into the depth her true nature had been driven by other people's expectations. So far down, it seemed, that she couldn't find herself—only in the books and in the lined faces of the people who came and went and were beautiful because they showed emotion—maybe also because they weren't very safe.

Merrin would be what most people would call a Goth. She didn't at all see herself so, considering herself more an artist—a bohemian—and a witch, than the trendy catchphrase "spike" terminology. Her hair was dyed raven-black, and it hung down her back to her waist in its customary plait and the front of her head was shaved from her ears and across her forehead in the custom of the ancient Druids.

She loved deep-red lipstick, and lots of eyeliner to accentuate her pale grey eyes. She was adorned in silver jewelry that spoke of her sense of spirituality—silver pentagrams and ornate rosaries—that hung from her neck as a statement. Several rings and multimeaning charms dangled from the many piercings on her ears. She wore multiple layers of black clothing in textures from leather to linen, chunky lace-up Doc Martens over thick socks and mesh tights, and this was all covered, against the cold, by her worn but still-snug duffel coat.

Her greatest love was the small Celtic triscele tattooed on the back of her left hand.

Merrin's upbringing had been one of abuse and neglect. Her mother had moved regularly from place to place as each boyfriend became a disaster. As Merrin had grown older, the boyfriends had taken to more than shutting her out of the apartments at night.

She'd never stayed in any one school for more than six months so she had made no deep friendships and her grades had reflected her sense of abandonment. She'd dropped out when she was fourteen years old and had run away from home at the same time, risking the streets and the squats, and trusting in her well-earned sense of self-preservation to keep her safe. She had been right. Other than the offers of junk or rough sex (neither of which came close to enticing her) Merrin established a life for herself and slowly came alive to the possibilities of her own creativity.

Now, at twenty-four years old, she had a part-time job at Dimity's serving coffee and sometimes working behind the counter in the bookstore, a small, but light and airy studio, just off the canal down Napier Lane with its market stalls and ever-present odors of Lebanese and Chinese cooking, marijuana, incense, and other, less pleasant, less identifiable scents hinting at poverty and neglected buildings.

Her place was all decked out *Merrin-style*, with a wall full of books on every subject from mythology, folklore, and fantasy, to Yogalates, Yeats, and the Dancing Wu Li Masters. She had her pens and her paints and lots of paper, a battered old fiddle that she'd picked up at a pawn shop but hadn't yet learned to play, and a collection of music that defied cataloging. She had enough money to go to Mary Flannery's Tavern one night a week to listen to whatever live gig was playing and drink a pint or two, to train in Kung Fu with some guys down at the dock early on Sunday mornings, and to cover what food she bought to cook at home. She was happy being alone most of the time, except when she remembered the one time she had been really in love.

She'd taken off from the city once, just under two years ago; she'd met up with a band of Travelers at Flannery's where the musicians among them had played a session. When they'd started the gig the tavern had been almost empty.

She'd been aware of staring at this one guy in the band all through the set but, oh boy, he was something else! He had this long, foxy-colored hair tied in two plaits like a Celtic warrior or something, and almond-shaped green eyes that seemed to hold an entire conversation with her while he played the hottest fiddle she'd ever heard. He'd come over to her at half-time and had asked her if she'd share a pint of Guinness with him. They'd talked for the whole fifteen minutes until the others in the band called him back to the stage.

During their second set the place had begun to fill with locals, mostly doing a lot of drinking and dancing because the Fíanna really rocked the house. By the third set she was so far back in the crowd that she couldn't see the fiddler anymore. The band finished to whoops and calls for more, but started packing up anyway.

Merrin was just putting on her jacket, about to leave, when Willie squeezed his way through the bodies and plonked himself down on the stool beside her.

Are you goin' then? he'd asked.

I gotta work tomorrow, she'd lied.

Will you stay a little while? he'd asked.

Well, maybe just a little while, she'd answered.

The people he was with were leaving the next day, but he'd stayed the night with Merrin and in the morning he'd asked her if she wanted to go with them. She'd dropped in at the shop later on and asked Dimity if she'd mind if she had a few days off work and could someone go by her place and water her plants for her?

"No problem," Dimity had said. "I got you covered, girl."

That had been early spring and they'd gone south, traveling the older roads in a big old double-decker bus. There had been eleven of them, plus Merrin. It had been a journey of magic, with the most otherworldly people she could have hoped to meet.

She had thought for most of the journey that she could have stayed with them forever, but as days turned into weeks she began to yearn inexplicably and passionately for her little studio.

It became an almost unbearable homesickness that didn't make any sense at all.

Willie had sat her down by the fire at dawn one morning and told her that stuff had come up and that everybody who wasn't at the core of the group was supposed to go home and he was really sorry and he loved her heaps. She'd cried but she'd told him she was glad, too, and she explained how she'd been feeling. *I know*, he'd said, *that's Hunter makin' it all right for you.*

She didn't know then what he meant, but she did know that Hunter—who seemed as much a leader among them as did the small, older woman named Brighid—was full of magic and had probably laid some kind of spell on her. They'd turned the bus around and headed north for the midsummer solstice.

At a small seaside town just outside the city they'd stopped for the night, and Willie had taken her to the local tattoo parlor and gifted her with the triscele tattoo.

They'd dropped her off outside her door, promising to come by whenever they passed through.

She had thought she might cry forever when they left, but she never did. She was just left with a warm glow. She fell asleep that first night—her first night alone for weeks—with a smile on her face and the hand with the tattoo on it resting on the pillow where she could see it when she woke up. Her job was still there easy, and all the plants had been looked after really well.

Chapter Two

Kathryn rang off and Merrin sighed as she flipped her cell phone shut. *Well, I'm excited*, she thought to herself as she finished wrapping the last of the collection of presents she'd gathered for Cat's birthday, thinking how much more fun it was to open five packages rather than the obligatory one.

She had scoured the junk shops for days looking for just the right collection of bits. She'd found a pair of 1960s shoes all covered in diamantes that'd look fabulous if Cat ever dressed up in secret, a lock-up diary that'd never been used, a big kick-ass black jumper, that'd probably reach her knees, knowing how cold her friend got out there in the backwoods.

At home she'd rummaged through her music collection and found her Loreena McKennitt's CD called *A Book of Secrets*. That had the song "The Highwayman" on it and she'd once read the lyrics aloud and Cat had loved it, so she taped a copy for her. And lastly, even though Merrin figured Cat'd never wear it, she wrapped a little silver pentagram that she'd treasured for years because it had been the first one she'd ever bought.

She stuffed all her packages into her backpack, along with everything else she figured she'd need for the day, locked up her little studio, and set off into town on her battered old mountain bike.

Merrin had known Kathryn for two months, ever since they'd literally and metaphorically banged heads down at

Dimity's. It had been their only meeting ground in all that time. They didn't socialize in the same circles—to anybody else the two women were an utter contradiction.

MERRIN CAME HERE EVERY DAY. It was her main haunt. Two days a week she made coffee and organized for the guy out the back to make the snacks. Just last week Dimity had also given her Sundays taking the sales for the bookshop—a major plus for her wallet.

This morning wasn't one of those days. She had nothing planned but a whole "Cat" day, so she sat out in the courtyard in the sunshine of a warming morning. She sighed aloud. *This is no place for a witch*, she thought restlessly as she sugared her first coffee of the day, her pile of presents occupying the chair beside her.

Every now and then, like now, a yearning to be back on the road overwhelmed her. She was used to the deep places where wonder dwelt, and memory was art because the Travelers had showed her real magic, where love wasn't about impressing or fear or possession.

She chuckled at her train of thought and poured a second spoonful of sugar into the thick, black coffee. Still, you never knew who was going to turn up here and it was likely that one day Willie'd just waltz back in on her life. She wasn't pining—it'd been too long ago to be anything other than a very cool reflection.

Kathryn was her current project—her Lost-Cause-in-Transition. The first time she'd met her was on a day off. Merrin had been sitting on the floor, her head bent sideways, reading the new titles that had arrived the day before and that had just happened to end up on the bottom shelf among the Zs—an entire collection of Zimmer-Bradley's *Witchworld*, a masterpiece of a collection, three of which she hadn't read before. She had stood up with her treasure and had banged hard into a woman who had been poised above her, leaning over the same shelf.

Merrin was all set to rant in her most abusive language, but then she'd looked into the other woman's eyes. *Lost*, she'd thought.

"You okay?" she'd asked instead.

The top of her head had collided with the other woman's chin and a tooth had cut into her lip, which was beaded with blood.

"Ow!" said Merrin as the woman pulled a tissue from her handbag and pressed it to the wound.

"Th-okay;" she'd mumbled. "You okay?"

"Yeah," Merrin grinned. "Can I buy you a coffee?"

The woman was staring wide-eyed at Merrin and had taken a step back from her. "Ah, sure . . ." she'd answered, attempting to hide her embarrassment, realizing she was making the younger woman uncomfortable.

"You go on out back," Merrin suggested, "while I pay for these." She slapped the three books together in delight. "I'll be right out."

She'd paid for her purchase and walked out into the leafy courtyard and had found the pale redhead sitting at one of the tables beside the wall.

"What'll you have?" she'd asked.

Kathryn hadn't looked up. "You don't have to buy me a coffee. It's fine, really," and she proceeded to open her own book, seemingly dismissing Merrin outright.

Lost Cause is also a bitch, thought Merrin. "Lost Cause," she said aloud.

"What did you say?"

"You're a lost cause, girl."

"How dare you . . ." Kathryn began, attempting to sound disgusted, but unable to think of a retort.

"Whatever . . ." said Merrin. "I'll get my own coffee then."

She turned her back and walked over to where Lyn was frothing milk for a cappuccino. "Short black?" she'd asked Merrin.

"Yeah, thanks Lyn, and stick it on my tab, okay?"

Merrin went and sat on her own as far away from the Lost Cause as she could. She took out the Zimmer-Bradleys and spent a few minutes deciding the order in which she'd read them.

"I'm sorry."

Merrin looked up from reading a back cover.

"I'm really sorry," said the Lost Cause.

Merrin sighed. "You wanna sit? I'm Merrin, by the way."

Kathryn pulled out the chair, dropped her bags off her shoulder and onto the ground, and sat delicately.

Merrin watched her and created all kinds of instant and plausible scenarios of the other's past lives, her current situation, her possible bank account figure, whether she smoked when she was nervous, and whether she saw a shrink on a regular basis, maybe for depression or anxiety. She also wondered, because the Lost Cause was as thin as a pole, whether she maybe had an eating disorder. She reserved her full assessment for the moment, though wondering why she always did this stuff, and in seconds—whether it was actually a psychic gift or her own way of keeping to the high ground. *It's all Sun Tzu's fault*, she thought, keeping a straight face all throughout.

"I'm Kathryn Shilton," holding out a hand, which Merrin shook vigorously, just as Lyn shouted out the number for Kathryn's coffee.

Merrin slid out from her chair "I'll get that—mine's probably ready to go as well—just wait here, okay?" and she did a little hop-step over to the counter where her number was about to be called. She took both coffees back to the table.

"I'm sorry if I seemed rude before," Kathryn apologized again as Merrin placed the mugs down.

"Which time?" replied Merrin.

"What? What do you mean?" Kathryn looked devastated, and Merrin suppressed a grin.

"In the shop or out here?"

"Was I rude in the shop?" Merrin didn't suppose that Kathryn had realized that she'd been gawping.

"I wouldn't *want* to look like you," said Merrin straight out.

"I'm lost . . ." Kathryn had looked seriously concerned.

"You were staring at me like I was a freak."

"What do you mean you wouldn't want to look like me? What's wrong with the way I look . . . that's not what I meant anyway. Now who's being rude, huh?"

"Then why? And you look like some kinda life that I wouldn't want to have, that's what I meant."

"Argh," growled Kathryn. "Whatever . . . !" And she put her book in her bag as though to leave. Merrin grinned.

"Hey! That is just *so* much better!"

"You did that on purpose," huffed Kathryn.

"We can talk about that later, okay Cat? So what do you mean that's not what you meant?"

"What?"

"In the shop. The look?"

"You look just like someone I met once. This woman who really eeked me out. She was older than you, but it was . . . yeah, I guess it was freaky looking at you. I never forgot her, you see?"

Merrin thought about the image of herself in the mirror in the bathroom that morning when she'd put on her make-up. She knew she didn't look like other people, but that didn't matter. She'd worked hard to find out how she really wanted to appear to the world, and she was years beyond caring if people couldn't recognize what she wanted to say, so it came as a bit of a surprise to think that someone as straight as this woman knew her maybe-double.

"You're kidding, yeah?" said Merrin flatly.

Kathryn toyed with her coffee mug, the past event resurfacing in all its detail. "No. When I was younger I met this woman—a fortune-teller—you look so much like her that the resemblance threw me."

Merrin waited, and observed, while Kathryn sipped her coffee, then sat looking into the depths of the mug like it was an oracle. This didn't equate with the picture of the woman that she'd earlier gauged Kathryn to be. *Fortune-teller?* It wasn't that she disbelieved her, it was just that she so didn't come across as the type.

"Earth calling Cat-woman!"

Kathryn laughed suddenly with her brow all knitted up, like she was really sad and there was nothing funny.

"Why are you calling me that?" She looked at Merrin with tired eyes, and Merrin realized that there was probably more wrong in the Lost Cause's life than she'd been able to intuit so far.

"Cause it's cool?" she shrugged.

Kathryn just looked at her for a minute, then nodded all serious-like. "It is kinda cool, Merrin." Then she shook herself.

"Wow!" she exclaimed. "I haven't thought about her for years!"

"More, then." Merrin, settled back for the full story, rolling a cigarette and lighting it with an old but precious Zippo that she'd scored when someone had left it unguarded on a table at the tavern one night.

"A psychic. Her name was Bridget or something. I'd gone up north with my folks and my cousin Amanda the year I finished high school—we've got a place up along the coast there for holidays—and the first night there Amanda and I borrowed my dad's car and we went into the town to one of the local nightclubs. There was a group of backpackers at the table next to us, and we overheard them talking about some people that they called Travelers."

Merrin got a rush all over. She was instantly all ears. Talk about serendipity!

"Anyhow these two girls were saying how one of them was telling people's fortunes, reading Tarot for money. They both said she was really weird but mega worth the bucks.

"I'd always had a deep-down secret interest in all that—not that I'd admit it to my family or Martin or such . . ." (Merrin reassessed again.)

"So I leaned across to their table and I said I was sorry to eavesdrop, but it sounded like it might be fun to get my fortune told. She's scary, said one of the girls, but the other just giggled. They were down by the pier yesterday, she told me. You can't miss 'em—they've got this big old crappy bus and there's a whole bunch of 'em. They might still be there if the rangers haven't found 'em yet."

Oh my God—it's them, Merrin thought to herself, not wanting to miss what Cat was saying.

"I asked how I'd recognize the fortune-teller, and the first girl described her."

"So you went?" But even as she said it Merrin thought to herself, *Of course she went, duh!*

"Yeah. Next day. On my own."

"And . . . ?"

"Like I said, she looked like you. She wasn't as, ah, elaborate with the jewelry, and she didn't wear any make-up, but she shaved the same front bit like you and she had lots of plaits, not just one—or were they braids?—doesn't matter. Same face; same face exactly. Now do you understand?"

"Well? Did she do you a reading?"

"A short one. Nothing really—just cryptic; just stuff that seemed all metaphor."

"What?" Merrin encouraged.

Kathryn thought about it. "Ah . . . She'd said. 'Nothing is as it seems. Everything will change because you will change everything. Stuff like that.' Then she repeated, 'Nothing is as it seems.' She'd shaken her head and reached over the cards and had taken both of my hands. That's when she spun me out utterly . . ."

"*What* did she say, Cat?"

"She'd said, 'You've forgotten what you knew about yourself, haven't you?' Then she said, 'That'll be ten bucks.' I said, 'Is that it?' She said, 'You wouldn't believe me if I told you.'

"What wouldn't I believe? I asked her, but she shook her head. 'Just pay me and go, okay?' she said.

"I pulled ten dollars from my wallet. She picked it up, got up from the table, and walked away from me to join a group of eccentric-looking people camped by the bus.

"I'd muttered, *Bitch, rip-off,* under my breath. She'd looked back at me over her shoulder and called out, 'Do you believe in magic, Kathryn?' Then she got on the bus. I left really upset."

"Why? Doesn't sound like she told you much."

"I never told her my name, Merrin."

Chapter Three

Kathryn came into the café like a black cloud, muttering to herself under her breath, occasionally baring her teeth, looking around for Merrin.

"Wuhoo!" exclaimed Merrin as she caught sight of her friend. "Happy . . ." The words died in her throat. She wasn't about to comment on how long she'd been waiting, knowing that all that time Cat had probably been stuck in traffic.

"Merrin . . ." moaned Kathryn as she approached the table.

"Aw, c'mon and let me look after you!" Merrin was gleeful and conciliatory at the same time. "Now you just sit and let Aunty Mezza get you a cuppa, girl!"

Kathryn sat down, still feeling huffy after the stressful drive, to see a chair piled with packages wrapped in brown paper that had been painted all over with stars and moons and cats and smiley faces. She grinned.

Merrin arrived back with two coffees and an almond croissant with a candle alight at its center.

"Don't you dare . . ." began Kathryn.

"Happy birthday to you . . ." Merrin sang. Kathryn attempted to glower but could not hold the face. She was, after all, exactly where she wanted to be, with her best friend in the world, who actually meant what she was singing.

The other people in the café soon joined in, and Kathryn merely ended up grinning from ear to ear as the whole odd assortment of patrons cheered her. That to most of them she was a stranger was irrelevant.

Merrin sat down after Kathryn blew out the candle and piled the packages on the table. "Open them—go on and make a mess!"

She unwrapped the gifts delicately, one by one. Her realization of the thought that had gone into every unexpected gift made her cry. When she opened the little box with the pentagram in it she felt at once confused and charmed that Merrin would think to have included her in such a way.

"I know you probably won't wear it—or the shoes . . ."

"No! I mean yes. I don't know about the shoes, unless Martin and his mother think up some really lousy dinner for tonight, but the necklace?" and she promptly put it around her neck and did up the clasp.

"I'll be right back." She stood up and headed for the ladies room without waiting for a reply from Merrin. Once inside she looked in the mirror at the talisman she wore. The sight disturbed her.

This is not who I am, she thought, while at the same time experiencing an eerie recognition that it was exactly who she was. She took the pentagram off and felt like the Kathryn she was when she was with Martin; she put it back on and felt like someone she didn't know but thought she'd like to. She repeated the process again and again. In the end she left it on. Before she left the bathroom she mussed up her short red hair just a little.

Back at the table Merrin asked her what her plans were for the day.

"Haven't got any. I suppose I ought to contact Martin to find out what he's organized so I know what time to be home."

She pulled out her cell phone and dialed Martin's office number. The phone was answered by his secretary, Jenny Sutton. No, he's in a meeting at the moment. Yes, he asked me to let you know that dinner is scheduled at his mother's for 8 PM and to please be dressed when he arrives home as he'll have to catch the later train as he has several appointments that will keep him busy longer than usual. Yes, I'll inform him that you rang.

"Hmm." She hung up and dialed her mother. She got the answer-machine, which said there was nobody at home right now so please leave a message, and "if that's you, Kathryn, have a lovely day, sorry I can't catch up with you until later in the week, love you heaps, so does Dad, so . . . happy birthday, darling!"

Merrin sat quietly while she watched the emotions like unrequited ghosts that played across the other woman's face ever so subtly but obvious for all that. Minutes passed. Kathryn put her elbows on the table and leaned her chin in her steepled hands, looking at her friend but saying nothing.

Merrin had the situation sussed, but she just leaned back in her chair, closed her eyes, and raised her face toward the sun.

"What did you do on your last birthday?" Kathryn asked eventually, having realized that she didn't even know when that was; Merrin certainly had never told her, but, she thought with slight horror, she'd never asked.

"November 30th," Merrin gave the date as though reading Cat's thoughts.

"I'm sorry."

Merrin just shrugged. "Ah, what did I do? Oh, yeah! In the morning I worked here and the gang bought me this humongous breakfast and we ate cakes and ignored as many customers as we could—not the regulars, mind you—and Dimity played all my favorite music until I finished work just after one. Then I went down to the dojo to see if anyone was hanging around and had a bit of a spar with Jasper Queedy and Stephan and some guy who'd only just started training whose name I forget. Then . . . I rode the ferry over to the zoo and wandered around there for a while, telling the animals stories about the wild places, and then I went home.

"Later I went to Mary Flannery's and struck up a conversation with some real Irishers who were out here backpacking, and we all ended up singing along with the band who were playing some trad folksongs." Merrin laughed as she remembered. "Shit, we musta sung 'Dirty Old Town' about fifty times in a row! Oh, and I beat Lilly Read—she's always there—at a game of pool."

"Did you get any presents?"

"I bought myself a fiddle from the pawn shop! It's very cool—even has its own case and all. I just got to learn to play it one day."

"Didn't you used to go out with a guy who played the fiddle?"

"Willie. Yeah. I was just thinking about those times this morning while I waited for you. I guess that's why I bought it, huh?"

"You don't go out with many guys, do you?"

Merrin snorted and dug around in her pack for her tobacco pouch. She rolled a thin cigarette without answering.

"Well?" asked Kathryn. "Is there something I don't know? Are you seeing someone you haven't told me about?"

"No. No one. Most guys don't like my look. Not that I care too much. But most guys also hear a different kinda music than me."

"Like the magic and all?"

"Especially that. Most guys think the stuff that interests me is kinda spooky and embarrassing, and they'd rather be with girls like you."

"Hrmph! What are you on? I'm *boring*! I wish I wasn't, but it's the truth. It's years since I did anything interesting except sneak here."

"Why do you do that, Cat?"

"What?"

"You know. You put yourself down. You sneak around buying books for fuck's sake! I mean, what kinda sneaking around is that?"

Kathryn fingered the little pentagram at her neck and felt herself going red in the face. She'd steered well away from the topic of Martin/Martin's family/Martin's friends/her family for the whole time she'd known Merrin.

"Have you ever felt like you just have to please the people around you? Like you owe them yourself?"

"*What?* How can you *think* that!" Merrin spluttered.

"Well it's like that for me. I can't really articulate it all that very well. It's just that . . ." Kathryn hadn't thought this through—it was like she was swimming with sharks even broaching the deep place with another person.

"I'm adopted, you know."

"Yeah, you told me," said Merrin.

"My mother and father didn't believe in pretending. I've always known, just like I've always known I was privileged. Neither my mother nor my father ever said aloud that I ought to be grateful, but I felt it from them. I used to sense so much that a great deal of my childhood was spent listening to people's conversations without them needing to speak a word."

Merrin even breathed softly so as to not disrupt Cat's train of thought.

"The people at the schools knew I wasn't the Bolton's daughter by blood but by law—and by money. When I was young I used to hate being adopted because there was always this way people had of look-ing at me that made me feel like I was a pretender. So I always felt like a lie. And I ended up needing to fit in with what was expected of me because, like, how easy would it have been to be rejected if I showed tendencies that had maybe come from my blood parents?"

"Didn't you want to know who they were?" Merrin had wanted to know who her father was, except her mother wasn't sure.

"I asked my mother when I was about ten years old. She said she'd try to find out the details for me. She never came back to me on that one. I was quiet for about four years, then I asked her again. She said I'd been abandoned and that there weren't any records, but that I was such a pretty baby that I was their first and only choice and that they'd never wanted to adopt another child after they'd brought me home because I was so bloody special and . . ." Kathryn felt ridicu-lous. She was crying without even having realized it.

". . . and that would have been okay if I'd felt it from either of them, but I didn't. I hardly ever saw them."

"But what about Martin?" asked Merrin. Kathryn just looked at her. Merrin got the picture. "Oh, shit!" she said.

There was a moment's uncomfortable silence until Merrin, in Merrin-style, piped up with, "Hey! More coffee?"

Kathryn was glad for the change of subject. "Sure."

"I'll organize it, but don't you go anywhere 'cause I've got a question . . . actually I've got a couple of questions, and they're not nosey so don't look so ooey like that."

Kathryn felt as though any more coffee and she'd start to shake, but she was also feeling as though a door had opened somewhere inside her and it was okay to talk about all this with Merrin. She got up and joined her friend over at the counter and asked Lyn if she'd please put the Loreena McKennitt tape on because it was her birthday present.

"Cool," said Lyn.

"Cool!" agreed Merrin.

The late morning sun had moved away from where they'd been sitting so they gathered their belongings and moved tables. The slight wind had a feeling of snow, even though it was almost a month and a half into spring.

When they'd settled, Merrin continued where she'd left off. "Okay, three questions . . ."

"Shoot," said Kathryn, having recovered her composure.

"First question: What happened to the telepathy thing where you heard people without them talking? Is it still there?"

That was the last thing Kathryn had expected, and she did a doubletake. "Whoa! What?"

"You said . . ."

"Yeah, I know what I said. I just have to think about it, is all. Shit, I don't know, Merrin. I don't think it's still there at all. I didn't even remember about it till it just slipped out before."

"Well, I'm really curious, so think about it."

"N . . . no, I don't figure it is still there. I think I stopped listening somewhere along the line."

"This is still question one then . . . So if you were so fucked-up how come you went to the university and did what you did instead of maybe studying business or becoming a professional wa-wa or something, or do a How To Be a Good Wife degree?"

"Ouch!"

"No offense, girlfriend!"

"Sure. Because I always loved to read and I figured that I had a good imagination and that with structured training I could write books that'd make other people as happy as reading had made me."

"Okay. Second question: What would happen if you didn't turn up at Martin and Martin's mom's birthday dinner?"

Kathryn just sat there. She looked at Merrin with almost horror.

"Well? What would happen?"

"I, uh . . . I have no idea." She felt slightly sick at the very idea.

"I mean, what would happen if you just phoned him up at work and said I don't want to do that for my birthday?"

"He'd tell me it was all planned and that I couldn't do that to everyone who'd gone to so much trouble on my behalf, is what he'd say," she replied softly.

"Okay." Merrin adjusted herself in her seat and leaned across the table so that she was almost in Kathryn's face. "Third question: You wanna hit the town with me tonight for your birthday?

"We go shopping for you on *your* credit card this afternoon, and we spend a whole freakin' lot of *your* money on clothes and stuff that *you* really like, even though you mightn't know you do till you try them on and I tell you how good they look, and we go do whatever. We maybe go to Mary Flannery's and drink pints and eat chips and play pool and dance and maybe flirt with some guys . . . Then you get a taxi all the way home 'cause you'll be in no condition to drive, and Martin can pick the car up tomorrow or you can catch a taxi back into town and do it yourself."

She took a big, deep breath. "Or you can sleep over on the swag I've got in the closet, and we can talk like girls until morning about *me!*" And she grinned.

"Oh," was all Kathryn could manage for a moment. "So that was the third question, was it?"

Merrin roared with laughter.

KATHRYN FELT LIKE SHE WAS standing on the edge of a precipice and the wind was howling from all directions and that the enemy was closing in behind her and that she was standing right beside herself telling herself not to be so stupid—look what she stood to lose?

And she let herself fall.

And somewhere apart from where most people call the real world a goddess sensed something alter that was not of her doing—felt a ripple, and raised her head to scent the air.

Chapter Four

The Brotherhood of the Eclipse—

Michael James Blacker was raised in the Christian Identity Movement—a radical, hate-based fundamentalist community. He'd been accustomed to getting his own way since he was young—the youngest of three brothers—Ryan, John Junior, and himself.

He was highly intelligent and excelled both academically and as a valued member of his track and field team. His father had heavily influenced all three of his sons; his mother, not at all. She had long ago relinquished any delusions of significance—the capacity for cruelty that was the inevitable consequence to shirking the fulfillment of the role that had been demanded of her from the very first day after pledging her marriage vows had cowed her completely. Who could respect that?

By the ages of six, seven, and nine years old, all three boys had learned to shoot several different firearms. They were taken on camping expeditions with John Senior and his associates every second weekend, for the express purpose of hunting wild game and turning the boys into men.

The family was deeply devoted to their religious congregation with its racist and highly moralistic ideology, and any deviation from the strict doctrines of the Church brought about swift, and often brutal, retribution.

Michael was unaware that his true nature bordered on the mystical, so he could never understand his early fascination with the more Satanic and demonic concerns of the sermons delivered to the Fellowship by their pastor. He was, however, given a free rein to read anything he wanted as long as this did not contravene his Bible studies.

By the of age of twenty he had pored over many books, both acceptable and apocryphal, that related to the Roman Catholic Church and its history, from its so-called conception in post-Diaspora, post-Hellenistic Greece at the altar of an Unknown God, and its subsequent vindication based upon the vision of Constantine, to its institutionalization during the Council of Nicea, its dissemination, and the blanket-authority that led to the Crusades and the subsequent Inquisition. He took special interest in the Knights Templar—their rise and demise—and the so-called, mysteriously powerful Order of Zion, the Masonic traditions, and all forms of ritualized Western Mystery Traditions. He was interested in orders of angels (both exalted and fallen), demons and demonic possession, and the Church's stand against heretics of all kinds, including witches, those considered to be dabbling in satanic debauchery, and the whole range of the so-called Black Arts.

His study taught him about such men as Moses de Leon, da Vinci, Copernicus, Giordano Bruno, Eliaphas Levi, Richard Flood, Abra-Melin the Jew, Dr. John Dee, James Crook, the celebrated European occultist Cornelius Agrippa von Nettesheim, and the compacts of these men with Satan or Satanism.

Michael James Blacker subsequently embraced Roman Catholicism, an act that outraged his family and led to a complete and irrevocable alienation between them.

Michael's avid hunger for all things theological was fueled by a fascination for what he understood to be *evil*: anything not acceptable to Church doctrine, but particularly that which was deemed *magical*.

To understand his enemy, Michael James Blacker studied many variations of the arcane, from Paganism in general through to the ways of worship associated with the Church of Set, the training involved in modern Magickal Orders, the rituals and beliefs of Wicca, the relationship that Witchcraft embraces with certain "gods," and any and all practices of spellcrafting.

IN HIS MIDDLE THIRTIES MICHAEL had an epiphany, and the Brotherhood of the Eclipse was conceived.

He formulated an entire training protocol for his would-be army of God, which included a general congregation embracing men, women, and children. He named them The Church of the Penitents of the True Faith. To the eye of the public this was all there was to it—yet another cult of extremist Christianity (although on stage, in front of the gathered flock, their leader was a gifted and charismatic orator).

The Penitents of the True Faith did, however, attract many individuals and groups jaded by both conventional and, particularly, modern liberal trends toward the acceptance of what these few considered as degenerate, even as abomination.

The cult that Michael created was a mix of high ritual such as was employed by the Roman Catholic Church prior to its "modernization." They excluded, of course, such heathen concepts as the Virgin Mary, holy days, sainthood, and a Holy Ghost, but continued the use of the sacraments of confession (albeit public) and communion as necessary incitements to piety, and revived the art of exorcism, the practice of which had been so bizarre as to become headline material on more than one occasion, due to the constant fetish, on the part of the press, for the infiltration of what were known as "fringe spiritual movements"—cults.

The Brotherhood reinstated the Sabbath at sunset on Fridays, and introduced the symbolic Sacred Feast calling upon the Blood of the Lamb and therefore introducing meat as the body of Christ, rather than bread, and chalices of good red wine.

The congregation enthusiastically endorsed the need for extremes to control sin and the hungers of the flesh. Women were encouraged—or forced—to embrace full body coverage and the wearing of scarves or headgear, and children were, once again, raised to see evil in the merest of pastimes, and to have their behavior modified by the threat of hell (the descriptions of which were right out of the text of the visions of Zoroaster).

There was the backing of a created clergy and the dangling of the carrot of advancement into these ranks for any man who acknowledged only the rights of the adherents who had undergone the rigors of its harsh penance practices (which included extreme fasting, public flagellation, public confessions for the slightest transgressions, full emersion baptisms on a regular basis, a community spy network aimed at disrupting those employed in pursuits deemed evil) and who had agreed to the strict code of behavior that Michael coined "The Sanctity Code."

This code standardized a formula for the recognition of what was termed "abomination": *That which represents abomination includes the mistaken concept that women have equal rights to men, all forms of homosexuality, the right to abortion and euthanasia, the Darwinian theory of evolution, the denial of the existence of demonic interference in the decisions of both the individual and the masses, freedom of speech, the right to protest, sexual intercourse outside of the sacrament of marriage, illegitimate children born of such union, the idea that all things were created equal, any religion that denies Christ as its Savior, any religion practicing idolatry or pagan rites, including even those who claimed to be Christians but who adhere to the old European heathen practices such as Christmas, Easter, and ritual or worship on the day of the Sun (Sunday).*

They included all branches of Islam, Hinduism, and Buddhism in the latter category.

Blacks, Jews, Gypsies, or any indigenous groups were considered subhuman. All other non-whites were painted with the same tar.

Michael's project was financially backed by a small, but extremely wealthy, umbrella company of investment speculators who cared nothing for Michael's ideals. They had earned their fortunes through the recognition of the gullibility of the general public. The Church of the Penitents of the True Faith had reinvented the practice of tithing—10 percent of the weekly income of all members of the congregation was put into the coffers of the Brotherhood, and 3 percent of this money was paid to their backers on an annual basis. This amounted to quite huge sums.

It took four years for the congregation to number in the thousands and to have an established television broadcast and a small periodical newsletter.

They were localized in one country, however, but it was not Michael's intention that this should remain the case.

It was a Christian Identity Movement with a grand façade.

From within the ranks, the highly charismatic Michael chose his elite—his Inner Sanctum called the Twelve. These were all hand-picked, well-educated, highly motivated, and ambitious men (some with military backgrounds, well-versed in the use of weapons and high explosives), most of whom had exotic tastes and were capable of extremes. To these few Michael explained his vision: a world under their control, ripe for the taking—God's Chosen Few. This could be achieved only through the eradication of the wave of deviation associated with the acceptance of magic and mysticism of any kind (liberal consciousness embracing individuality, summoning demonic intervention into being through ritual practice, exalting anarchy and disorder).

Michael and the Twelve—deemed the Brotherhood—agreed that it was the allowance of these practices that had led the world into a moral nadir—they would not be tolerated. They set their sights on the establishment of an Inquisitional Tribunal, a thing that the Roman Catholic Church had demoted to toothlessness in the twentieth century. Its aim: to infest government, educational, medical, legal, and media establishments, and to thereby reintroduce the True Faith.

Michael James Blacker had discovered and become fixated by one particularly elusive group known only as the Travelers. There were purportedly several hundred of them. They had a reputation for being *otherworldly,* and it was rumored that they were from an unknown and ancient race.

The information conjured images of werewolves and vampires and other creatures out of fable. So far the intelligence that the Brotherhood had collected had pointed to an inexplicable yearly congregation of these people in a town on the far northeast coast.

It was discovered that one family, the O'Neills, hosted these gatherings year after year on their property, several miles outside of Worthington, the nearby resort township.

They had recruited one of the Twelve to infiltrate the family by courting the love of their only daughter and her two children, whose father (or fathers) was rumored to have been a member of the Travelers. This recruit was Phillip Adler, but he took the name Owen Riordan to endear himself to the family's Irish roots.

The deception was never discovered. The O'Neill's daughter was "handfasted" to Phillip, who became known as her husband. Through her he learned of the true abomination that the Travelers represented, and the part the O'Neills played in continuing the protection and mentorship of these demons, generation after generation.

Phillip was ordered to extinguish the O'Neill line at the time of the summer gathering—not so much a warning as a statement. Phillip/Owen set fire to the house in which his wife and her children slept. It was an old weatherboard, two-story ramble that literally exploded as the petrol-soaked veranda was set ablaze.

Phillip was recalled to the Brotherhood, and after suitable penance and purification was embraced back into their ranks.

Chapter Five

The Twelve gathered in a beige and glass executive suite on the fourteenth floor of a five-star luxury hotel in the heart of New Rathmore's central business district. They rarely conferenced at the same hotel more than once in a year, but Michael James Blacker had a definite preference for Brampton Terrace, with its immaculate view of the river and the botanical gardens where the World Heritage-listed Museum of Natural History nestled among the well-manicured adjacent parklands.

Two of the Twelve were stationed in close proximity to the door into the suite, the slight bulge in their well-tailored suit jackets hinting at the Glock 9mm pistols that nestled in standard law-enforcement-issue shoulder holsters, while the other ten men, along with Michael, sat at the long maple conference table with their laptops open.

Instructions had been issued to the hotel reception desk to hold all calls, and the cell phones of all except the security men had been switched off.

The meeting had been underway for two hours, and the objectives had been discussed down to the most minute detail. An Old Testament-style "scorched-earth" pogrom was to be instituted initially against all known heads of pagan practices, in a series of smash-and-burn paramilitary-style attacks on homes, the establishments where these groups were known to gather, and the retail outlets that sold products and icons used in their practices. Individuals were also targeted—those who were recognized as public representatives or sympathizers.

A large network of the city's skinhead community had been commissioned to aid in the pogroms at no cost, except the supply of weapons, ammunition, explosives, and necessary equipment. The connection between the Brotherhood of the Eclipse and the leaders of these groups was sealed tight. Both knew the consequences of leaked information, and an honor system as stringent as the Samurai code of *giri* ensured the success of the series of operations.

The list of targets was extensive: an A to Z of the city and outlying district's Occult and New Age movements. Included on the list was the Petro Societé d'Ayida Wedo, a group practicing Voodoo that its followers referred to as Vodoun. It was led by a woman, Mambo Julienne Morres, who had been granted the *asson*, a symbolic representation of the woman's initiation, by the founder and head of the Vodoun religion in the country, Mariani Bizango, before the latter had moved out of the area.

Michael Blacker knew very well the true nature of the religion of Vodoun, but played his followers fully into the superstitions supplied by the sensationalism of the B-grade movie industry in the mid-twentieth century: snake-worship, necromancy, zombification, devil-worship, animal sacrifice.

He was horrified at the data he had researched on this whole setup. A black woman from a third-world Caribbean country seduced a Japanese scientist and trapped him into a marriage. They apparently had a male child, but no one seemed to know his whereabouts or anything about him. There was obviously plenty of money on the scene because the cult had seventeen prime acres at Teagan Grove, on the outskirts of the city, that had been bought back in the '70s, and there were several dwellings for the believers and their families to live in, plus a huge temple (called a *hounfor*) where they held their rituals and sacrifices.

The fact that the authorities did nothing to stop this, nor to prevent the group from advertising its dates of worship in the religious services section of the New Rathmore Times put the place and the people on an A list for extermination, along with a huge coven of witches who had been holding seasonal sabbat rituals in a public park up along the northern beaches, the leader of which had been interviewed on chat shows and written up in several women's magazines as "The New Face of the Witchcraft Movement," she being blonde and attractive, and a young single mother with a boyfriend, rather than the stereotypical hag.

The A list included not only groups that the Brotherhood labeled as "Satanic," but those that fitted several of the criteria in the Sanctity Code, specifically women who refused to know their place in the scheme of things, and who spat in the face of Christianity by their very blatancy and carnality.

The meeting concluded at just after five in the evening with twenty-four sites and three individuals formally targeted for the following week.

Michael gestured with a tilt of his head toward Brendon Chapman, the only skinhead who had been admitted into the Twelve. Brendon considered himself to be Michael's shotgun and never let his master out of his sight. Michael tolerated, and encouraged, this devotion, knowing full well the vast network of connections, and respect, that Brendon commanded amongst the city's youth.

The gesture resulted in Brendon phoning room service. He ordered a lavish selection from the menu beside the television—enough to satisfy all present.

"Food's on its way," he pronounced to the other men.

AFTER A QUIET PRAYER AND the consumption of the more than adequate meal, the Twelve were disseminated to their various operational command centers, after first making contact with the leaders of the white supremacy groups assigned to each.

That same night Michael Blacker, accompanied by Daniel Thurman, Brendon Chapman, and Richard Dobbs—three of the Twelve—

met at the headquarters of the 7th Division Unit of the Movement for a White Aryan Nation, a fully-decked paramilitary squad of right-wing, supposedly Christian, extremists, on the preorganized mission to destroy the Vodoun temple.

They arrived at 2 AM and set sufficient remote-detonation plastic explosives under or around each of the dwellings, to create maximum destruction.

The group cleared the area and one of the cars drove off, putting several miles between its occupants and the property, before making a call from a public phone, warning residents at the Vodoun site that they had ten minutes to evacuate.

From the vantage of a ridge on the perimeter of the adjacent state forest the unit watched as lights blazed in the housing compound and cars took off at high speed. People could be seen though, dressed in ritual white, heading unhurriedly toward the hounfor.

Twelve minutes elapsed. Ron Enger, his face blackened with camouflage paint, looked toward Michael.

"How long do you wanna wait?" he asked softly.

"Fuck it," Michael replied, bored already.

Ron signaled to the two men in charge of detonation.

In grotesque syncopation the buildings and homes blew apart, igniting gas supplies and flammable materials, and sending blasts of skyrocket fire in all directions. The fourteen men of the 7th Division Unit whooped and cheered at the sight but were rendered rapturous as the main temple exploded in a fireball and the bodies of some of those who had chosen to stay were catapulted across the compound like blazing satellites.

"It begins," Michael whispered dramatically to the three men crouched beside him on the damp, rocky outcrop.

"Praise the Lord," whooped Ron, riding the thrill for all it was worth.

Whatever, thought Michael to himself.

He returned to his own hotel before dawn, sleeping fitfully until just before noon. He phoned into headquarters to ascertain that everything was on track for the second night, then settled down to watch the news broadcasts on the television just to be sure that the impact of last night was given its due.

He turned it off with a satisfied grunt and spent the rest of the afternoon writing up his sermon for the following night.

IT WAS LATE AFTERNOON WHEN finally he stood and stretched, his discourse completed. He wandered into the bathroom and splashed cold water onto his face, looking into the mirror above the basin and running his fingers through his hair.

He'd been told by more than one woman, usually the ones that he paid for, that he reminded them of some kind of graceful animal. He was very lean and tall, with dark brown hair, pale skin, and eyes of a decided baby-blue. He had schooled himself to what attracted others, and his cultured, well-groomed appearance was the result of many years of calculated strategy. Most people considered him utterly charming.

HE WANDERED BACK INTO THE sitting room of his suite and over to the window to take in the sunset panorama of the parklands and the city.

A crowd was milling just off the joggers track that ran beside the river. He was curious as to what had drawn their attention.

As several people moved away he saw what had so intrigued them.

There was a huge circle of—what were they? Crows or ravens? Who the hell knew the difference? They were holding some kind of council on the grass. There must have been hundreds of them, and the trees nearby were full of them.

Michael's neck tingled as he observed the phenomenon. En masse they seemed to turn and look toward the hotel. Michael pulled the drapes shut, closing out the weirdness.

It was nothing. Still . . . the thing had unnerved him for a moment, and he couldn't work out why. He was tired. He needed a drink.

Chapter Six

The Wild Card—

Vincent Tanaka was born November 29, 1969. His mother, Mariani Bizango, was known as La Prophétess. She'd raised Vincent with a full understanding of the ways of her ancestors, but also to have his own mind—to have a deep reverence for whatever became his understanding of the sacred.

His father, Fujiko Tanaka, an ethnobotanist, was born in Hawaii in 1942, a third-generation Japanese-American, and he'd grown up pulled between two cultures—the Japanese heritage of Shinto and the Bushido art of the sword, and the Westernized culture of post-war America. He'd introduced his son to the martial arts at the age of five and had trained with him whenever his workload allowed until Vincent left home to attend the university.

Fujiko Tanaka had been commissioned by the United States government in 1965 to research rare plants in Haiti. While living on the island, Fujiko met and fell in love with Mariani. He'd married her, without the permission of his family, while still living in Port au Prince. They'd subsequently moved to the United States, but had received a cold reception—the now common interracial marriages being still taboo at that time.

The couple emigrated in 1968 and, due to Fujiko's credentials, were unequivocally welcomed by the academic community in New Rathmore. Fujiko was employed by a rapidly expanding medical research institute, and Mariani had presented herself to the nearest university anthropology department. She was given a post as a guest lecturer on the culture and religion of Haiti (this being a rare opportunity for students to learn directly from a traditional practitioner) while, at the same time, establishing the country's first hounfor, in which devotees could serve the Loa, and the traditions of the Vodoun religion could be practiced and understood.

Vincent was their only child.

MARIANI AND FUJIKO SEPARATED NOT long after Vincent left home to study. It was an amicable separation as Fujiko had, for many years, been returned to the field to research possible sources of medicinals deep in the Amazon rainforest, while Mariani had incurred increasing spiritual responsibilities that kept her constantly occupied. After the separation she left the city, leaving the established hounfor in the hands of those she had trained. She had moved to the northeast coast, where the climate was tropical and the ocean was close to her current temple-home.

Vincent studied law, but dropped out of university before completing his degree. He had been brought up to be a very free thinker, and he became more and more disenchanted with the way the world worked, with a justice system that seemed doomed to serve only the wealthy, and with a morality of greed that was causing ceaseless destruction of natural environments.

He had a deep reverence for all life, gained through his understanding of both Shinto and Vodoun, and he'd set out to learn about as many variations of the sacred as he could explore. The more he learned, the more attuned he became to the *kami*—the Loa— with whom he shared his world.

He had been a perennial wanderer for several years. He traveled in a fully outfitted van (a gift from his father), and although he had never left the country of his birth he sensed the whole earth. He had not had many girlfriends—his introverted nature, his restlessness, and the call of something he sought not to name causing him to seem somewhat aloof—although no one had stayed around him long enough to realize what he was really like.

Recently, however, he had spent time in one area: inland from where his mother lived.

VINCENT HAD HIS CAMP ON a ridge just beyond the hiss (in the wet season—the roar) of a waterfall that ribboned 300 feet into a pool at a place called Violation Gully.

At the forested edge of the only natural clearing near his camp he had constructed a small stone shrine and erected a Torii made from slabs of discarded wood that he discovered at the site of a house demolition. He'd brought them to the camp, sanded and oiled them, and erected them in the traditional way of his father's ancestors as a gift of honor to the kami of the area. He trained for two hours every day, firstly with katana and wakazashi and then with the staff. The practice calmed his mind and honed his reflexes—each move requiring tranquillity in accord with perfection—mushin.

His thinking place was a flat rock that jutted out over the pool, where he could feel the mist from the falls like a blessing on his naked body. He played the sacred Batá there at dawn, a ritual to the day in honor of the Mysterè, and the mournful, mystical chacuhachi at dusk, to the kami of the night.

Vincent was 5'7" tall. His skin was a deep coffee-bronze, both from suntan and because of the mixed blood of his heritage. His head was customarily shaven, the rest of his body all but hairless. His slight build was an illusion, masking the strength, stamina, and agility of both his body and his mind. In public he liked to hide his shape in baggy T-shirts and black fisherman's pants, and he usually covered his head with a cap. He avoided people's eyes in the street and, as a result, hardly anyone noticed him except in passing.

Only during the rituals performed at the peristyle of Mariani's hounfor would he, a devoted member of the Societé, allow himself to lose his dislike for crowds in his passion for the music and the dance.

VINCENT WAS VISITING HIS MOTHER'S place, helping her and Francis and Danielle Corrin build the five-foot high dry-stone wall running along the path from the small public parking area to the hounfor. It was meant to meander. Small alcoves featuring tropical native plants, wooden benches, shrines, and statuary were scattered along the path, giving the whole a *journey* feel. Many visitors, from students and academics to mystics and indigenous guests, both local and international, came here seeking to understand the religion and its practices, and to meet and interact with the initiates.

Mariani's houngan was Harvey Dessallier, whom she had helped to gain admission into the country. He was a brilliant young photographer whose work depicting the many faces of Vodoun had taken him from Haiti to Havana, and from Havana to New Orleans, where his work was seen by a New York art dealer who had secured him an exhibition in her home city. It was a knockout opening, and the reviews guaranteed Harvey a three-month run, during which time he made extremely large sums of money and sold his story to one of the most prestigious London magazines.

The money for the article had funded the journey of the rainbow road that most Haitians only ever dreamed of taking—to the west coast of Africa. The ensuing exhibition—shown in London, Paris, and, subsequently, Port au Prince, at Harvey's own expense—linked his people's present history to their ancestral past.

Mariani had kept strong ties with her relatives in Haiti, and Harvey had contacted her three years earlier, when he had traveled with the Peace Train (a group of indigenous representatives from many lands), taking photographs for a future compilation. He had fallen in love with the easy-going culture and had requested Mariani to go guarantor for him. His residency was granted easily due to his fame and, of course, his money.

He now took over a lion's share of the administrative responsibilities of the hounfor, giving Mariani more time to devote to teaching new pupils, while still being sufficiently unburdened as to allow time for his photography to continue.

HARVEY TOOK THE CALL ABOUT the bombing. In a state of half-shock he took in all the details that the hounsi in New Rathmore provided, including all information that the police had acquired to-date, which apparently was not much as the perpetrators had covered their tracks with professional alacrity.

That it had all the hallmarks of a hate-crime seemed beyond question, however, especially considering that another series of blasts had destroyed the home of a well-known witch on the affluent northern beaches foreshores on the same night, using similar explosives. The authorities were looking into the current whereabouts of several hundred known antagonists.

At the Teagan Grove community, eleven people had chosen not to heed the phone call warning them of the impending attack and had, instead, gone to the peristyle in defiance. Six were dead and three were in intensive care, having received severe burns. Amazingly, two initiates were thrown clear, with one suffering only a broken wrist, and both were still hospitalized for shock and severe lacerations.

Harvey hung up the receiver slowly. He had taken note of everything that he had been told. He walked calmly out into the early afternoon sunshine and along the freshly created wall with the notepad of information held before him like an offering.

Mariani saw him first and was about to ask if he'd come to call a tea-break when she saw the look on his face. She dropped the shovel that she'd been using to turn a small patch of ground in preparation for planting and ran to him just as Vincent and the others noticed and realized there was trouble. Harvey placed his notes in the Mambo's hands and began to cry.

Mariani and Vincent booked the 4:15 flight to New Rathmore, which arrived in just over an hour. They were met at the airport and driven to Sandon, a quiet, leafy suburb on the edge of the city where several of the Societé were being housed by close family members.

Chapter Seven

The Sídhe—

The Southside still reflected the glory days. Narrow cobbled streets and alleyways wound in and around the docks where the rum carts once plied their trade directly off the riggers. It was a maze.

Willie sat alone atop a wide concrete plinth recently erected to support one of the pylons of the MacLean Street Bridge—one of the oldest, still operative bridges in the city, built entirely of convict brick: small, red-mottled numbers scored with the marks of their makers in a bid for creative immortality.

He remembered the voyage here, during the Troubles. He recalled when he and Rory and Brighid, along with hundreds of others, had been manacled and herded below decks, where they were bunked five to a bench, and allowed on deck only intermittently; where rats the size of cats harried the living and mutilated the dead; and where scurvy, dysentery, and typhoid all claimed their victims. The journey had taken months, with the transport stopping at Gibraltar, somewhere in the West Indies, South America, and the Cape of Good Hope, dropping off prisoners, doomed to slave-like labor, at most of these destinations.

He and Rory and Brighid had been on their way to the Great Summer Gathering of the Tuatha Dé Danann at Teamhair, their old stomping ground. They'd traveled all the way from Sligo in Connachta when they'd got caught up in the skelter. The Crown had laid down strict curfew laws disallowing the people to be out of doors between sunset and sunrise.

The village where they'd intended to spend the night was in flames on the horizon. They'd raced toward the place and had nearly tripped over the crowd. The townsfolk were all hiding behind the hedges. Many had been severely hurt and some were dying, and all of them were terrified. There was a lot of praying going on with the *Hail Mary, full of Grace's* being mumbled constantly.

Willie had grabbed one lad by the arm and asked what had happened, and the boy had told him the king's men had come riding into town just after dark and had started torching the whole bloody place. A few of the older lads had done a theft in Dublin and had picked up some weapons. They'd started in on the riders. Two of the troopers had been shot before the lads took off. No, we don't know where they went. No, we don't know if they're White boys.

Brighid had started right in working her gift on the dying. "We can't stay," Willie told her.

"Shut up and see about getting them moving," she'd hissed. "They can't stay here—they'll be found."

He and Rory were organizing the people to move when down rode a couple of hundred coppers, or king's men—they didn't know which—all armed and ready for the kill. In the end there wasn't anything to be done, and the three of them got caught up in the net.

They'd been manacled and set to walking in a convoy all the way to Dublin, where they were shunted off to Kilmainham for several weeks. The prison had compounds set up for containment, and the authorities took all the people's names and details and the like, and, Willie had supposed, they got condemned and sentenced to something, not that there were any trials. *I don't think*, he recalled, *that justice had ever had anything to do with any of it, at least as far back as that stupid bastard Dermot MacMurrough, who'd sold us all out around seven hundred years before by giving the English the bleedin' front door key to the country.*

Everybody had been crowded in together. Only the magic that the Sídhe could work under the circumstances—and that was just a wee bit—kept the three of them from being separated.

They were sent from Kilmainham Gaol to Cork, where they were herded onto the ship, the *Brampton*, along with a couple of hundred others up for transportation. She set sail early in November of 1822.

Needless to tell, Willie's people weren't ever meant to cross the water at all, but like it or not, the Folk had been going here and there all over the bloody place—to Canada and Argentina, America and the Caribbean, along with other immigrants and convicted transportees, for at least a couple of hundred years, taking the little mysteries and their magic with them wherever they went.

He and Brighid and Rory managed to stay as close as they could through the first years in a harsh, god-forsaken country (which it was then) even after they'd been granted their freedom tickets.

Then they'd started on the traveling.

Over time they met up with the others—it always seemed like they could smell each other out from a hundred miles away—until they'd formed the core of their particular clan that was still together. Only Rory ended up leaving and going back to Eire, and even though most of the Folk have said they'd do the same some day, it seems their business is here for however long the Blessed Ones see fit.

Hunter found Willie and Brighid first. He was the living magic of the homeland that this land embraced.

They'd found Black Annis and Trevor, and then Matt and Raven, and then they'd picked up a few of the Lost along the way. Hunter met a beautiful woman whose born-name escaped them all but who was recognized straight off as a powerful fey, and as much of a changeling as could be found among the mortals. Hunter, it was, who originally introduced her to the clan and told them her name was Puck. He always said it was the world's wildest trick to sneak her up on him like it did.

The two of them were the only merging of Sídhe and the people known to not only have conceived, but given birth to a living child—

they named him Robin—in fact the only other situation in a thousand years was Jack, who was with them now too. Both he and Puck took the dreaming of the Quicken Brew and made it through to live the magic all the way into forever.

Along the road they picked up Rowan and Gypsy and Alan. All Lost. All of them shining with what was left of the legacy of the Fáidh.

THEY'D ARRIVED BACK IN THE city the day before yesterday and had set up home down in the abandoned part of the underground rail that they'd always used whenever they came through.

Once they were all warm and snug, Rowan and Annis and Willie took off to Mary Flannery's to see about getting a few gigs. Tom Doddy, who runs the place nowadays, was so pleased to see them, remembering the crowds they'd pulled, that he shouted them a meal and a couple of pints as well as set them up for Thursday night—tonight—for their first gig, and then the Monday, Thursday, and Friday line-ups for next week if they were staying that long.

"Sure to be," they'd assured him.

Yesterday, apart from getting well stocked up with fuel against the cold, a good supply of food, and other things they figured they'd need, Hunter, along with a few of the others, had driven the bus to a pay-by-the-week garage that would keep it out of harm's way until they took off again.

THE WIND OFF THE WATER was bitterly cold, but it was beautiful where the last of the river idled shallow and dark into the sea. The day was all sun and shadow with bit-like cloud, very high, causing an almost strobe-like effect on the water, even through the tarnish of the city's perennial haze.

Willie stood and stomped his feet to get the blood moving and leaped down onto the straggly grass verge. He climbed the almost vertical incline onto the causeway that led beneath the bridge alongside the river, and started the long walk toward home. He was sad to see the garbage of so many people's lives littering the edges of the walkway. Lots of people who had nowhere safe to be and kids who were new to the streets came down here to hang out. There was evidence that people came here to do a fix or to drink goon where the cops weren't likely to harass them easily because they couldn't get the wagons down the steep decline. He passed old supermarket carts, plastic and more plastic, beer bottles, and the ever-present take-away containers. Sad. It all seemed so careless. It was all headed for the river sooner or later. As long as Willie had been coming here it had been like this. He'd twice done a major rubbish haul-out, but what was the point? It would all be back again within a week.

He sniffed with disgust. It had been okay nearer to the water. His greatest sense was olfactory. Others of the Fair Folk had hearing or sight or touch gifts. Most of the time he loved smells, but not now. Up here he wore the full insanity of the city, and his gift was more like a curse and he yearned to be back on the road to open places where the spirits of the land wafted their pleasure to people like him.

The small magics that were always around each of the Folk hovered right in close to Willie as he walked, all too aware of the desolation of their contemporaries struggling to survive amid a plunder of concrete and glass and cold, cold steel, and the constant day that smog and electricity caused that never allowed the night to show off its glory.

He skipped up off the causeway and onto the street. He walked all the way past where the ferries ply the harbor and down to the end where Bank Street turns onto Wharf Road. The arteries leading off Wharf were like a maze of rabbit warrens—narrow cobbled lanes and alleyways that could disorient anyone who didn't frequent the area regularly. Willie took turn after turn, his senses drawing him inevitably closer to the old section of City Rail that had become obsolete twenty years before, except for the moving of the huge containers unloaded from the ships and shuttled down along the docks

where all the warehouses were. His shortcut took him onto Copperhead Lane, right past Dimity's.

He'd started thinking about Merrin, not realizing that she was
out back of the shop with Kathryn. He thought about going to visit
her but worried that he'd interfere in whatever was currently happening for her. She was one of the Lost and she'd traveled with them
awhile, but the circumstances surrounding the deaths of the
O'Neills that summer had put an abrupt halt to wherever their relationship had been heading. It had certainly put a stop to any more
Quickenings.

The whole phenomenon of just how many of the fey people,
called the Lost by the Sídhe, were either being born or were just waking up had given the Folk great hope for the future of the world, and
for the magic that was currently hanging on for its life where it had
once flourished as the lands had flourished.

It had been driven mostly into the secret places though, for at
least a millennium, just to survive.

Not only were the people waking up, but they were also putting
out signals and shine, remembering the old ways and making it so
much easier for the Folk to find them, so much easier to love them.

Merrin had been the first woman in a couple of hundred years
who had floored Willie with her intuition and her humor and all. He
thought he might even love her. He'd talked at length to the others
about letting her stay even despite the ttroubles, but it had been an
all-round no, except for him. How bad was the timing?

THAT HAD BEEN SUCH BAD shite. The hunt for the killer or killers that
Hunter had initiated just after the Autumn Equinox had yielded
nothing so far except to lead them here. The police had found very
little that would incriminate anyone, and when Robert and Shauna,
the last of the royal O'Neill line, had mentioned Owen, whose body
wasn't identified within the ruins of the aftermath of the fire, they'd
said they'd look into it, but there was no knowing if he'd been con-

nected to it, and did they know if he'd been there or away somewhere at the time? No, they hadn't known for sure.

Robert and Shauna O'Neill had taken the Quicken brew, understanding the danger to people of their age, but they hadn't made it.
They'd covered their tracks, in case death had been the result of their
desperation, by letting friends believe they were going to Ireland for
a long overdue visit and they didn't know when they'd be back,
which was understandable under the tragic circumstances, and
they'd left the caretaking of the farm in Puck's official name, so
there was no one for the police to inform if there had been a breakthrough.

It had been left for the Folk to seek their own justice.

There were eight clans of Tuatha Dé in this country alone, each of
them known by a totem from the ancient homeland. Five of them,
numbering in all seventy-three people, were ranged around the city
now, forming a kind of psychic dragnet.

Three of the clans were warrior clans—Clan Broc, named for the
Badger, Clan Mac Tíre, for Wolf, and Willie's clan, Fiach Dubh, the
Raven clan. The other two clans involved in the net both had the
Sight in one way or another. They were Clan Dobharchú and Clan
Ulchabhán, named for Otter and Owl.

Aw, fuckit, Willie thought, turning around and backtracking the
way he'd come. He had a chance to be with her—he knew he did. He
knew she'd really liked him—what were the odds that maybe she'd
still remember him and not be with some other guy right now?

He grinned as he walked. Odds were always even, weren't they?
Just depended on whether you thought about the immediate picture
or the grand plan. *Luck o' the Irish*, he whispered under his breath as
he turned the corner of Bank Street, into Napier Lane, and up to the
boarded-up shop front that hid Merrin's place.

He slipped the latch on the rickety gate that opened onto a narrow
walkway between two buildings and that led to the small patch of
space that Merrin had transformed from a concrete nothing to a
courtyard, with hundreds of potted flowers and herbs, and with two

old washtubs, painted red, that were filled with spring vegetable seedlings. She'd rummaged up an assortment of benches, bits of lace-like wrought-iron salvaged from abandoned turn-of-the-twentieth-century houses left to rot after the suburbs became popular, and other sculpture-like oddments that she'd either vamped up with paint or left to the lichen. It was like a riotous Zen.

Her studio had once been the stock-house for the shop. She'd told Willie that it had been really *dero* when she'd originally come to stay. She'd heard about it from the guy who'd been squatting there who'd offered her a night or two's refuge from the street not long after she'd left home. He'd been really old and sick and had disappeared just a few days into her stay and had never come back. She could guess what had happened.

No one had ever come around about rent or anything, and unless the developers took it into their heads that the area was maybe about to turn a profit, which was like so absolutely doubtful, it was hers.

Willie could sense that she wasn't home just by the stillness in the air. He wrote a quickly scrawled note saying, *Hi, it's Willie, the guy from the bus. The good lookin' one*, and then he wrote that he was in town and that he'd maybe see her at Flannery's if she felt like catching their gig.

Then he screwed the note into a little ball and stuffed it into the pocket of his jacket because he knew the rules: *Don't interfere unless you're invited*, and the only way that ever happened was a look in the eye from the person, face-to-face.

Willie sighed and started back the way he'd come.

"Ark, ark." Two fluff-feathered youngsters were perched on the fence of the little track between the two buildings. One cocked its head quizzically and fearlessly, catching Willie's gaze with its one white eye.

"Yeah. Fark-awl . . . I hear ya," he said as he passed them.

He wandered back through the labyrinth of lanes and alleyways and arrived at the big, rusted industrial door that led down into the now-defunct and derelict Bank Street Station. It appeared to be securely locked, but that was just a glamour that the Folk had laid. Willie put his weight to the bar and slid the door open just enough for him to squeeze through before he rammed it home behind him. He was in a black so absolute it had weight. He reached into his pocket for his flashlight and headed down.

He could hear the sweet, sweet strains of the distant rehearsal even from here. *Damn, those acoustics are good*, he thought. He played with the beam of the flashlight as he descended the four flights, taking in the ridiculously boring gray-green paint flaking from the walls, that had once been standard State Rail issue, and the little ceramic tiles that had mostly fallen onto the cement stairs, causing his boots to crunch with each step.

He came out onto the cavernous platform that still held the distinctive smell that all train stations have, and walked across to the edge where he jumped easily down onto the tracks and followed them into the maw of the tunnel, picking his footing carefully through the fallen-in façade that littered the ground with lumpy rubble. A few yards up ahead of him he saw the flickering glow of unseen candles, kerosene lanterns, and a healthy fire that warmed out from a wide, square entrance onto the service bay. The music was actually softer here than it was at a distance, and he could hear the easy fangle of an accordion offset by both the bodhrans and Puck's guitar. He smiled as he navigated the remainder of the distance, thinking how much better they sounded with his fiddle to inspire them.

Chapter Eight

Vincent had anticipated that he would be horrified. That's not what had happened. He felt something, for sure, but the sensation was more like distraction.

He'd gone with his mother and the others. The burned and gutted buildings were still smoking, and there was a strong police presence. Detective Inspector Greg Reilly was expecting them. He was heading the investigation, and he approached the members of the Societé as they worked their way across barricades and toward the center of the compound. Vincent stood to his mother's side as the inspector talked to the gathering, informing them of updates and asking questions that could aid the department in its findings. There was a team poring over the place and everyone that spoke to the company was generally very sympathetic, but there was something wrong with Vincent's ears and everything that was being said was kind of muffled and meaningless.

He made what he hoped were appropriate gestures and feigned an interest that he just didn't feel. It may have been, he thought to himself, that the dead and the injured were no longer there, but he thought he would have felt at least some of the residue of the night of violence as he'd always been extremely, sometimes uncomfortably, aware of the ghost-like emotions that tended to linger after any significant event.

There was something else.

He stayed with the others until they became deeply absorbed in a discussion with the inspector that didn't seem to require his participation, and then he wandered off to be alone.

He passed the mess. Oh, the mess! But he continued walking until he'd wandered far enough into the surrounding forest to no longer see or hear the people.

He sat down on a high rock and entered into a state of mushin. It seemed that he could hear other voices, although there was no one near. He attempted to concentrate, but he couldn't work out what they were saying, and that frustrated him because he had the overwhelming sensation that he was meant to be a part of the conversation. He listened harder. He could hear music—a kind of foot-tapping rhythm completely out-of-place with either the surroundings or the drama into which he'd been thrust.

A man was speaking with a soft, deep voice in an accent that he could not place until he realized that another language was spoken.

Vincent let himself drift—the state of mushin distracting him from attachment to the experience, and the voices were right beside him. This was too weird, but he stayed with it.

"WHO THE FUCK ARE YOU?" The challenge startled Vincent with its clarity, and he opened his eyes to find himself somewhere else.

He was on a bare mattress in a firelit cavern that, at first glance, appeared man-made. Then he fainted.

HUNTER AND BRIGHID AND THE others stood staring with astonishment at the collapsed figure that had simply materialized in the room.

Vincent recovered in a few moments, opening his eyes to a ring of faces.

"What the . . ." was all he could manage.

"Welcome to just another bloody reality," said a small, fortyish-something woman with a multitude of dark braids, tattoos on her face, and eyes as pale as clear water. She was obviously less intimidated by the manifestation of this compact, dark-skinned, slightly Oriental drop-in than the others. Hunter laughed throatily, but everyone else just looked confused.

Vincent sat up.

"Why?" was his first question, as he rubbed his face and head briskly with both hands.

"Would you like a cup of tea?" asked Puck.

"Ah . . . sure. Thanks," he replied.

He looked around himself. He was in a large concrete room filled with an odd collection of very ratty furniture, including several mattresses, indicating that it was most likely that many (if not all) of the present company actually slept there, with some curtaining to provide privacy to whoever, and the cooking setup of a camp.

Hunter helped Vincent to his feet. As he touched the young man he experienced a slight electrical jag that ran into his hand and up over his wrist. *Curious*, he thought, not knowing what they'd got here.

He led him over to one of the couches where everyone was congregating. The infirm sensation that Vincent had initially felt was rapidly withdrawing, and he felt his chi flow more strongly with every pulse. By the time he sat down he was alert and intensely focused on everything around him, and highly charged, as though the air here was cleaner and clearer than anything possible in this day and age.

Hunter went through the formality of introductions.

"And you are . . . ?" he finally asked.

"Vincent. Can anybody explain what just happened 'cause I haven't got a clue."

Hunter sat forward, his arms folded on his knees, his waist-length dredlocks, all littered with small black feathers, falling over his shoulders, the tattoos on his cheeks and forehead and chin only barely discernable against the darkness of his skin. Vincent was aware that the big man was not trying to intimidate him by this closeness, and his very strangeness seemed inexplicably comforting.

Hunter studied the unexpected visitor. He had the same shine about him that the Lost exhibited, but he wasn't one of them. He was like no one that Hunter had ever met—some kind of random warp in the weft of the loom—and he exuded a rich, powerful scent, vital and keen, like a cross between cedar and highland stone. Hunter was convinced that this was no mistake. Their guest had magics all around him, both familiar and exotic.

The fire in the converted forty-four-gallon drum crackled as the burning wood settled, sending a small fountain of sparks into the quiet air.

Brighid and Puck came around from the kitchen area bearing a tray of steaming mugs of tea and a large platter of dark bread and creamy cheese. They deposited them on the slabs of wood resting on several plastic milk-crates that served as a coffee table between the assortment of chairs and couches. Brighid sat down beside Vincent, close enough to have made anyone else uncomfortable, but he just looked at her and grinned—he liked what her face said to him. Puck curled up on a couch with a small boy of about three or four years old who had been introduced to him as Robin. The others were quiet.

"I get the feeling you're a Sending," said Hunter at last.

"Agreed," Brighid responded with no hesitation. A few *mmms,* and *that-seems-rights,* were mumbled by the others.

Vincent ignored them, looking directly at Hunter, who had the blackest, most fathomless, animal eyes that he had ever encountered, refusing to be distracted.

"And that is . . . ?"

"Can I ask you to tell us about yourself first? I know it might seem pushy but it's important, to be sure. This kind of thing—you popping in like you did—well, it's not a thing that happens on a regular basis, you know." Vincent saw the twinkle in the eyes that informed him that Hunter could see a funny side to this that he couldn't yet recognize. Oh well.

"You first," he said.

"No," replied Hunter.

Vincent pulled back from the challenge. He picked up a mug of tea and sniffed it. Brighid burst out laughing, and this time the smile actually reached Hunter's mouth. The realization of what this whole setup must look like to anyone unfamiliar with the way of the Travelers struck them all.

Vincent turned to Brighid, a pained look on his face. "It's okay," she soothed. "Willie smells his food too, don't you Willie?" which only sent her off into more laughter. He couldn't help but smile.

The seriousness returned to his face. "There's magic in this place," he said.

"I know," she began, "so tell . . ."

So he did.

They asked him to explain when he spoke of unfamiliar things. They asked unexpected questions intermittently—not so much about him as the way he saw things, what inspired him, why he chose to be so much alone, his relationship with what he explained as kami.

When he'd told them as much as he could he wasn't at all empty—which was what usually occurred when he spoke more than half a dozen sentences. He realized it was because they'd kept asking questions that mattered, but hadn't once pried.

"Now your turn," he said, folding his legs under himself, feeling very comfortable among them.

"We're fuckin' fairies!" piped Willie, and everybody groaned. The strange, bird-like girl who'd been introduced as Black Annis pulled her thick green sweater over head and proceeded with a full-scale woolen assault. Willie feigned terror and rolled off the chair onto the floor, squealing, "No! No! Don't hurt me Annis, no! No!" Annis promptly leaped onto him, growling, and rubbing the sweaty old jumper into his face. The small boy named Robin took the opportunity to join what appeared to be a great game.

Hunter sighed and returned his attention to Vincent. "We don't use the 'f' word," he said patiently.

"What . . . ?"

BRIGHID TOOK ONE OF VINCENT'S hands and began to explain. By the time she had finished the telling of it all, both the child and his mother were sound asleep, curled up on one of the sofas, the drum had been refueled twice, and everyone except Hunter, Brighid, and the Rowan were busy doing something else.

Vincent sat quietly. He took it all in. He believed everything she told him.

"That's why we think that you're a Sending," said Hunter.

"That's the only thing I still don't get," replied Vincent.

Hunter's voice was very deep but surprisingly soft for such a big man, and Vincent found that he had to constantly lean forward slightly to be able to hear him.

Hunter told him about the Lady, and about the Travelers' sacred connection to the land, and about the killings of the last of the line of the O'Neill family—the descendants of one of the families of ancient high kings and self-designated guardians of one of the gathering places—and he wondered if it had anything to do with Vincent's sudden appearance because that was the only thing he could make out of all this.

Vincent explained why he had come to the city, an unnerving sixth sense informing him that there was no such thing as a coincidence.

Hunter must have heard him thinking because he stood and stretched, saying, "My conclusion also."

"Will you stay with us until this thing pans out?" asked Brighid.

"Look . . . I have to think about this first. It's not that this isn't the most amazing thing that's ever happened to me because it is. But I hate the city—I hate the city big-time."

"Your choice."

"No, I somehow don't think it is," Vincent looked at Hunter, who merely smiled.

"I've got to contact Mariani though. She'll be really freaked what with me just wandering off and being gone—she's good, but I don't think that even La Prophétess would figure on this one thing—how long, by the way? Do any of you know what time it is down here anyway?"

"It's around three," said the Rowan.

"What? Morning or afternoon?"

"Afternoon."

"Okay. I gotta go. How do I get out of here?"

"I'll take you," Rowan offered. "I used to live here before I joined the Folk."

Black Annis was the Rowan's girlfriend, and she insisted on joining them. Once up on the street they took Vincent to the nearest phone booth, where he dialed his mother's cell phone and assured her he was all right and that he was on his way there now.

"We're still at the hounfor," she informed him, "waiting for you to come back from wherever you disappeared to."

"You wouldn't believe me if I told you," said Vincent.

"Don't bet on it," Mariani replied.

They took the ferry to Morton Cove, then the bus the rest of the way. They arrived at the scene just before 4 PM. Mariani eyed the two who arrived with her son, noting the clean-cut, clean-shaven appearance of the man, who was dressed casually in a dark blue sweatshirt and jeans and who had his arm draped around the shoulders of a ragged girl in army surplus khakis with steel-capped, lace-up boots and short hair dyed the colors of a parrot, with several elastic bands tying it into little tufts all over her head, and looking like butter wouldn't melt in her mouth. Mariani sensed something about the two strangers that she couldn't quite recognize. *Mysteré,* she thought to herself.

Vincent introduced her. She shook hands with them both and felt a warmth and a friendliness that quite took her breath away. She grinned at the parrot girl, who grinned back, slightly raising one eyebrow at the shine that surrounded the woman.

Annis turned to Vincent. "We can't stay. We got a gig on tonight."

"Where?" asked Vincent.

Rowan gave directions to Flannery's. "Can you make it later?"

"I'll try," he assured them.

Mariani looked at him and wondered for a moment how he could possibly consider going to a pub with these obvious strangers and determined to discover what was going on, but then she realized that Vincent did nothing without good reason and without free choice.

The other two left. Vincent turned to his mother. "Hey, Maman."

"I trust you, Vincent," she said. "Some time you tell me, okay?"

He looped his arm through hers and they joined the others, who were heading toward the cars for the trip back to the house where they were staying.

There was so much that had to be done, from funeral arrangements and ceremonies, to organizing temporary shelter for the members of the Societé who had had their homes destroyed, to dealing with the cops and the insurance company and organizing the cleanup and rebuilding of the premises. They'd already agreed that no one would drive them away.

In the small room he'd been given at the back of the house, Vincent put his few essentials into his backpack and replaced his daisho in their heavy, black silk carrying case. He walked through to the large, warm kitchen, where the people were working on laptops and telephones, and among themselves with notebooks and lots of coffee and talk. He kissed his mother on both cheeks.

"Will you keep in touch?" she asked.

"I don't know what's going to happen."

"I'll know anyway." She smiled, patting his hands, which rested on her shoulders. "*Se byen?*"

"*Se byen,*" he assured.

He gave her shoulders a brief massage and a final squeeze before readjusting his gear on his back. All eyes were on him as he walked through the screen door and onto the back porch, closing the door quietly behind himself.

No one in the house asked Mariani what was going on—there was too much else to attend to without wondering what the wild boy was getting himself into.

Chapter Nine

The Otherworld—

Hunter was disturbed. He took himself away from the others, deep, deep into the darkness of the tunnel.

He leaned his back against the wall and closed his eyes. He seemed asleep but he wasn't—he was gone.

The world into which Hunter stepped was night. He ran in the body of a large gray wolf, his amber eyes adjusting to the intense darkness. He moved easily and soundlessly between huge trees. He leaped gnarled and ancient roots and forced his way through the thick bracken and underbrush of the densely forested mountainside.

He broke cover and padded along the very edge of the high escarpment that looked down into a gorge some five hundred or so feet below. Around him moved silent shadows—some were aware of his passing for this was their natural home, and Hunter was the one among the many—but others, flitting in and out between the worlds, had no idea of where it was that they had come or just what the huge wolf represented.

On the highest point of the cliffside a finger of rock jutted out above the abyss, seeming suspended by nothing, crowned by a single monolithic standing stone. It was to this that Hunter loped and sat, tongue lolling from the corner of his mouth, waiting.

The shape of a woman moved from the darkness of the stone's shadow, a cloak of moths surrounding her insubstantiability. She moved across to Hunter and took his head between both hands, her fingers melting deeply into the thick fur ruff, crouching as she did so.

"Hunter," she acknowledged, with a voice like the rattle of wings.

I don't know what I'm looking for, he thought.

"Look for the Unseelie and a man who resembles both a Roman king and a Roman priest," she replied.

Can't you give me a name and a phone number? He asked.

The woman laughed. "He didn't give it to me." Irony. He should have known. "He's going to give himself away, and I know enough to know what music he hears, and it isn't yours, Hunter . . . and it could never be the music of the Unseelie Court, for he detests the very thought of it, just like he detests the ones who worship him."

Just tell me—is it Owen we seek? Is he responsible?

"There's no such person," she replied, "and it's a way of seeing the world that is our enemy."

Both na Dobharchú and nUlchabhán clans picked up a metallic taste to the air in the city that reeks of polluted magic.

"It's them all right. Have pity for the mysteries that have been so misused. The Unseelie knows well the ways to twist the pattern from a beauty to a scream, for he is putrid and the one who he has touched—mine—has many who love him for he lets them play with fire."

We will find them. Hunter had no doubt—he couldn't afford it.

"Just do not be found first." And the thick cloud of moths fluttered wildly around her, obscuring any semblance of familiarity. They flew off in all directions, into the night, in search of whatever moths seek. Another wolf howled from a long way off, and Hunter heard it. He was alone beside the stone.

Chapter Ten

The ravens were all there, in Kathryn's backyard, high up in the branches of the gnarly walnut tree that had only just begun to bud with the promise of spring. They were very quiet, very quiet.

Had their charge run away from home? Because something had been wrong with her when she had left that morning, that's for sure, and she had not yet returned. And couldn't they all just feel it?

It wasn't like she hadn't gone again and again, a hundred, hundred times before, but none of those times had this morning's feel when she had left the house and driven away. None of those times were today, and the smoke should be coming from the chimney. All knew it. And she was their collective responsibility.

Ruffled feathers and disturbed thoughts. The mid-afternoon shadows reached out across the demesne and no light flared, no chimney smoked.

As though a beast had begun to climb to take the weakest amongst them, or the children, the fiach took flight, spooked by the telepathed sensation, only the sentinels making any sound at all—calling a warning. As they settled they knew: She had to be found. Two of their finest warriors, Beatha and her beloved N'ar, chose to scout the way that she had gone.

They had traveled very far, becoming momentarily disoriented when they'd finally tracked her pattern to the city, because the place was a mess of sensations, an utterly unfamiliar assault.

They'd alighted in a park that bordered a river for just a wee spell before the hunt continued. The sentinels of the territory into which they'd flown had been aware of them the moment they had crossed the unseen border and had spread the word to the four directions, so that within minutes several dozen others had surrounded the pair, demanding to know their business. Beatha and N'ar duly told them.

The flurry and rattle of several hundred pairs of wings, along with a multitude of vital communications and conversations, erupted within the branches of every tree in proximity to the visiting warriors, while two hundred and forty-three representatives of the city's many tribes received invitations and winged their way from the four directions. This was common courtesy, but uncommon numbers.

The country ravens absorbed the gossip and told, and retold, the urgency of their journey, and it took until the arrival of the Copperhead Road enclave before a solution was confirmed.

"She with the Spirit-Girl," said M'ohra, one of the Copperhead fiach, "and she seemed to be miffedy and angsty when we were there."

"Who is Spirit-Girl then? Is we to worry her about be?" asked Beatha.

"Oh no! Oh no, she's cool. Within her blood the raven runs from the ancient-of-days, easy to see 'tis."

"Is safe she is with the Spirit-Girl we must understand?" N'ar asked this because he knew that Beatha would have done so and he had not yet spoken, which was a shameful thing.

"Is better, for her remembers, is," said M'ohra.

"Ah-h!" Many voices responded to this understanding.

"We got to get her back though." N'ar was anxious because he knew the city wasn't safe for people.

"Wait, wait," said T'arn, an inner-city Elder, deeply respected by all who knew of him, who held honorary status within an unprecedented five tribes. He was an intelligence carrier of the highest order—had been for many years—and possessed an uncanniness for recognizing danger. He commanded respect even with such a hushed demand.

"Can do nothing, anyways," said M'ohra, who was silenced with a look.

"Wait, wait! Is something wrong around here, feel it?"

Several humankind had stopped to watch the business undertaken by the council of huge ravens, but that always happened when the necessity for a gathering in a public place occurred. The collective mind of hundreds of birds linked to place the focus of the Elder's tension. It was not among the onlookers.

"Oh . . . sick is feeling," groaned T'arn. He turned his gaze upward. There! A face in a window, high up in the citadel across the road from the park. A tall man stood looking down at them from behind the glass, and yet still he sent out messages.

"Predator is?" asked Ana'harm, the huge warrior who guarded the western edge of the park's boundary, following the Elders' train of emotions.

"Is predator is!" T'arn hissed, wondering how one man could send so strongly from such a distance.

All turned in the predator's direction. He must have seen, for he pulled the eyes of the window closed and could no longer be seen.

He had been sensed, this threat to the living magic, for a very long time, but his face had not been tagged before. What had radiated from him though, as he'd watched from that high place, was just like the cold, cold farmer with his cold, cold shotgun, aimed and cocked a thousand-fold.

"But also," said M'ohra, once everyone had calmed down and the chatter had started again, "is the Travelers be here again so is all right also, yah?"

"Is not their time to be though," responded T'arn, shocked. The Travelers came only in winter. Everybody knew that.

"Is!" M'ohra and her companion Rorl exclaimed this simultaneously because both of them had seen the Willie-with-the-Red-Hair that very same day.

"Arl," said T'arn very slowly, understanding the implications of a much bigger pattern on the loom than merely this, and this, and this, all separate.

Go C'av'arn is a must, he decided to himself.

"Go C'av'arn with the news then," he announced.

Everyone n'a'arked their agreement with this wise outcome. C'av'arn was their Dreamer. No one knew how old she was—she'd always been there. She had the memory of what this city was before the humankind had come, and it was said she had the Sight so strong as to foresee what it would be when they had also gone from here. She held the legends of the ancient-of-days and told a story like no other Fiach Dubh known the length and breadth of the land. C'av'arn, the White-Eyes.

C'AV'ARN WAS ALSO THE QUEEN of the Bentley Fort High School, one of the most prestigious feeding-grounds on the upper northside.

The conspiracy of ravens that flew there late in the afternoon included the warriors from Kathryn's demesne. An envoy had already respectfully informed the Dreamer that T'arn and the others sought an audience, so she was preened (not that it mattered to her all that much at her age) and glossy when they arrived. The whole was told.

C'av'arn listened to them, and through all the worlds. By the time the enclaves had completed the telling she had traveled far and arranged the tapestry.

She spoke in the language of people mostly nowadays. She had long ago mostly forfeited the old tongue for the power of cross-species communication. The price she paid. So she spoke slowly, haltingly.

"The word I wish for you to ponder upon is 'carnage.'" She looked around the group to ascertain that they understood the meaning of the word, but the others were eerily silent.

"As of always has we been to guide the dying through that dance, though is not all we do, yah?" She glinted with ancient humor. There were clickings of laughter at the intimation of their many talents.

She became serious almost immediately. "So it seems it is to be here that this charge is laid upon us once again, and I never thought to see the day . . ."

She wandered off in her thoughts and memories, returning with a judgment. "The human world, or so it seems, hasn't changed according to need. Some insist on being stupid."

"Who is the man who is bad?" asked T'arn.

C'av'arn turned her ice-white eyes upon him. "Magic's bane." The sorrow in her voice was unmistakable.

"Is a part in 'carnage' we is?" asked Beatha humbly, not yet fully aware of the meaning of the term.

"Finally," the Dreamer replied cryptically.

"Sending back we will, with what we is to do for sure, say?" asked N'ar.

"The walnut tree is a hazel, when a hazel we have not," said C'av'arn.

"Ah-ha'a," rorled the many, understanding the symbolism and the sacredness of the hazel in all of the stories.

But, "Kathryn we must protect is said!" exclaimed N'ar, not fully understanding the implications to which the Dreamer alluded.

"No!" the Dreamer demanded, with a voice that none would dare to disobey. "Kathryn," *by what a silly name, when true name is a power*, she thought to herself, "must *Kathryn* protect! No one else! For if she cannot then she is no longer of any validity!"

Silence was the most disturbing sound that the ravens could make. They made it soundlessly, and all realized what the Dreamer meant. "The walnut tree must the walnut tree tribe protect, for there will come a gathering for sanctuary, and there, also, will the gathering be found . . . and *there* will we be what we are destined to be remembered as having been," she glared around the gathering, striking superstitious fear into the very young.

T'arn told them, "We is Remembers. Our Lady is our blood and bones, and we do Remember her when we need her to be *is*. Yah! Is so."

"Is so," agreed C'av'arn. "Walks-Between-the-Worlds is the Fury and the Frenzy," she paused as she remembered older battles. 'And Kathryn will call her because that is why we keep her safe. Her geas was set within her blood and she was moved . . . and she was sent to live among the Lost, *not* to make her weak, but so that she would surely know the strong when it was big enough *because* it is a new thing, precious all the more so.

"But others are also in the pattern. So much better then," she reassured the visitors.

"Like Willie-with-the-Red-Hair and the Dark Man and the others is? And is the Spirit-Girl, yah?" Beatha added knowingly.

"And us," agreed C'av'arn, liking very much this perky little country upstart. "And one who is not known about at all. The mysteries speak of him, and love him say, and say he is a power but a secret."

"Then is it home is it that we must go and say what?" asked N'ar.

"Home . . . for now," said the Dreamer compassionately. "Say what is known and watch the day. And protect the tree, yah?"

She stretched her glossy wings for all to see.

"And last I ask another thing," and she projected her voice to be sure that all would hear. "Is forty who must come to here and learn the things I know. And not tomorrow, but when it is decided."

"That is very little time," said T'arn, aware of how fixed and territorial the members of the tribes were like to be.

"Is enough. I want them *now!*" C'av'arn hissed, knowing it would happen, and that training up new Dreamers wasn't exactly the thing she thought she'd be doing at her age, but knowing certain outcomes that required this to be so. She turned to Beatha. "You is one for me?"

"I get to fight, is?" asked Beatha hopefully.

"Is, and more, you want it,"said the ancient queen.

"Yah, I stay, sure!" Beatha agreed, not realizing that her life would change forever as a result, but willing nonetheless.

Chapter Eleven

Martin didn't raise his voice, but the undertone of rage and disbelief when Kathryn told him she was doing something else caused her stomach to clench and her hands to shake.

He'd hissed on and on at her, calling her immature, fickle, a right bitch. That was after about fifteen minutes of explaining to her that she couldn't possibly mean it; what a joke, ha ha; that he expected her to behave herself after all the trouble people had gone to—catering had been arranged, gifts had been bought; was she premenstrual?

He asked where she was. She said, "I'm all right, doesn't matter where I am." He'd asked if she was at home or somewhere else, and she said she was at a café in the city. He'd said he'd send a taxi to pick her up, and she said, "You're not listening to me and no, I've got the car anyway." He told her she was a fool to take the car into the city. He'd warned her that if she didn't get over this and change her mind she was on her own because he'd not do this to his family. She'd said, "I don't give a shit, right now, what you do." He'd said, "Fine, I'll just take back my apartment in the city, and you can just bury yourself in that silly country house whim that you wanted so badly, you selfish bitch, and yeah, happy birthday for that too."

She'd disconnected and shut off her cell phone without hearing where else this was leading.

Merrin had left her to make the call in private. If Cat decided to change her mind she didn't want to be any more influence than she had already been. She sat over on the bench by the French doors, talking to a sweet guy named Jess about whatever came to mind whilst keeping a subtle watch in Cat's direction.

Mezza! She thought to herself, *what have you gone and done?* But she'd felt really right when the suggestions had poured out. Typical, she sighed.

Kathryn sat quietly, shaking. *Well, you brought that on yourself, you fool,* she thought. *How naïve am I anyway to not say what I thought at the beginning?* She felt guilty—that was definitely the emotion—guilty, and relieved. She'd never had an argument past the word "but" with Martin. She'd let it happen. She'd been the good mouse. No wonder he was angry.

But.

She slipped past the emotion to a deeper place and thought about how he had spoken to her. She recalled that he had always spoken so if she'd seemed belligerent toward his plans. He'd even, in the beginning, told her how she should behave during sex, for goodness sake.

And in the deep place was anger. And two voices. The first agreed with the guilt, backing up Martin's words and telling her how stupid she'd been to let her life get to this.

Then the second voice told the first voice to shut-up. Then it was silent; silent and curious. It was as though a secret, knowing smile dwelt there, and it was like something thinking—she could sense its thought: *What're you going to do?* No ifs, no becauses, no maybes.

A slow-moving calm killed the first voice.

Kathryn looked at the impotent cell phone lying like a limp thing in her hand, and she gently dropped it into her bag. She looked across at Merrin and the two locked eyes.

"Oh . . . my . . . *God!*" she squealed loudly. It slipped out. People turned to look at her, smiling because it had been an epithet of sheer exultation.

"Wuhoo!" Merrin erupted. She kissed Jess on the cheek, said, "I'll see you later, bye," and bounced toward Kathryn, who was up from the table and hugging her friend, grinning like a crazy woman.

Merrin didn't ask what had gone down on the phone because she didn't really want to know right now. *It just would have been shit, that's for sure*, she thought. She knew though, from her friend's behavior, that the plan was on.

THE TWO LEFT THE CAFÉ and Kathryn suggested some places to shop. Then she wrinkled up her nose and said, "Nah, changed my mind," headed for an ATM, and withdrew five hundred dollars.

"Wow," Merrin commented dryly as Kathryn fanned the bills.

"You want some?" she asked.

"I don't want your money, bitch," Merrin teased.

"This is nothing, that's all."

"You loaded then?"

"I've been a very good cook and an exemplary housekeeper and an adept bookkeeper and errand-runner for a very well-paying boss." She said it in such a way that anyone other than Merrin might have thought it quite funny, and she smiled a bitter smile as she stuffed the money into her wallet.

"Ouch."

"Yeah, well . . . So where do you get your haute couture?"

They wandered through the labyrinth of Southside streets and lanes, stopping at Merrin's favorite pre-loved-clothing boutiques. Kathryn had traded her pale sweaters for the big black wool jumper that Merrin had given her while they were still at their first stop, leaving her rejected cashmere to the thrift shop.

After just over an hour Kathryn had picked up a dozen or so bits of clothing and necessities that made no sense to her friend, *but hey*, thought Merrin, *it's her birthday—what if she has strange tastes?*

They carried the few packages through the deepening chill of the late afternoon, along a route becoming clearer to Kathryn the more often she came to this part of town, and they picked up some Chinese take-out around the corner from Merrin's studio.

When they finally arrived in the backyard, Kathryn's mouth opened in sheer surprise. It was truly the most beautiful place that she had ever seen. *So much for being poor,* she thought.

Merrin fished the latch-key out of the fish tank that had once been a small bath tub but that was now painted brown. She kept it hidden there, drowned under the profusion of green plants floating on the face of the water. She bent down and opened a yellow plastic container of fish food and sprinkled the contents onto the surface, where several guppies and a couple of goldfish rose to feed.

Kathryn looked at the building. It was a very old place—she guessed that it maybe dated back to the early 1900s. It was built of hand-made red brick and had double doors of solid-looking wood that would open only slightly because of the riot of potted plants that filled the courtyard.

As Merrin slipped the key into the lock Kathryn goose-fleshed all over her body.

"Someone's here," she whispered.

"Wh . . . ?" Merrin spun around.

"I can feel someone here."

"You're freakin' me out," said Merrin in a soft hiss. "If you're in there I'm gonna break your legs!" she yelled, as loudly and as deeply as she could, grabbing hold of a small hatchet that rested in the corner between the door and the bench where she kept a store of wood.

Kathryn took hold of her arm. "Sorry. I feel silly—it's gone now."

Still holding the hatchet like a weapon Merrin cautiously turned the tarnished doorknob and opened the door. She scanned her place. There were windows on two sides of the building and dust motes were floating lazily down the light from the uncurtained panes.

Everything was normal.

"Shit!" She exhaled, not realizing she'd been holding her breath. "Some psychic, Cat!" She chuckled with relief as she opened the door just enough for Kathryn to squeeze through.

"Phew," exclaimed Kathryn as she walked into the huge store-house. She dropped her bags onto the floor beside the door and pulled it shut behind her. "That was so weird!"

"You okay?' Merrin asked, propping her weapon against the wall.

"Yeah, I'm fine—the feeling was out there though, not in here. I'm fine—that was so weird." She shook off the remnants of the sensation. "What were you going to do—sever them to death?" Both women laughed; Kathryn, because the image was so funny and Merrin, because she knew just exactly what damage she could inflict with an axe.

M'OHRA, RAOUL, AND KH'BAR WERE perched along the old TV antenna atop the deserted building next door looking down at the arrival of the two women. Kh'bar winged off to pass the news along to T'arn and the others, while M'ohra and Raoul stayed behind to call in the night and stand sentinel.

M'ohra knew it wasn't them that Kathryn had sensed—the red-haired Sídhe had left the traces of his pattern all over the yard, and she had known. She had known.

Splendid, is excellent! She fluffed her feathers with pleasure. Things seemed to be progressing rather nicely.

ONE CORNER OF THE STUDIO was graced by a small hearth. At some time or other the help must have slept out here. Merrin had cleaned out the rats' nests that had blocked up the chimney in the desperation of her first winter. She hurried across to it now and lit the solid-fuel fire-starters before piling on the kindling like a crossword puzzle. Once the split packing wood was well ablaze she added denser wood, and soon the chill from the early evening was driven from the room.

She lit a few candles and chimed, "Let's eat!"

"Absolutely. I'm ravenous." Kathryn pulled off her thick coat and piled it onto the floor as an immediate cushion. They ate in the fading light, not bothering to talk, comfortable in each other's company.

Kathryn looked around as she chop-sticked noodles from the carton to her mouth. It was a huge space with a riot of assorted furnishings including, in the far corner, a double bed that Merrin had converted into a four-poster, draped with muslin dyed in various shades of scarlet and red, the bed being piled high with a tangle of blankets and pillows and a patchwork, multitextured duvet.

There were stacks of books, odd sculptures and knick-knacks, and many candlesticks holding a variety of sized candles, mainly of honey-colored beeswax. There was an odd lamp that looked like a ball of clear party-lights that were attached to a bank of four car batteries on the floor beside an overstuffed wing-back chair.

"What's that?" Kathryn gestured, between mouthfuls, to the odd tangle of wires and lights and aluminium foil.

'There's no electricity," explained Merrin, "so they're all old brake-light bulbs from across town at the junk-yard. Dan, who works there, collects them for me. I rig 'em up to the batteries when I'm on a marathon read and my eyes get too stressed from candle-light."

"S'cool," admired Kathryn, truly impressed.

"I only need to get the batteries recharged every couple of months if I'm careful, too."

"How do you take a shower if you haven't got power?"

"Dimity let's me use her place sometimes; sometimes Lyn. Otherwise I've got a tap outside, y'know."

"In winter?" Kathryn was horrified at the thought of the freezing water.

"I heat it up on the burner, silly," Merrin chuckled as she stood up.

She walked to where a large crate or box, covered with a sheet of what appeared to be black silk, stood against the east wall under the window. On the surface was a pair of shiny brass candlesticks, their candles evenly burned down, a selection of deep blue glass bottles, jars, and small bowls, what looked like a flat copper disk, a very impressive mirror within a carved, dark, highly polished wooden frame supported by the statue of a ceramic leopard, a pair of daggers, side by side—one with a black hilt and the other appearing to be made of horn—and a brass dragon-looking incense burner off to the side.

Merrin lit both the candles and then went about the rest of the studio lighting several more, transforming the interior of the room from gloomy to glowing.

"What's all that?" Kathryn looked toward the mysterious things upon the silk.

"My altar," Merrin replied, picking up the containers from the coffee table.

"How come?"

"I told you, I'm a witch."

"Of course you did, duh!" Kathryn fingered the little pentagram at her neck wondering if there were ramifications to it.

"Okay." She stood up and put her hands on her hips. "So give me the grand tour; show me where everything is so I don't feel like a visitor!"

"The grand tour it is," said Merrin with pomp. She walked the few feet to the back of the building, carrying the empty cartons.

"This is the kitchen. And we don't ever throw away these in this house," she added, twiddling the two pair of disposable wooden chopsticks. There were a table, and several shelves against the wall, filled with an assortment of canned goods, glass jars full of dry-goods, mismatched crockery, and a quaint old jug holding knives and forks and other bits.

"You don't leave any food in packages or boxes either, 'cause sure as shit any rat within ten blocks'll find their way in here to get at it."

There were a two-burner gas campstove on a crate attached to a gas-bottle, an unemptied bucket of water with a few plates still half submerged in its murky depths, and a couple of towels hanging on hooks.

"And we don't buy any perishables when the weather's warm 'cause there's no fridge." She showed Merrin the old-fashioned wire-mesh cupboard that was used to store bread and cheese and milk.

She turned, grinning, toward the bed. "That's the master bedroom, but you'll have to take the smaller guest quarters," and she pointed toward the couch, "which doubles, as you see, as an en suite living room. There's no bathroom, but there's a really cute chain-pull mother outside, across the garden, attached to the old shop."

Kathryn groaned.

"So how about you make tea before we get ourselves ready to do the town?" Merrin suggested, as she stoked the fire.

"I'm on it!" Kathryn headed to the kitchen.

Merrin put the CD *Prayer Cycle* into her portable player and the voices of Alanis Morrissette and Salif Keita haunted the room as they sang the first track on the compilation album.

Merrin picked up Kathryn's coat and hung it on one of the assorted hooks in the only built-in cupboard in the room, which had once been used for smoking bacon and now served as Merrin's extensive wardrobe. While she was there she pulled out her swag, a couple of spare pillows, and a sleeping bag, which she deposited on the couch. She grabbed a few of the several dozen cushions that occupied a large part of the floor and plopped them down in front of the hearth just as Kathryn brought over two mugs of Irish breakfast tea.

They sat down happily. Merrin raised her mug to Kathryn. "Happy birthday for real, yeah?" she said, clinking mugs with her friend.

"You're not kidding," replied Kathryn, realizing what she had done today. "We going out?"

"We sure are." Merrin lifted her mug and sipped her tea before reaching over and turning off the music. The two women sat in the silence for a few minutes.

"It's quiet out there tonight," said Merrin, not realizing that she spoke too soon.

"Mmmm," replied Kathryn, smiling.

Chapter Twelve

They took turns to wash in basins full of warm water. Merrin sat before the mirror on her altar applying make-up like an artist. Kathryn had scrubbed her face clean of hers and determined to stay that way, which would be the first time she had done so in years. She had no idea how ethereal she looked without it.

She dressed in some of the odd assortment of clothing that she'd picked up that afternoon. She wore a kilt in the McLeod tartan that someone had shortened and added extra buckles to, complete with a leather belt that had its own pouch.

"Damn!" said Merrin when she saw what her friend had scored. "How did I miss *that*, bitch!"

Kathryn chuckled. She had no idea if she looked good or if she looked very silly, but she had seen some rock singer one time wearing something like this and she remembered thinking *I wish* . . .

She threw on a plain cotton T-shirt with the big black jumper over the top and put her own boots back on. She didn't even look in a mirror. She really didn't care. She was ready before Merrin.

"You want to take the car?"

"Let's do the bus instead," replied Merrin, "just in case you want to do some shots of the old *uiske beatha*." Kathryn asked what that was and Merrin said, "Whisky, silly."

"I don't drink much."

"Doesn't matter if you don't but it doesn't matter if you

do tonight, either, 'cause we'll take the bus and it's your birthday, yeah?" Merrin didn't have a license, but she'd never driven a car anyway and wasn't about to be in any position to own one, so there was no point.

She finished putting the final touches to her clothing and re-plaited her hair. She was content with the outcome. She extinguished all of the candles except for two that were in squat, safe holders, and put a mesh fire-guard in front of the banked-up hearth.

THEY CAUGHT THE 117 BUS to Geraldton Park at seven-fifteen that evening to ensure they were at Mary Flannery's early enough to get a table near the dance-floor and the band.

As the bus turned the corner into George Street the traffic slowed right down. Both women stood up in the almost-empty bus and wandered down the aisle to claim the seat right behind the driver so that they could see what was causing the delay.

Way up ahead, in the clubbing sector, about a block or so from the Courthouse, the blue and red lights of what appeared to be several vehicles were glittering in the night.

"Traffic's being diverted," the driver called over his shoulder.

"What do you think? Accident?" asked Kathryn.

"No. Look. There's a couple of fire trucks there with their ladders up . . . Yeah, there's a lot of smoke. Looks like it's coming from the upper story," he replied, craning forward over the wheel.

The bus crept, moving with the traffic, until they could actually see the fire, which had intensified and was licking savagely from two of the windows on the second floor of the building.

The driver leaned forward over the wheel, squinting. "It's Utopia, I think. Gay club."

Police cars blocked the road and the traffic was being detoured down Harvey Drive but not before the occupants of the bus saw several ambulances and police cars and many bodies laid out on the pavement at a safe distance from the inferno. There were injured everywhere, some being treated by paramedics and some being cared for and consoled by friends or people who had just happened to be at the scene at the time. A large crowd of spectators was being contained by barricades, and the press—including a couple of hovering helicopters—was obvious everywhere.

The driver turned on the radio to his left and switched channels until he found a local news station. The reader announced that a suspected bombing had taken place at an uptown gay nightclub and that up to twelve people were confirmed dead and several dozen had been injured, some seriously.

"You're kidding," he said. "A bomb, huh?"

Merrin shivered.

They turned onto Harvey and followed the traffic as it detoured several blocks out of their way. It was eerie on the streets.

Groups of men, mostly with shaved heads and big jackets and boots, were strutting with what seemed to be real purpose. As they drove along Valley Avenue the men could be seen pouring down the steps toward the underground railway station.

Other groups of more ordinary men were standing in occasional clusters of up to twenty to a group, deep in conversation, all along Valley and well past the crossroads of Fleet and Mersey.

There was a protest on the steps of St. Mark's Cathedral, mostly women, all with hats and scarves on their heads, and most carrying placards and banners proclaiming themselves as Right-to-Lifers. The cathedral was closed and there was no press anywhere, so what they were doing there, instead of their usual chanting sit-ins at known abortion clinics, and at that time of night, made no sense at all.

"Has someone declared Nutter Night and I wasn't told?" The driver was getting edgy; he didn't expect an answer, and the bus dawdled along Mersey.

"I'm just glad we didn't take the car," Kathryn replied anyway, feeling sick at the thought of having to tackle the roads with all this happening.

He chuckled and agreed. "Name's Max, by the way" (the girls introduced themselves). "You get nights like this though, sometimes, like there's something in the air, you know?" Kathryn didn't but Merrin nodded.

By the time they'd branched off onto the Collins Street overpass the traffic had cleared. The trip to Geraldton Park that normally took ten minutes had taken forty.

Merrin stood up, putting her hands on the back of Max's seat. "Can you let us out next stop?"

The bus turned the corner into Yeats Street, the street that the tavern was on that ran parallel to the park itself, and straight toward another scene.

"Holy Mary! I'm glad my bloody run's just about over," exclaimed Max. "You sure you're getting out here ladies?"

"Yeah," said Merrin. "Hey, thanks Max."

"For what?"

"For caring," she replied, as he pulled in to the curb and opened the automatic doors.

"Well take it easy," he called, putting the bus into gear. Both women waved as he drove off.

Geraldton was an odd mèlange of cultures and ethnicities all jumbled together, with the Glasgow Arms sharing the street with the Taj Mahal Curry House, several strip clubs, an all-night laundromat, a run-down Handi-Mart, several massage parlors, a Japanese bathhouse, Mary Flannery's Tavern, and a Lebanese take-out.

Believe it or not, the only seriously unsafe place was the park itself. The local council had erected tall floodlights several years ago in an attempt to dissuade people from carrying out illicit trade within its darkened corners, but someone had kept shooting them out and they'd finally been given up on.

Every gang, from the local yakuza youth to second generation Lebanese, from the Irishers and the Vietnamese to the very rich kids slumming from the Northside looking for party favors, did their scoring and their dealing from set territories within the one-and-a half-square-acre badlands.

Merrin came to this part of town once a week, regularly, but she never walked on the park side of the street.

"SHIT!" SHE TOOK IN THE scene of mess and chaos, pulling Kathryn closer as though to keep her safe.

There were two police cars, a wagon, and an ambulance across the road from Flannery's, where the pedestrian crossing connected with the park. People were milling around everywhere, trying to see what had happened.

The two women walked straight ahead to the tavern, paid the two dollar cover-charge that was required when there was live music, and walked into the relatively quiet lounge area, too early to know what band was playing.

They went up to the bar and Merrin called out to the woman working the Thursday night roster.

"Wendy Wu, hey!"

Wendy turned and waved, and finished pulling the beer for the patron she was serving.

Merrin and Wendy had hit it off the night she had found the tavern. Wendy's folks had entered the country from Vietnam on a leaky, rusted, overcrowded boat at the height of the Khmer Rouge regime and had been granted permanent refugee status. They had remained very firmly entrenched in what was known locally as Little Saigon, but Wendy had been sent to a midcity public school, so she had a broad local accent.

"Hey Merrin, s'up? They still full-on out front?"

"Hey Wendy, this is Cat." Wendy was only five foot nothing so she bounced up onto the bar, sitting sideways to reach Kathryn's outstretched hand. "Hey, how doin'?"

"It's her birthday," Merrin offered. "Big night out. And yeah, there's a real crowd outside. Do you know what's going on?"

"Bad shit. Three hookers got cut up real nasty-like by some hit'n' runners."

"No."

"Yep. One's dead, and the other two won't be doing trade any-more—they were messed-up in a major way."

"Any idea who?"

"Eddy out front said he'd heard they were a couple of dozen real-ly straight-looking dudes. Out for some sick kicks by the sound of it."

"Oh my god!" said Kathryn, disgusted.

"Yeah. They left notes pinned to the clothes of each of the girls with 'Whore' written on them."

"Who'd do that?"

"Who knows? Freaks, holy rollers, an *I Hate My Mother* confer-ence. But the thing is, the seven o'clock news said that heavy-duty shit is happening all over the place tonight, like all the loonies had marked the date in their diaries or something, yeah? You want Guinness?"

"Yeah, I'm game—never had it before."

"You're kidding," said Wendy.

"Yeah, Guinness for me as well," Merrin added. 'So who's got the gig here tonight, Wendy Wu?'

"Fíanna, an Irish . . ."

She didn't finish. The look on Merrin's face said it all.

"You know them, huh?" said Wendy, not really a question.

Merrin put some cash on the counter; her hands shaking.

"Merrin?" Kathryn watched the changing expressions on her friend's face. She'd turned pale.

"I'll be okay, just give me a minute. What time are they playing?"

"Nine's when they're supposed to start." Wendy looked worried; it wasn't like the Goth girl to get angsty.

"Are they here yet?"

"No."

"Okay." Merrin looked meaningfully at Kathryn.

"Okay!" Kathryn beamed. "Some night this is turning out to be!"

"Looks that way," and Merrin burst out laughing.

Over in another part of the city Michael James Blacker was seated at a table with several of his men. They had a large map of the city up on a plas-screen and were marking off their targets for the night. It would be three or four in the morning before all the heads of command reported in. Apart from the two morality hits they'd also organized for two individual homes to be taken out, Our Lady of the Sacred Heart Catholic Church in the western suburbs, and a shop in the inner city selling occult supplies.

So far he was very pleased with the efficiency of the operations. Tony Ryan had been monitoring the emergency frequencies for most of the night and nobody had any idea. There was plenty of press coverage, but it was far too early in the crusade for anyone to put it together as being somehow connected. By then the Brotherhood would have set up their scapegoat anyway.

Sooner or later I'm going to want to let it be known to the public that the New Inquisition has begun, mused Michael, in a moment of foolishness. He dismissed the thought immediately as a momentary weakness of the ego.

Chapter Thirteen

The two women found themselves a table close to the dance floor before the crowds arrived that would inevitably turn up for a live gig. While they waited for the Fíanna to arrive Kathryn filled Merrin in on the phone conversation with Martin. She was past any of her earlier angst: words like *husband* and *have-to* and *your mother* all dissolving and blowing away, replaced by a sense of herself that was new—freer and cleaner than she could remember. She knew what she was doing. It was her turn to cut in on Merrin's train of thoughts and keep her preoccupied until Willie arrived. It was having an okay effect, too, because Merrin had calmed down while Kathryn rambled on.

At one stage Eddie, bouncer and all-around problem-solver for the tavern, had gone up onto the stage, taken a mike, and informed the patrons that if any of them wanted to leave, the cops had gone and the street had quieted down heaps. A few people who looked like they might have business in the park had picked up and left.

Kathryn let her gaze wander around the once-splendid old pub. The floors were wood and were kept at a high sheen, and three of the four walls retained the old gaslights from before electricity had been installed. The bar was original, too, by the look of it, and other than the mirrors that lined the back of it, there was an entire section of wall devoted to the World Cup Series Finals since its inception. Most of the place was done out in deep forest greens and warm browns. Over against the west wall, opposite the bar and at right-angles to the stage, there was a huge fireplace, with logs ablaze in the grate. Much of the crowd, beginning to build now that the band was due were warming themselves, sitting on the benches provided for such events, and talking and laughing as if nothing in the outside world could possibly be a problem.

Just after 8.30 PM an entourage entered the lounge from the back entrance. Five men and two women went straight to the stage. There was a reserved sign on a large table off to one side and three other adults—a woman and two men—and a young child, piled into the waiting chairs and deposited their coats and bags and extra instrument cases.

Merrin went all quiet. She sat holding her Guinness with both hands as she and Kathryn watched them enter.

Up on stage the wild and ragged bunch of Fíanna members set up their equipment and tuned their instruments. Merrin knew them all. There was Black Annis, who'd dyed her hair different colors since the last time she'd seen her—very Goth-looking otherwise, with pale make-up and lots of black around her eyes, wearing a coat that looked like it had just come off a Matrix set, over knee-high lace-up boots, thick black tights, a skirt that would have exposed most of her had the tights not been there, a long-sleeved black T-shirt with the anarchy symbol painted on it in green, and a pair of short, white lace gloves that looked like they could be from the Victorian era (which they probably were). Puck looked like a Botticelli angel, with pale red hair and white-on-white-on-white layered clothing, while Andy and Trevor just wore jeans and sweatshirts. Matt was typical in his top hat and Mummers outfit looking like a Rom, all darkly handsome with a gold earring glinting from under his long brown hair. He knew how he looked, and he knew the effect he had on women, which was, after all, his intention.

And there was Willie. He had on baggy old jeans, heavy, black workman's boots just showing beneath the hem that obviously dragged at ground level, and a woven brown shirt that looked as though it had been a part of a forest somewhere, over which he wore a brown leather vest that had seen better days. His hair was tied in its warrior braids which shone like autumn under the stage lights, and he had small silver rings in both earlobes. He looked just the same.

He took his fiddle from its case and began tuning it. He was deep in concentration for a minute or so before he looked up and out into the room. Merrin.

His arms went to his sides, and he mouthed something that she thought was, *Well I'll be fucked.*

He gently laid his fiddle on top of its case and walked across the stage before jumping down onto the dance floor, heading in her direction.

Merrin stood up carefully and covered the extra few feet. Without words they seemed to flow into each other's bodies: Merrin winding her arms around Willie's neck, and he wrapping himself around her and nuzzling into her hair. They stood like that for all of thirty seconds before Merrin pulled back to look at him. She grinned. Willie kissed her lightly on the nose and asked if she might just hang around until after the gig.

"I figure I might," she said.

"Well then, I think that's a grand idea," he replied softly. "So you'll be here when we're done then?" As if to confirm that she really would stay she pulled him to her by both his braids and kissed him deeply. The question hinted at much more, and the shining in his eyes told her that he was as pleased to see her as she was to see him.

He turned and hopped back onto the stage. Merrin's smile was beatific as she walked back to the table.

Kathryn, on the other hand, was staring from the group sitting at the reserved table to the band, and back again, obviously in some kind of distress.

"What's wrong . . ." Merrin was disturbed by her friend's agitation—the night just kept getting crazier and crazier.

Kathryn didn't answer. Her breathing was shallow and rapid, and she was paler than usual.

Merrin looked over at the Travelers. There was nothing about them that should cause Cat to be this upset—sure, they mostly looked like a cross between the Rom and street people, but, shit, she thought, Kathryn had been coming to Dimity's long enough to have encountered all kinds of interesting individuals.

She sat down in confusion, waiting for an explanation. She pulled her tobacco from her backpack and rolled a thin cigarette, being casual; letting whatever it was that was going through her friend's head right now run its course. She lit her cigarette and looked over at the stage, watching the band complete their sound check with the guy who was doing the desk. She turned back to Kathryn to see if she was okay, but she was still out there somewhere—transfixed.

"Earth calling Cat," she joked, leaning over the table to touch her friend's hand. Kathryn flinched and looked away from the astonishing scene briefly. Her face had gone a sickly white, and her pupils were dilated with fear. *Whoa,* thought Merrin, *there's something really eeky goin' on here.* She was hoping this wasn't something out of control, like maybe epilepsy, but figured it might be better to just wait and see whether it'd pass on its own.

She tried to imagine what was going on in Kathryn's mind, but it was impossible.

MERRIN SIMPLY COULDN'T SEE WHAT Kathryn saw.

Sure, she could see the people, but across the faces of all but a few of them Kathryn watched a dance of ghostly—but obvious—creatures, other than human. And they weren't fixed; they kept changing. She was seeing boar and bear and hare, fox and owl, otter and crow, and lynx and hound, and more and more and more. They just kept morphing and shifting. Not only were they superimposing over the faces of the strangers, but they were *around* them. Shadows; real.

Kathryn had no idea what was happening, but she was terrified; afraid that she was hallucinating, afraid that she'd just fallen off the world somehow. Then in walked two more.

THE TALL, HEAVY-SET MAN had skin as dark as leather or bark. He was bundled up to look like a mountain in an army surplus great-coat. He had long, black dreds that fell almost to his waist, gathered at the back of his head by leather ties—the sides of his head were clean-shaven, and the whole thing gave him a pointed, feral look.

Beside him was the woman who had told her fortune when she was younger. This alone was too much overload. None of it made sense. That she was here—that any of them were here—it just didn't gel. It was all too much of a coincidence.

She looked around the pub, but no one else seemed to be taking any notice. Surely they could see. But no—the crowd was moving to take up tables closer to the stage; people were chatting and laughing, smoking and drinking, like it was just another night.

The big man and the woman who looked like Merrin caught sight of Kathryn and Merrin at the same time. They stared at Kathryn with what seemed like shock, and with equal intensity.

Kathryn saw, superimposed over the big man, the very clear images of three things: a many-tined stag, a pale wolf, and a crow or maybe a raven, and each beast was distinct and separate unlike the others of their company. The dark-haired psychic, with the hundreds of braids, looked just like an ordinary, if unusual-looking, woman—almost a relief. But as she watched her, the woman smiled a slight and impish smile, and shrugged her shoulders. She shook her head, as if to say no, not that simple and, as if willing it to happen, she changed.

Kathryn was faced with the vision of a raven with white eyes.

IT WAS NOT, HOWEVER, A one-sided experience. Hunter and Brighid hid their shock and confusion very well. It hardly ever happened that they were unprepared for the way the magic could trick you into thinking that you knew it all. But there, strong and clear, overriding the humanness of the woman seated beside their dear friend Merrin, was the image of a white doe, thought lost to the mortal worlds—relegated to the ancient legends by those who still remembered.

"Was it there when you played fortune-teller?" Hunter asked out of the corner of his mouth.

"Well I would have known *then*, wouldn't I?" she replied caustically.

"Ah, Flidhais," said Hunter.

He turned slowly to face his companion. "Gentle. Gentle, Brighid. Don't you go spooking her, ceart go leor? All right?"

Brighid turned her crystal-bright gaze on him just long enough for him to regret his slip of the tongue, but he grinned at her.

"CAN YOU SEE THIS?" KATHRYN turned to Merrin, her voice shaky with panic.

"What's happening, girl?" Merrin asked carefully, initially wishing that this weird shit wasn't happening, whatever it was, because they were supposed to be having a good time, then feeling decidedly responsible for her friend's well-being.

"I . . ." Kathryn turned a pale green at the corners of her mouth, and all color left her face. Then she slid gracefully from the chair, folding to the floor, unconscious.

Brighid and Hunter walked over to the two women quickly and purposefully, just as Merrin leapt from her seat before any of the pub's employees noticed. Hunter picked Kathryn up in his powerful arms as though she was air and spirited her past the others, creating a glamour of invisibility as he moved. They went straight out into the alleyway at the rear of the building.

The fog outside was as thick as pea soup. A fine drizzle chilled the night air, but it was clean and invigorating, the cobbles glistening in the light that spilled from the building onto the ground. The alley was a world away from the twentieth century—a soft place.

KATHRYN CAME TO AFTER ONLY a few minutes, still cradled in Hunter's arms, with Brighid's hands warming her temples and filling her with a sense of comfort and safety. Rowan had followed quickly behind the escape, and he knelt beside Merrin. Worry was written onto both their faces with frowns and silence.

Kathryn opened her eyes to the same disorientation that had caused the anxiety attack. She wanted to scream.

"Go gcumhdaí is dtreoraí na déithe thú." *May the gods guard and guide you.* Hunter spoke the ancient blessing just above a whisper.

"Flidhais?" queried Brighid, knowing beyond doubt anyway.

"My, ah . . . my name's Kathryn," and she attempted to crawl out of Hunter's arms to gain some semblance of composure.

"We know," said Hunter, just as Jack came out of the back door.

He held out a small shot glass filled to the brim with golden liquid. "You better drop this down in one go," he smiled warmly.

"I don't . . ." she mumbled, looking at his normal, everyday, human face.

"Oh, I think you do," replied the light-eyed woman. "I'm Brighid by the way." She looked in Hunter's direction. "The big man here's known as Hunter . . . and this is our Rowan," nodding at the only straight-looking member of the troupe.

"And Jack," said the older man, softly spoken, wearing well-worn Levis, a flannel shirt, and a red bandana tied around his head keeping his long steel-gray hair off his face, who had only the hint of something coyote-like fleeting around the edges.

Kathryn hesitated before taking the glass from his outstretched hand. She downed the fiery dram in one gulp. It warmed all the way to her belly and then spread out through her body like a blast of summer. It didn't take away the images, but it certainly lessened the disorientation. Then she realized that if she looked at Merrin and the guy beside her, the hallucination wasn't there.

She turned back to Brighid.

"What can you see?" Hunter's voice sliced through her disorientation, and she slowly turned her gaze toward him.

"When I look at you? Stag," she replied. "And raven. And wolf." She looked at Brighid. "But you made it happen—I saw you do it on purpose!"

Brighid chuckled. "Was I that obvious?"

"You called up a raven with white eyes. And it's not there now, either."

Oh, Brighid . . . , Hunter sighed. She merely smiled innocently.

"And when you look at Merrin?"

"Merrin's Merrin," and she turned her attention toward Rowan, "and you're whoever you are."

"Good." Hunter helped her to her feet.

"Did someone drop a trip into my stout?"

Hunter and Brighid both chuckled. "Nothing quite that simple," he told her.

"Get a grip, mo fían iníon," said Brighid. "You can see us, is all. C'mon. Let's get you inside where it's warm. And don't freak out. There's nothing wrong. I simply did not see you properly the first time we met, is all. Must have been all the pollution from that family you were sent to."

Kathryn was about to ask her what on earth she was talking about, but instead she allowed herself to be led inside to the table where the others were waiting.

The band was already playing—a traditional reel with two bodhrans, an acoustic guitar, an accordion, the uilleann pipes, a low whistle, and the fiddle—and the small dance floor had about thirty people crammed onto it, all thoroughly entranced.

As far as Kathryn was concerned, the stage was packed. Five of the seven musicians seemed to be a morph of human and animal, while the other two looked completely human. Amorphous shapes danced around all of them, however, radiating an ecstasy and enthusiasm that finally caused Kathryn to smile. She found that if she moved her head really slowly the nauseous, disorienting sensation was less intense.

"You know we all see the same when we look at you," Hunter began, as young Robin wormed his way into Merrin's lap.

Merrin was taking this all in her stride, figuring she'd been set up by the déithe—her gods—somewhere in all this, sensing what the others were seeing (she always had—the magic had been with them from the first time she'd encountered them).

"What do you see?" asked Kathryn.

"A white deer," he replied. "And do you know what that tells us?"

She shook her head. Merrin, still supporting Robin, who was curled up like a puppy, reached her arm around her friend's shoulders and giggled. She was not looking at any of them: her eyes, and those of Willie, were sending sizzling telepathic messages, easy to read, over the heads of the dancers.

She butted in on the meaningful conversation. "Hey Cat—is he just a fox or what, huh?"

"That's exactly what I see anyway," said Kathryn, raising her eyebrows, knowing what her friend really meant.

"So?" continued Hunter. "Do you know what that means to us?"

"No . . . Why do I get the feeling I'm out of my depths with all this? Sorry. Please tell me. I mean, when you say what does it mean to us—fine—but what I want to know is what does everything that's happening here mean for me? And why me?"

"Can I tell you a story?"

"Does it help?"

"It's a start."

"Then I'd love to hear it, but you'll have to talk louder because I can't hear you very well over the band."

"He can't talk louder," said Brighid. "It's not in his nature. It's dangerous for him to raise his voice."

Kathryn was lost again.

"Let me?" Brighid offered. Hunter shrugged his shoulders.

She cleared her throat. "There once was a great man named Fíonn Mac Cumhaill. He started a whole thing going with the Fíanna, which is where the band got its name . . ." She smiled and nodded.

"Well, he was in love with Sadbh, daughter of the Munster king Bódearg. Around that time a nasty old sorcerer had a bitch with just about everybody, but especially with Fíonn because he was a bit of an all-round achiever—could have been a jealousy thing. I got the news secondhand, yeah?—and just to ruin everybody's good time he placed a curse on Sadbh that condemned her to a life in which she could exist in either the form of a woman or a doe.

"Sadbh never knew when the spell would take effect or wear off and this, as you can imagine, was heartbreaking for Fíonn, as he never knew when he would be able to catch a glimpse of his love.

"One day he was hunting on the lower slopes of Benbulben when a rustle and a movement in the undergrowth caught his attention. He crouched down low and crept forward to investigate.

"As he parted the bushes in front of him he was amazed to find a hidden clearing that was walled on every side by stout blackthorn bushes. In the middle of the clearing was a young, beautiful white deer nurturing a newborn baby boy. She spoke straight into Fíonn's mind, saying his name, and seeking to have him understand that the child was his son, that she was Sadbh.

"Fíonn gently picked up the child and held him closely. Sadbh explained that she could not break the spell anymore and was doomed to stay in her animal form forever. They spent the rest of that day together, and at sunset he watched as Sadbh disappeared into the forest leaving him holding his son. He named him Oisín, which means 'small deer.'

"And forever was right. The longer Sadbh lived the more Other-worldly she became, and as time passed she learned to come and go between all the worlds and so became a treasured guardian of the magics. She became known as one of the déithe, and different people knew her by different names and she was often known as Flidhais . . ."

Kathryn interrupted her. "That's what you called me earlier!"

"Are you listening, or am I talking to myself?" replied Brighid tartly.

"Don't give her a hard time," Hunter growled.

"Yeah, well . . . anyway shall I finish the story?"

"Please," said Kathryn.

"So anyway . . . the more Sadbh lived between the worlds the more she learned the ways of shape-changing—woman deer, deer woman;

you know what I mean—and that way, over the years, when she took a fancy to the idea of gifting herself the pleasure of a lover, she'd take on the form of woman for a while. She managed to take many lovers and to bear special children who had the true Sight. Like you."

"But . . . whoa! Are you trying to tell me . . ."

"Not trying at all," Hunter interrupted. "There's no try involved."

"Then . . ." Sweat broke out in tiny beads, and her eyes widened like a trapped animal.

"She gets it," Brighid patted the forest god's hand.

"You're kidding," piped in Merrin. "You mean she really was a Lost Cause?"

"I'm not necessarily buying any of this," said Kathryn.

"Well, it is a bit quirky," Brighid admitted.

"You mean . . . my mother . . ."

"That's exactly where all this seems to be pointing. Look around you, Kathryn. How do you explain what's happening?"

"I can't. But it's never happened before. Why now?"

"Can I interrupt?" asked Hunter.

"If you must." Brighid rolled her eyes in Merrin's direction.

"Do you know if your family were your family by blood?"

"Of course they weren't!" Brighid sniffed. "Even I know that."

"Can she answer for herself, woman?" The look on his face caused her to smile angelically.

"No, they weren't," Kathryn spoke just above a whisper.

Brighid was about to say something to Hunter, like I told you so, but knew he wasn't in the mood, so she decided against it—for the moment.

"So, why now? Was that what you asked?" And Kathryn nodded, not quite trusting herself to speak.

"It's because of what we are. And believe me, there aren't many of us."

"Then what are you?" She sorely needed another drink as the last one had seemed to soothe her anxiety, which had mounted again despite her, and she turned to Jack before anyone could answer. "Could you possibly get me another one of those wonderful small glasses of whatever it was you gave me out the back?"

"It's her birthday," Merrin offered with a glint in her eye.

"My treat then," he said warmly, heading off to the bar.

Kathryn turned back to Brighid. "Hmm. So then . . . ?"

"We're Sídhe." She didn't elaborate, and there was a moment of uncomfortable silence.

"Like . . ." Kathryn was lost for words.

"Like nothing, girl. Sídhe. The Fair Folk. Tuatha Dé Danann and all that."

"What? Like in the books? The myths and folk-tale-type Sídhe?"

"Thank the déithe she didn't say . . ." Gypsy didn't finish. *Phew!* She thought.

"Shh!" Rowan cautioned. Merrin chuckled, remembering the times that Willie had used *that* dig to get a reaction, but Kathryn didn't catch on.

"Well, most of us here are," continued Brighid. "Well . . . maybe not Puck, or the Rowan, or Alan. And Jack's not and neither's Gypsy. And certainly not Hunter."

"But . . . I can see more of the animals in Hunter's face than any of you."

"I'm a god," Hunter told her with a straight face.

"No shit." Kathryn wondered if she'd had a nervous breakdown after the phone call to Martin and whether she was really in an observation ward somewhere and this was all some medicated dream.

"You just can't help bringin' that up," said Brighid, hands on her hips. Hunter smiled a smile to melt the heart of any woman, showing perfect white teeth—if not slightly elongated incisors.

THE BAND FINISHED ITS FIRST set to whoops and cheers and overwhelming applause. They placed their instruments on specially prepared stands and all came over to the table for a fifteen-minute break.

Everyone was sitting around, introducing themselves to Kathryn and hugging Merrin with groans of glee at seeing her again, having pints and sharing out packets of crisps, when a man walked into the lounge with a pack on his back, a staff in his hand, and what looked like the tsuka of a Japanese sword peeking out from a black cloth case slung over one shoulder. He saw them and waved.

"You made it!" shouted Matt and Annis almost in unison.

Kathryn and Merrin turned to see the slight, bronze-skinned man, dressed in loose black clothing, as he walked across to the table. Kathryn felt physically overwhelmed.

Rowan grabbed a spare chair from close by and pulled it over for Vincent.

Matt introduced him to the two girls.

"So," Hunter spoke softly to all present. "The odds just got slightly more in our favor every which way."

That's all well and good—whatever you're talking about Hunter, Kathryn thought to herself, as she observed Vincent Tanaka as he sat and deposited his backpack beside him on the floor, *but if you're all who you say you are, then what's he?* Because although Vincent's appearance was that of an ordinary, if somewhat exotic, young man, around him crowded abundantly more of the shifting magics than all the others put together. It was as though he was calmly living with an entire ecosystem. Was he aware of it? She couldn't tell. His face gave nothing away. He was probably the most compact and peaceful-seeming person that she had ever encountered.

Kathryn needed to get hold of herself. Concentrate. What had Hunter just said? Something about odds? Was she included in the analogy?

Chapter Fourteen

uesdays and Thursdays, my daddy works on the newspaper that him and the boys put out once a week. That's always good for me 'cause I get to go the long ways home. Mama thinks I'm shootin' hoops on these days 'cause I'd get in so much trouble if they knew about the books.

I've got the third one from the Wizard of Earthsea *series called* The Farthest Shore, *and Sally Plessing's got the whole* Narnia *lot for me for when I'm done with this one—only I'm wishin' it's never gonna finish 'cause this's got to be the best of 'em so fars.*

I'm walking down Wentworth and I take the track that turns down to the lake. I've always got the old boatshed to myself on Tuesdays.

I love this time all by myself—I get to be anybody I can imagine, and no one's gonna be around if I get to talkin' out loud.

I'm thinkin' it's lookin' like rain—the wind's pickin' up and the sky's as gray as dirty water—so I'm makin' my way through the backroads as quick as I can.

I get to hearin' this yip-yip from off the track. There ain't nobody lives there. I better keep on goin', but the yip turns into somethin' soundin' high and in pain. I can always sneak. John Junior reckons I sneak better'n all three us boys.

There's nothin' but scrawny trees and ragged old bushes this close to the quarry so I can see a fair way ahead. Up by the edge of the old machine shop—that's ain't had no one go near it for donkey's years—is the burned-out shell of some old car that's been here forever, seems.

The noise is comin' from the other side. Dog noises. I go round and there's this cute little bitch, that might be made of a whole dozen different breeds, that's got a bit of chain around her neck that's stuck on the barbed wire there.

She sees me comin' and she starts in on shakin' all over and tuckin' that feathery tail 'tween her legs and lookin' as scared as you could imagine.

"S'okay girl." I'm soft-talkin' cause she's lookin' pretty freaked out. I keep on to sayin' it over and over—"S'okay, s'okay girl. S'okay. I won't hurt you," and all the while I'm soft clickin' my fingers.

I get to her and I don't know if she's glad to see me or if she wants to bite me, so I just hold my hand out real slow so's she can sniff me and know that I'm just a kid like her. She don't even look a year old, all soft brindle brown and gray.

"Hey, you are a pretty little thing," I say, "yes you are, you a pretty girl then? You a pretty little thing." And that tail comes out from where it's hidin' and starts in waggin' like crazy.

I don't know how long she's been here, but she's poorly. The chain's gone and dug itself into her neck, and it's got all dried blood on it where she's tried to pull herself free.

I don't try to get her clear first off. I pull my water bottle outa my pack and pour some into my hands and, oh man, she's so thirsty. I keeps to talkin' all the while, and I don't let her drink too much 'cause I know you're not supposed to if you're real real thirsty.

I just kinda sit down beside her and rub her fur a little, movin' closer to the chain all the time. She settles a bit. I'm real careful when I dip my finger under that chain, but it loosens easy—she's been pullin' all the wrong way.

I slide it offa her neck fast as I can but she still squeals 'cause it hurts her. "S'okay," I say, "S'okay, you're a good girl, ain't ya? You're a good girl, yes you are." And she comes up real close and nuzzles me and settles right down there with me.

"You wanna come with me, huh girl?" I say. "You wanna come home with me?" Seems like she knows every word. I swear she's smilin' with that soft little face and those big dark eyes.

I stand up and slap my thigh with my hand, and she gets up too. I figure the book can stay down the bottom of my pack until Thursday 'cause this little girl's got some lookin' after to get done.

I'm walkin' in the back gate and I been callin' the dog Sally since we start-ed out for home, and she's lookin' at me every time I say it like that was her all along and I first had to understand her when she told me.

My daddy's got two dogs of his own—they're called Andy and Flint—and they're his good dogs but they don't like anybody 'cept Daddy, and he keeps 'em locked in their pen 'ceptin' when he takes 'em hunting.

They're goin' off like crazy when me and Sal walk across the yard. She's up close to my side 'cause she don't know they can't get out.

We get up to the back door and walk on into the kitchen. Daddy keeps the bag of dry food for his pitters down beside the stove in a plastic drum.

I keep talkin' to Sal while I scoop some o' that dog biscuit into a ice-cream container, and she gets into it like she's starvin', poor little thing, while I fill her up a bowl of water from the sink.

My mama comes into the kitchen and just stares at the two of us. "Get it outa here!" she yells at me. "You get that dirty, filthy thing outa my kitchen." I ignore her. What's she gonna do?

"You betta get that outa here 'fore your daddy gets home," she says. She's thinkin' I'm gonna jump at that but I'm not. I figure I'm old enough to have my own dog now and I know it.

I take Sally right on past her, and we go upstairs to my room. Ryan and John Junior's not home either so I just get myself settled and pull out my home-work. Better I get it done when they're off doin' somethin' else 'cause they always like to make me feel like a girl 'cause I don't mind bein' at the books.

Sally settles real easy on my bed. I better wash her tomorrow sure—she'll look so pretty then that even my mama won't mind her.

IT'S LATER. I HEAR THE screen door bang shut on the porch. *I hear my mama and daddy talkin'. Next thing Daddy's bangin' open my door and sayin', "What the fuck you think you're doin' boy?"*

"Daddy, I found her . . ." I start, but he don't wanna listen. He tells me to get down the stairs now. I'm out the door when I hear Sally yelp in pain. He's got her by the scruff of her neck right where she was bleedin', and I say, "Don't

Daddy, no . . ." And he hits me over the head with his free hand and near pushes me down the stairs.

"Get out back!" he yells.

I don't know what to do. "I can look after her Daddy." I try to get him to listen, but he's not takin' any notice of what I'm sayin'.

He's got a rope down from the hook on the back door. Sally's strugglin' and I wanna kick him to make him let her go. I can feel her. She's so frightened and he's hurtin' her so bad, but I can't help you, Sal, I think at her. Soon as we're outside you run, girl. I'll find you. I will. I promise.

I'll run away, I think. I can't let him send her to the pound or anything. She's mine. We love each other. She's my friend.

But that's not what's happening.

Daddy's tying her up to the garden tap outside the back door. Mama's watching from the kitchen window with that look on her face that she gets when no one knows what she's thinking.

"You stay there by that bitch," says Daddy, pointing to Sal. I kneel down beside her, just figurin' we're gonna do a runner. I'm pattin' her and strokin' her, and she's lookin' at me with those sweet eyes.

Daddy comes out from the kitchen unstrappin' his hunting knife from the leather belt sheath he keeps it in.

"Time you learned," he said grimly. "You gotta start this sooner or later—might as well be now."

My throat's all dry. He's holding the knife by the blade, wantin' me to take the handle.

No . . . I wanna scream. No!

"You do it quick like me and the boys showed you," he says.

"No," I say. "She's mine." And I hold her close.

He hits me on the face, and Sal pulls away scared to death, makin' the wound on her neck open.

"You do what I say or I'm gonna make that fuckin', filthy mongrel thing suffer so bad . . . and God's gonna know it were your fault 'cause you was too much a coward to make it easy for her."

I'm shakin' and I think I'm gonna wet my pants I'm so scared.

He's standing over me.

"You got to three," says Daddy. "On three you take this or you get up to your room and outa my way."

His pitters are going crazy over in the cage.

"You know I'll put her in there with them don't you?"

I take the knife from his hand 'fore he starts to countin', and I'm gonna be sick, I know I am, 'cause my daddy always does what he says he will, otherwise he says it's lyin', and that's a sin.

I've still got one arm around Sally's neck, strokin' her. She's lookin' at me and she's real scared, but she trusts me.

I can't scream. Only girls scream. I wanna scream so bad that my mouth tastes like metal till I realize that it's blood from where I bit my tongue.

"One," says Daddy.

"I love you," I whisper to Sal close up. Don't you cry Micky, I think to myself, but it's too late 'cause this is too hard, and it just starts happening.

"Shit," says Daddy. "Two!"

"I'm so sorry," I say as I pull the razor-sharp hunting knife across her throat.

Blood spurts out all over me.

"Good boy," says Daddy, takin' the knife from my hand and pattin' me on the shoulder afore he walks back into the kitchen.

She's dying and I feel like the bottom just fell outa everything.

"S'okay," I say softly. "S'okay. You're a good girl, ain't ya, huh?" But I know she's dead.

Then . . .

MICHAEL JAMES BLACKER AWOKE SCREAMING. The moment of the dog's death had felt like he'd fallen into her eyes and drowned. He was dead, not her. His hands and arms were alive with her blood and he felt it get absorbed into his own skin; into his own body so that she was a part of him. It had seemed like a holy thing.

His body was drenched with sweat. It had been years since the recurring nightmare had made his life a misery. He'd grown out of it; had forgotten it.

He sat up, breathing heavily, and looked at the luminous digits on the clock at his bedside—3:23 AM.

He threw back the covers and switched on the lamp, swinging his legs over the side of the bed, gaining back the control.

"Dear God," he whispered. "Dear fucking God."

He fought to drive away the after-effect of the dream. The remembering. He fought off the memory of all the times he'd had to go hunting with his father and his brothers and his father's friends, and how, for the first two years after Sally, he'd been made to cut the throat of every beast that the hunters brought down. Every one of them had looked at him; every one of them had drenched him in their blood and died inside of him. Every one of them had drowned him more, and none of it was holy at all, just a kind of penance for what he'd done to Sal.

He became so proficient at pretending that he'd whoop and holler like the others. It was easy. It didn't matter. None of it was real. He worked so hard at it that by the time he was eleven years old he came to believe himself.

And the door shut tight, oh yes it did. Amen!

There was no point trying to get back to sleep. What he needed right now was to get down to the Church Meeting Hall, where the Brotherhood had their offices, and ascertain any updates from night two.

He'd only had three hour's sleep but, he thought, I can catch up when I'm dead.

He went into the en-suite bathroom and showered and shaved. He dressed in a casual black, cashmere high-necked sweater over which he strapped the brown leather, standard police-issue shoulder holster, his Versace slacks and jacket, black socks, and highly polished, soft leather loafers. Wallet, money-clip, cell phone, keys, 9mm pistol. All where they should be.

Michael had spent years cultivating both his appearance and an accentless voice, eradicating his upbringing and his *good ol' boy* background. No one knew anything about either his family or his past.

He had changed his surname to Blacker when he was of an age to do so legally, but by then neither his family or anyone from his earlier years would have recognized him anyway, had he knocked on their door and said who he was.

He took a final check in the bathroom mirror. He phoned out for a cab and left the apartment at 4 AM.

The night was foggy and the streets were all but deserted on the drive across town to headquarters. As usual, though, as Michael looked out of the window he could see them. Sporadic and shifting, blending with the shadows away from the street-lights and the all-night neon where they thought they were invisible, the unmistakable forms of animals and beasts that made no sense. This was how he knew that his work had just begun, because all of them, and he had first spotted them over a dozen years ago, had been summoned into the world as an off-shoot to the workings of the dark arts—all of them were demons. That was sure in Michael's mind.

He thought of this Sight as a gift from God: God's way of letting him know how much cleansing lay ahead. He realized that no one else saw them, and at one time he had, in a moment of self-doubt, wondered if perhaps he was crazy. He had suffered for that thought with an almost crippling guilt and had spent days and nights in the privacy of his room, in self-flagellation, to atone. He had not gone there again. Doubt was a disease.

The cab rounded the corner into Armidale Road and pulled up alongside the curb in front of the ultra-modern, tinted glass frontage of the Church of the Penitents of the True Faith. Michael paid the driver and stepped out of the car.

As he walked along the path that led to the rear of the building his movement activated the motion-sensitive lighting, illuminating his passage. He was monitored every few yards by state-of-the-art security cameras.

He slipped his pass-card into the lock of the office door, punching in his four-digit access code beside it, and let himself in. There

was a skeleton crew of six men sitting around the computer termi-
nals with cups of coffee, relaxing, except for Brendon who was on his
cell phone and writing frantically on a notepad. He looked like the
night was wearing him down, and Michael figured that, God-botherer or no God-botherer, Brendon was sure to be running on something that he'd snorted again because he was also wired and chewing
on his mouth as he listened to the caller. He gestured toward
Michael, but Michael just signaled that he'd get to him later.

"Everything gone quiet?" he asked of no one in particular.

Ron Fenney, a burly man in his middle forties, ex-military with a
nasty attitude to anyone he considered his inferior, raised his hand
without turning from the monitor.

Brendon clicked his cell phone shut at the same time, saying, "I've
got stuff," but Ron told him to shut the fuck up and wait. Michael
suppressed a smile. Ron had a real hard-on for being top dog, and as
far as he was concerned Brendon was a weasel and would probably
fold if things got hot—the guy was just too damned religious and
too into speed. Ron wasn't in this for the hype, and every one of the
others in the Brotherhood knew it. Michael trusted him.

"Cops just reported into Central that they've finished up at that
Selena Woodford chick's little shoppy-thing over on the bay," he
said, as Michael pulled up a chair beside him.

"Nothing?"

"Nada."

"No connection to last night?"

"Oh they know there's a connection, sir."

"What about the club and the bitches?"

"Nah. Not a clue. Too far apart," and he laughed.

Tom Delaney lit up a cigarette and rolled his chair over from his
console, drinking coffee from a polystyrene cup to help keep himself
alert. "You've got good boys out there, sir," he said.

Michael merely nodded. Things were looking tidy and he liked
that. "I'm going to want to keep things quiet tonight. No work on

the Sabbath and all that, all right? I want you to get the lists distributed for Saturday night's Eclipse early on the same day and not before. You onto it, Tom?"

"Yes sir."

"What you got?" He gestured for Brendon to sit.

"A group of loopers seen driving a bus into Shannon's 24/7 down on the Southside. Boys at Lucy's seen 'em come out, and two of their women was wearing the devil's star round their necks. The guys tracked 'em into the warrens, but . . ."

"What kind of bus?" interrupted Phillip, suddenly very awake.

"Crappy old double-decker, apparently."

"It's them," Phillip locked eyes with Michael, looking pale. "It's fuckin' them!"

"Calm down." Tom recognized the rising panic in the younger man's eyes and was disgusted. "You think they could've followed you here? Give me a break! You can't know it's them."

"Well, shit, 'course I'm not sure, but I'll bet there aren't that many loopers in the country drivin' that kind of vehicle." He was reacting with an edge to his voice. For all the penance, forgiveness, and cleansing he had endured, he still slept really badly knowing what he'd done.

"Whose boys are down that way?" Michael asked.

"Dan Taylor's," Brendon advised. "That was them on the phone just now."

"Bless you, son," Michael gently touched the young advocate's shoulder, and Brendon's knees went to jelly under the praise. "Please get back to Dan and ask him to have his men locate the group. Can you do that for me?"

"I'm on it, Father," he said reverentially, moving off to his desk to make the call.

"Fuckin' puppy," Ron snarled under his breath. Michael heard him, however, and the nerve under his left eye started to tick.

Chapter Fifteen

Hunter had been aware of the group of men standing outside the front of the club opposite the parking station. One of them had watched the bus the whole time as it pulled off the road, and when it stopped for Rowan to insert the access card into the slot that triggered the off-hours security gate.

The Travelers had parked the bus, unloaded and shouldered their equipment, and exited the building by the night door that led back onto the street.

The man who'd watched them going into the multistory car park attempted to be subtle as he alerted his companions, but the wave of excitation that they emitted—akin to blood-lust—was felt by everyone in the troupe of Travelers.

The men were laughing and joking among themselves, seeming to be merely walking in the same direction.

This was not good.

By unspoken agreement the Sídhe took the lead and abruptly turned down the first street leading away from their true destination. They proceeded to move through the winding labyrinth of lanes and alleyways in unobvious circles. It took about half an hour before their pursuers must have realized the ruse. Hunter wasn't certain if they'd lost them or whether they had simply given up the game.

Dawn was breaking up the last of the fog before he was certain it was safe enough to go home. Only when they were at their camp did he relax his guard.

Jack filled the kettle from the twenty-litre water container and put it on the gas ring to boil, while Gypsy and Matt set about preparing coffee for themselves and the others.

"We've got a problem," said Brighid dropping, exhausted, onto one of the couches. She watched as Hunter took Robin from Trevor's arms and deposited the sleeping child into his bed.

Merrin and Willie were helping Black Annis to store away the instruments, and Kathryn kept close to Merrin, feeling uncomfortably out of her depths in the strange surroundings.

"You figure they'll come back?" she asked of no one in particular.

"Come and get warm, Kate," Hunter said to her, adding more fuel to the fire. "Keep me company while things settle down." She came and stood as close to him as she could without seeming rude, very comforted by his presence in a way she could not describe.

Hunter allowed himself to send his awareness out into the pre rush-hour calm. He touched the minds of Fingal Pearce and Sweet Maggie, of the Clan Ulchabhán. They were both alarmed—Get out, they were saying. Get *out!*

Hmm, thought Hunter. Not likely. *Not me anyway, and knowing Brighid, not her either.*

"Seems we have a problem," he said to Brighid, who rolled her eyes like hadn't she just said as much?

WENDY WU HAD A RADIO in the room where she stole to smoke a cigarette every hour or so. She'd kept tabs on the news reports and passed along information regarding the wave of savagery taking place, apparently at random, throughout the city. But Hunter had known. Whether it was the work of one man or several was irrelevant. The pattern of the night, coupled with the burning of Vincent's family's hounfor and that fairly naïve would-be witch out along the beaches— same smell. How the bombing of a gay night-club and the mutilations of three sex workers fitted into the pattern was unclear right now, but that they *were* connected was beyond doubt.

Hunter dropped into deep thought, seemingly no longer aware of Kathryn's presence, so she moved away from the fire and sat on one of the chairs beside Vincent. His deep calm helped her to relax. He exhibited barely any emotion, but he wasn't cold or aloof. He just knew things. The animal spirits that moved around him did so with a sense of being in a safe space. She allowed her thoughts to take in the past twenty-four hours. Between waking up yesterday morning and being here with these people now, her whole world had been turned upside down. And still she kept her mobile phone switched off.

"I WANT EVERYONE OUT OF the city," said Brighid.

There were vehement protests from most of those present.

"This is not a suggestion," Hunter responded.

"Does that include you?" Annis stood with her arms folded across her body in an attitude of defiance.

"Not me and not Hunter," said Brighid.

"Why!" This from Matt.

Brighid *tsked.* "It's 'cause you smell too loud."

"Yeah I guess we do make a crowd." Annis grinned dangerously, exposing her small, sharp incisors. "But where do you suggest we go? A caravan park for fuck's sake? I'll not go far when there's trouble—you know that."

None of them wanted to go anywhere. They were quite prepared to hole up in the abandoned Underground until they were needed, and said as much.

"How long till you feel like you're dying, being out of the vitality and all?" Hunter took in each of the Sídhe one at a time. They were quiet. They all knew that well-being depended on being close to the elements, and that the magics that relied on them could not long endure without exposure to the sun and the wind and the rain.

"There's my place . . ." Kathryn stopped herself. *What was she doing? What if Martin . . . ?* She didn't let herself finish the thought.

"My place," she said clearly. "I live . . ."

"Yeah—Falconstowe, I know. But what about that husband of yours?" interrupted Brighid.

"How could you know . . ."

"A wee bird told me." The bright, pale eyes of the raven glittered. "It's a good place, though," she told the others. "Only an hour away if you travel out of traffic time."

"We can't risk taking the bus." Willie knew that those men were sure to have people stationed near the 24/7, but Merrin had the possible solution. "I can ask Dimity. She knows lots of people, and she's got the big delivery van. She's sure to be okay."

"It's too early to be asking anyone for anything." Puck came over to Hunter and he draped himself around her shoulders, kissing her pale gold hair.

"You coming to bed?" she whispered, a twitch to her lips.

"You go ahead, I just have one last thing to finish up," and he raised his voice a little, speaking to the others.

"Get some sleep everyone. In a couple of hours we'll see if we can arrange everything and get you out of the way in the middle of the day."

People started moving to their various corners, where many of the mattresses were shielded from each other by the positioning of furniture.

Hunter stretched and turned toward Vincent, who stood soundlessly to his side. The two exchanged a glance.

Without words it was agreed that he would remain in the city with Hunter and Brighid. It was what he was trained for.

Chapter Sixteen

Falconstowe—

The five clans of Tuatha Dé Danann and all their companions left New Rathmore within an hour of each other.

On the journey out of the city Kathryn checked her phone messages. Five. All from Martin, and each one more poisonous than the one preceding. The final message had been sent from his mother's place at 10:14 PM, after it had become obvious that she was a no-show. It was pure venom.

He was at the house when they arrived. Dimity drove the minibus along the dirt driveway calling *Uh oh* over her shoulder to Kathryn. He had two men with him, and they were loading furniture into a moving truck.

He stopped in his tracks, putting down the desk chair he'd been carrying, and stared as Kathryn and several unbelievably scruffy hippy types—total strangers—piled out of the bus into the early afternoon sunlight.

She looked different. How could twenty-four hours wreak such a change? These people must have given her drugs. Gone was the glamourous, tidy wife, a tribute to his success, replaced by this? She even walked differently—long strides—as she and some weirdo woman, who'd obviously shaved the front of her hair off, came in his direction.

They stopped in front of him, and Kathryn's face tilted toward him defiantly.

"What are you taking?"

"Everything I paid for Kathryn." He glanced at her, his eyes dangerous; hooded, no sign of remorse. "Who are these people?"

"My friends. I invited them." She had no idea what he might do. He was just as likely to lash out as he was to call the cops and try to use his influence to have her companions removed. Well it wasn't going to happen.

As the two faced off, the walnut tree behind the house exploded with jewel-bright blackness and noise as an uncountable frenzy of ravens took to the sky, ark-arking their intention. They landed again, as swiftly as they had erupted, in the foliage of the many trees around the front of the house. Several of Kathryn's company smiled.

"I want these people off my property, now!" Martin screamed, spittle flying from his mouth.

Predictable, thought Kathryn, unimpressed. *It's my place when I'm stuck here on my own and maybe come back to my senses, but it's his place when it suits him.*

"You go," said Merrin, ice in her voice.

"Wh . . ." he started, looking in her direction with a sneer.

"You go now," Kathryn repeated. "Take what you and your boys have already taken and go."

"I don't believe . . ."

Whatever he had been about to say was interrupted by the arrival of two more vehicles as full as the first. There were several women present now, but many men. Something about them made Martin's skin crawl. They all dressed like a bunch of carnies . . . But their eyes. When he looked around him he felt as though he was in the presence of wild animals and his nerve failed him.

He picked up the chair he had been carrying and threw it into the back of the already loaded truck.

"Let's go." He gestured to the two men standing near the doors. "Shut it up and let's get out of here."

"No argument from me," said one of the men as he closed the rear door of the truck, sending a wink in Kathryn's direction. This caused her to lift her eyebrows slightly as she realized that Martin had probably hired these guys and that they were just along for the money.

The two men got into the cab of the truck and turned over the engine, one of them waving out the window as they drove off slowly down the drive.

Martin came right up to Kathryn's face. "You'll regret this," he threatened softly. (The red-haired man and one who looked like a gypsy walked as silently as cats to stand beside him.)

"No. No, I won't, Martin."

He moved over to his Audi and pressed the remote that unlocked it.

"What is it they say?" He sneered as he slid into the driver's seat, "Oh yeah. I'll see you in court, Kathryn."

He pulled the door shut, kicked over the engine, and drove smoothly away from the gathering.

Kathryn waited until he was out of sight before turning toward her house. "Let's see what's left."

"Way cool, mo chroí." Willie ruffled her hair.

"Yeah," beamed Merrin. "You were pretty splendid, Cat."

Once inside Kathryn realized that the removals truck must have arrived only a short time before because the bulk of the furnishings were still intact. Martin had started with his own things, and most of what had been his away-from-town office had been dismantled.

"Is there much he can do to harm you legally?" asked Merrin, as the Sídhe and their entourage took up residence.

"No. That was all bluff," said Kathryn, lighting the slow combustion stove. "The deed is in my name. It was a birthday present."

Merrin laughed as she filled the kettle, looking out the window above the sink as she did so.

"Looks like everything's going on outside." The backyard looked more like a park than a garden, and several dozen people were out there building up a pyre of wood for a fire, making camp rather than inhabiting the small house.

"What?" asked Kathryn, wondering how on earth she was going to make coffee for the thirty-something people who had already arrived and the anticipated two more groups still on the way. She was looking in the cupboard where the neat, six-person plate settings were stored.

Merrin saw her friend's shoulders slump and realized what she was thinking.

"Hey, they're Travelers, silly! They'll have everything—relax!" She grabbed Kathryn by the sleeve, dragging her out to join the gathering, leaving a few people in the lounge room to light the indoor fire so that the whole house would be warm.

THE RAVENS WERE BACK IN the walnut tree, making like a crowd of raucous kids.

"Look at them all." Kathryn shaded her eyes, staring up at the turbulence of glossy black. "There's never been so many. It's like they know something." A finger of fear stroked the little hairs on the back of her neck while a kind of awe affected her deeply at the sight.

Annis overheard. "Oh, they know all right," she said, looking up into the ancient branches. "They're the Lady's lot." She breathed deeply of the crisp clean air and the heady scent of woodsmoke coming from the tine.

"And if they know, then she knows."

"Who are you talking about?" asked Kathryn.

Annis' hawk-like eyes looked distant, like she was someplace that no one else could see, and all the dancing wraiths of half-seen birds and beasts around her slowed right down to calm, so that Kathryn perceived them more clearly than she had done since this whole thing had begun.

"She's Mystery," said Annis in the end.

"And that's big," Willie added, sidling up to Merrin.

"What? Like a god?" asked Kathryn.

"Yes and no," said Willie.

"How so?"

"Well, that word always seems to be a something, you know what I mean?"

"Yeah, but . . ."

"So she's everything. So that's why she's the Mystery. It's better that way. You don't get caught unawares if you understand her like that."

"Hmm." Kathryn was the last person, right at the moment, to doubt.

Right then, the hauntingly beautiful sound of the uilleann pipes could be heard from the depths of the wood that led in to the protected reserve at the far end of Kathryn's property.

"Matt," said Black Annis, though no question had been asked.

Willie walked over to the back veranda of the house where the Fíanna had stored their belongings and took his fiddle from its case. He came and stood beside the fire and linked with the piper, lending the warm, rich beauty of his instrument to the ancient-sounding air. Even the ravens were quiet.

KATHRYN LOOKED AROUND HERSELF AT the people who were beginning to feel like the family she'd never known, at the property that hitherto she had detested for its isolation, and at the house that seemed like it was looking back and asking that she really see it, and her eyes stung with what she'd missed.

Within the next hour the other two clans arrived, but by then the Travelers had settled in like it was home.

From the woods, down at the far edge of the property, had walked a tall, fair-skinned Sídhe with jet black hair and black clothing, with a once-white T-shirt showing beneath his vest. He exuded a classic, androgynous beauty, hinting at a danger that had always attracted both men and women. He carried a pack over one shoulder and a bodhran, in its ancient leather bag, over the other. His hair and clothing were littered with debris from the forest, giving him an elemental and slightly feral cast as the others watched him walk into the light of the bonfire.

"Raven!"

Alan was first to acknowledge him. He had been one of the Lost, accepted by the Travelers several years ago, and he had loved this unpredictable Dé Danann almost more than life itself, missing him terribly every time he had gone away. He scrambled to his feet from where he had been sitting playing a like instrument—the one that his aunt had gifted him and that Raven had taught him to play—and threw his arms around the tall man. Raven held him distractedly, aware of the jaggle of thoughts that cascaded through Alan's mind but too curious about the unexpected gathering that had descended on the place where he had secreted himself for most of the past winter.

The others welcomed him wordlessly. They always did. He knew that. It still didn't make company any easier. Still. He was here now, and seeing Alan again was worth the crowd—for a while anyway.

LATER THAT NIGHT HE, ALAN, several of the men, and a few of the women—all members of the three warrior clans—sat away from the others, in Kathryn's living room.

It was Seamus Kelly who had pulled them all together because he, for sure, was going back if at all there was to be a fight go down. Puck had followed them when she'd heard the whispers and attempted to talk sense into the discussion, but there was no listening.

They were going back. That was that. And when Matt and Willie both agreed to represent Fiach Dubh, there was no keeping Merrin either.

"Then I'm coming if you're going," said Kathryn resolutely.

"It's not your war." Seamus still viewed Kathryn and Merrin as outsiders, human. It came with the clan—badgers were like that. "It's hers as much as ours," interrupted Matt. "It's her as has got the Sight."

"What's that got to do with anything?" asked Angus McLeish, Seamus' shield brother. "So she can see us? This is not about watching out for someone who can't protect themselves. We can't afford that or we might as well not have left in the first place."

Kathryn bristled. There was no way she would allow them to tell her what she could or couldn't do.

"You just watch your own fuckin' back," she said to everyone's surprise, Merrin's most of all.

"Well!" Merrin folded her arms across her chest. "Wuhoo, Cat!"

Seamus actually paled under Kathryn's look. "I never meant offense like," he offered. He was slightly confused by the woman staring him down. They all knew her for what she was but this didn't fit the legend at all. She wasn't supposed to be feisty. Still he didn't back down.

"What can you do? " he asked almost kindly. "I mean, what'd be the point?"

"I don't know," Kathryn frowned, "make sandwiches?" That cracked Willie up, and it was minutes before he could stop laughing.

"Shite," said Seamus, recognizing something in the air that informed him his objections were moot.

All together, twelve of the Sídhe—seven men and four women of the warrior clans, and one of the seers from the Otter Clan known as Selkie Duffy—along with Merrin, Kathryn, Rowan, Raven, and Alan, decided they were better off closer to the action than doing what Hunter and Brighid had suggested. At least Merrin and Kathryn didn't smell of the magic like the rest of them.

Black Annis laid back in the Rowan's arms, smiling to herself. *How long since some real action?* she thought. She hid her satisfaction with the outcome of the night's discussion, not because there was anything wrong with how she was feeling—but to savor the sensation that being a part of the Wild Hunt always aroused within her. Some very bad people, she was convinced, deserved to know her better.

Chapter Seventeen

Brighid and Hunter perched like birds upon the crenelated trim that bordered the rooftop of the forty-four story St. James building, looking out over the harbor as the sun rimmed the edge of the world with a slurry of gold. At that precise time a wind—the wind that always accompanied the moment—rushed out from the dawn and flew across the water, making its way onto the land to wash over those awaiting it like a benediction.

There had hardly been a day in forever that the two had missed receiving the gift of it. Very few humans actually knew about it, and to the bright god of the forests, and the little Sídhe woman, that was such a shame, for within that wind was the music of the world—just one song, one sound, but it was a wonder, and it was the garment that the Lady wore to remind the earth that she loved. Vincent, sitting slightly apart from the others, was one person who did know.

He needed the solitude to prepare for his day. He was deep in that state of mushin that allowed him to experience an unfetteredness from thought and involvement. He felt the wind, and a slight smile quirked the corners of his mouth as he reveled in its message.

He opened his eyes and hopped down from the turret-like cornice, landing lightly on the roof-top, cushioning the impact with soft knees. He walked a little way toward the center of the flat expanse and dropped his backpack to the ground before unbuckling the straps.

He pulled out a folded piece of silk, which he spread open to one side, then a rolled up length of black cloth, which he placed at the edge of the silk square. He then took the simple bag that he had slung across his back and removed his daisho. He laid the sword and the wakazashi, still within their saya, side by side, reverently, upon the silk.

He turned and bowed toward the rising sun and proceeded through a succession of warm-up exercises and stretches.

Hunter sensed him rather than heard him and half turned away from the dawn to watch, just as Vincent stripped off his sweatshirt before beginning his Qigong.

The young man stood very still with his knees bent and his arms forming a softly rounded arc in front of his body. As he focused he concentrated on his breathing, each breath becoming deeper and longer until he reached a place of seeming limit. He remained in that state until the sun had well and truly escaped the horizon and was falling softly and fully onto the three.

Hunter could sense the vibrant ki emanating from his companion. He smiled as he slid from his sitting place. He removed his big coat and a layer of warm things and walked over to Vincent as the latter began the slow sequence of movements that emulated certain animals and birds. Vincent's eyes widened as he recognized that what could have been misconstrued as fat, due to the bulk of Hunter's clothing, was in fact sheer power and muscle. He'd never seen a man as big in his entire life, and beside him Vincent looked like a child.

Hunter joined him for the pleasure of the movement. Vincent wasn't even surprised that he seemed able to execute each sequence with the precision of a master. It had been many years since he'd trained with his father, and he was very glad for the companionship.

As they wound down from the chi gong, sweat glistened on both men's bodies. Hunter put an arm around the shoulders of the younger man and thanked him before returning to sit with Brighid, bundling himself into his clothing. Vincent bowed formally as the other moved away.

"Should I be sayin' wow?" Brighid grinned. The big man simply beamed.

"Just watch. . ." he said.

Vincent went to the square of silk and took up the roll of black cloth, which he wound several times around his belly. When it was tied off to his satisfaction he dropped lightly to his knees, folding his wide-legged pants back over his calves.

He placed the palms of both hands on the ground. "To rei," he whispered, bowing to his sword. He first picked up the wakazashi and slid it into the folds of the obi, and then the katana, which he held vertically before himself before positioning it beside its companion.

Still in a kneeling position he turned to face the sun.

"Shinzen ni rei," he said aloud to that god.

He drew his katana from its saya and proceeded to execute a series of slow moves, strikes, and blocks, before replacing the sword in its sheath. Then he stood. He once again drew the katana and held it out from himself, sensing the flow of ki from his body to well beyond the tip of his blade. Both Hunter and Brighid could see this energy. It was like the life-force itself.

Vincent increased his speed, flowing effortlessly from one move to another, so the patterns of light that his sword produced mesmerized them. It was positively symphonic. An hour must have passed before he slowed, then stopped—calmly prepared to face whatever destiny presented.

THE THREE HAD ORGANIZED THEIR somewhat vague plan the preceding night, at around the same time as the others at Kathryn's farm had formulated their own.

It was simple, really. Go back to the bus. Hunter and Brighid intended to be captured by their pursuers of the previous encounter while Vincent planned not to be.

They had spent most of the day at Dimity's, talking about the events that had taken place for the others out at Falconstowe.

Dimity kept yawning. She had stayed until around 3 AM with folk she had fallen in love with right off. They had welcomed her as though she had been their knight in shining armor, gifting her with the choicest morsels of food and generally plying her with very elegant uiske beatha until she thought it appropriate to sober up for the long drive home.

Everyone had quieted down about an hour before she left, after a night of music and talking and general revelry.

"Anything unusual happen while you were still there?" Hunter asked, his gut instincts active as she spoke.

"Not so's I noticed." Then she thought about it a bit more. "Only . . . some of the people stayed in the house all night with Kathryn and Merrin and wouldn't come out when they were called to the feast. Nothing really."

Hunter looked at Brighid and sighed.

"What?" asked Dimity.

"One of them wouldn't have happened to have had long fox-colored braids hangin' almost to his waist by any chance?" Brighid didn't really need an answer.

"Yeah, that's right—the guy that our Merrin's sweet on. Why?"

"How many, did you see?"

"A few. I'd gone inside to use the loo and they were all huddled around the hearth in the living room. Dunno. A dozen maybe."

Hunter laughed a soft sound, kind of like distant thunder.

"They'll be coming back then?" suggested Brighid.

"What do you think?"

Dimity took a look at their good-looking companion, who had sat silently throughout the morning, drinking only water while the rest of them fueled up on the excellent coffee that her premises was famous for.

"Do you talk at all?" she asked without rancor.

"Just listening is all." He spoke so softly that Dimity unconsciously leaned forward.

"You from around here?"

"No."

"You known this lot for long then?"

"No."

"On holidays or just passing through?" She was beginning to get the picture. He wasn't being unfriendly, she realized, but my, he really was the most untalkative person she'd ever known.

"Neither, I guess."

Dimity sighed, her ample breasts lifting and falling with the depth of the breath. She turned her attention back to Hunter.

"So what's this all about?" She downed the last dregs of her coffee. "There was plenty of talk among your folk about trouble, and what with the news on the telly lately I can't quite shake off the feeling that you're involved somehow."

"It's unfinished business," said Hunter.

"Ouch! That sounds rather ominous."

"There's always hope . . ." Brighid added, as cryptically as ever.

"Hmm. Well, I'm here if you need me." She meant it. There was a quality to Merrin's friends that was a salve to her world-weary spirit. Dimity had gone through some major upheavals in her sixty-two years—the shop had been her salvation. She was still strong and walked taller nowadays than she had at one time in her past. She had what she called unfailing bullshit detectors, and had allowed them to guide her in her later life like she should have done when she was young, and they assured her of the straightforward sincerity of these people. She was never one to back away from a friend.

She had heaps of bookwork to catch up on, but before she left them she threw her van keys in Hunter's direction. "Knock yerself out. Leave them with Stewie at the front desk when you don't have a use for it any more. I can call Lyn if I get desperate."

"You get three wishes," Hunter smiled. Brighid dug him in the ribs and told him to behave himself, but Dimity hadn't heard.

Chapter Eighteen

They utilized the van just once, taking time to go to the market to stock up on supplies for the camp, knowing that sooner or later the others would make their way back into the city and reasoning that they would use the cover of night. They dropped the keys back at Dimity's just at sunset.

Following the trackways of the labyrinth across the Southside, the three kept as much to the dark as they could. A slow-moving mist crept in off the harbor, allying itself to their stealth. Most of the people they passed were oblivious to their presence—it was easy.

They wound their way down into the alley that ran beside the carpark. It was littered with junk and empty bottles and tins, several make-shift beds in back doorways and hidden up against the dumpsters—mostly of cardboard and scrounged bits and pieces—for those unfortunate enough to have no other roof. Toward the exit of the lane there were heaps of discarded wooden pallets and unclaimed crates—enough to provide an ample covey for observing the strip club (called Lucy's Bar) while they waited to see if the same men came back.

The three sat at separate vantage points, Vincent choosing the edge of the rooftop, accessed by redundant fire escapes still only just attached to a building adjacent to the 24/7 that had been boarded up years ago, marked for demolition and subsequently forgotten. Hunter assumed the glamour of one of the street people and huddled, seemingly drunk or stoned, in the doorway of a closed shop, while Brighid simply merged with the shadows.

It was she who spotted the group of five men, three of whom had followed them previously, mere seconds before the others. Hunter looked up to see if Vincent realized, but he was gone.

THE MEN ACROSS THE ROAD didn't talk. They headed straight for the entrance to the club, walking past the huge Maori who stood by the door, casually attentive lest his services be required. They were inside only long enough to return with glasses of beer.

The fog thickened as the night took hold. The men were having obvious difficulty seeing anywhere further than the entrance to the garage, and they were stamping their feet and shoving their hands not holding beers deep into jacket pockets in a vain attempt to keep them warm, therefore supple. Four of the five had their heads covered in warm woolen beanies, and the fifth wore a cap pulled down over his eyes. All of them, though, radiated agitation, and both Hunter and Brighid, their heightened senses on full alert, could smell an animal musk exuding from them even at this distance. Excitement. But from among the group there was another feeling—one of them was very afraid.

"What's going on?" Brighid moved silently and darkly to Hunter's side.

"Don't know yet. You smell 'em?"

"One of them doesn't seem to want to be here."

"I wonder why? The rest are pretty eager. I'm getting a closer look."

He took a battered old felt hat from one of the many pockets of the huge coat that he wore and pulled it onto his head to hide his dreds and shadow his face, even in the night. He stumbled from the shop-front, mumbling to himself, looking a little crazy and pretending to be very drunk.

He zigzagged across the road, half tripping over something unseen, and narrowly avoided the two-way traffic that blared their horns at him in disgust.

Once on the pavement he shoved his hands into his pockets and, keeping his head down, headed for the door of the club, coming up close to the pack of watchers as he did so.

They were constantly straining to gaze up and down the street, and he knew that he was right—they were back for the kill.

He stumbled behind them, weaving toward the entrance of the club. The bouncer raised his eyebrows as the big man approached. He could almost hear him thinking *No way!* as he prepared to block the entrance.

But Hunter stopped in his tracks.

He recognized the O'Neill daughter's ginger-haired husband.

He patted his pockets, pretending he had lost or forgotten something before turning back the way he'd come.

The heavy felt hat hid his eyes, which was just as well.

VINCENT MOVED BACK OVER THE rooftop and had leaped the narrow alleyway to land easily on the first floor of the ramp. He made his way across to the other side and over onto the adjacent rooftop that led into the warrens in the direction that Brighid and Hunter would lead their pursuers. He tied the wide pants close in to his legs to enable him to move unhindered. His katana was strapped to his back, even though he doubted he would use it, and he carried his staff easily.

Shadows, shadows—lithe and swift—surrounded him, all unseen, all alert to danger—earthy graces loving the man they ran with, creating a deeper darkness to protect him.

Vincent knew that he would defend his new friends—and he would kill if it came to it, even though it was his nature to attempt all other options.

The warrens were such that he knew he could keep to the high places for as long as he chose. For several hours during the afternoon he had ranged the entire area, remembering each twist and turn with unnerving skill, and so he was as prepared as he could be to stay abreast of the gang of men, just in case they pulled weapons.

As he looked back down the street he saw Hunter and Brighid emerge from the alleyway arm in arm. The men across the road pretended to ignore them, but they saw—it was clear that they saw. One man, head and shoulders taller than the others, removed his cap long enough to wipe the nervous sweat from his forehead. He had short-cropped ginger hair and a body-language that hinted at extreme danger. Vincent marked him.

Chapter Nineteen

Willie, Merrin, and Kathryn, along with Matt, Raven, Annis, and Rowan—all of Fiach Dubh—and five others from the Wolf and Badger clans, were crammed into Dimity's friend's old long-wheel-base Land Rover. Hunter's presumption that they would return the following night was incorrect—they took off quietly just before dawn on the Saturday morning and drove straight to Merrin's studio.

The Sídhe had argued among themselves for most of the trip back as to whether they should go and find Hunter and the other two and just rush the guys who were after them, taking them down to Willie's river place where no one was likely to disturb them while they discovered the reason they'd been tracked, or go to the ramp and follow them back to whatever lair from which they'd crawled.

"But why?" Merrin asked. "It could have been just a random guy-thing. Drunk guys in packs do that kinda shit all the time—follow people they don't like the look of just for the sake of the game."

"It was too weird," Matt assured her. "All that stuff going on in the one night. The bombings the night before. Those men at the club were just one of a whole bunch roaming the city. I figure there was purpose, sure as anything."

"Yeah, I guess. But why?" Down on the Southside there were many unusual-looking people. She couldn't understand what would have triggered them off.

Willie opened the window onto the courtyard and sniffed at the morning.

"No point worrying about it now. I'll figure it out afore too long. There's a 'why' for sure, and it's all connected." He was somewhat distracted by the soft butter glow of the light as it played on the red brick of the backyard and the buzz of insects busying themselves in Merrin's garden. All this seriousness wreaked havoc with his sense of priority.

Merrin moved to his side to see what had piqued his attention. As they looked out they noticed dozens of ravens rattling from the sky and coming to perch and flutter around the high points.

"You lookin' for somebody?" Willie called softly. He didn't disturb them in the least. If anything they seemed to settle.

"They know." Raven stood just behind the two, observing, and he walked out the door of the studio and sat down on the old bench beside the fish pond.

His long hair merged with his clothing, and a little silver harp glinted from one earlobe. The paleness of his skin gave an overall monochrome effect to the picture that wasn't even broken by the color of his eyes—gray as a storm.

Several of the corvids flew down from their vantage points to land around him, curious but unafraid, sensing kindred. One big, glossy adult perched itself on the back of the seat beside him, ruffling its feathers, seemingly content just to be there.

Kathryn came outside and sat down, and the bird never budged.

"I can see them all through you, you know," she whispered. Raven turned and directed his disconcerting gaze toward this attractive half-human woman without responding.

"Can you see me?" she asked.

"The Sight's not a gift we can all claim," he admitted. "What am I supposed to see?"

"Oh nothing, I guess." She felt slightly embarrassed and couldn't remember what had prompted her to come and sit with him.

"Some of us are just really old, Sunshine." He grinned and his whole face changed, becoming boyish and vital. Kathryn smiled back at him but stood as though to leave.

"Sit a while?" he asked, aware of her discomfort. "I'm just not used to too many people, even other Folk."

"I didn't notice what clan you came with to my place."

"There's the funny thing. No one. I was camped down at the base of the escarpment in that patch out back in the forest."

"I just met another person who camps out by himself." Kathryn smiled, remembering her first sight of Vincent.

"The guy with the swords that the others are talking about?"

"Mmm." They fell quiet. Kathryn thought about how often she'd been left by herself in her life, and just how much she was basking in the easy companionship of her new friends.

"I can't do it anymore." Raven looked down at his hands resting gently in his lap, as though studying an oracle.

"What did you say?"

"Couldn't do it much at all," he said.

"What?"

"What you were thinkin'."

"Oh . . . so you haven't got the Sight but you can read people's minds?"

"That's the trouble, yeah?" It struck Kathryn how horrible that must be considering that her own thoughts were ceaseless.

RAVEN HAD AN ABIDING MISTRUST for most humans. Alan and his Aunt Julie were the only two exceptions over the last decade: Julie because of an act of kindness after his release from a prison where he had spent seven hellish years of abuse after he'd been jailed for manslaughter.

He'd attended a horse fair and had seen a man savagely whipping one of the horses and had attempted to stop him. It had gone nasty. The man had turned his whip on Raven for interfering in what he considered his own business—Raven being an obvious outsider and looking like he did—and the Sídhe had retaliated, shoving the trader to the ground where his skull had connected with a rock, splitting like fruit.

None of the witnesses conceded self-defense when questioned regarding the incident, and Raven's attorney had been abysmal—pro bono, inept counsel.

Julie had found him wandering the streets of Paris. She was an artist and offered to pay him in accommodation and food if he'd sit for her. Something absolutely kind had shone from her, and he had agreed.

She'd taken him home to her apartment and had run him a deep, hot bath. He'd listened to her humming away to herself in the kitchen as she made them both soup.

He'd scrubbed at the grime that had encrusted his body until he hurt. He'd wrapped himself in an old pink towel that hung from the drying rack and wandered into the sitting room. Hanging from a hook on the wall to the left of the fireplace was an old, well-preserved bodhran. He'd taken it down and played it.

Julie had stood by the cooking range, spellbound, as he'd conjured images of ancient battles and ancient pride. She was as fey as could be and wondered at how right she was in thinking that this was not just some gorgeous guy that the gods had sent her way . . . the music was both haunting and otherworldly.

She'd been perfectly aware of the magic he evoked.

She'd wandered from the kitchen into the cozy, messy living room, and deposited the bowls of soup onto a table by the doors that led onto a small balcony.

"Come help me with the bread and things?"

He'd put down the instrument almost grudgingly and followed her through to the kitchen, where she'd deposited a plate of warmed bread, some cheese, knives and spoons, and a bottle of good red, with two old china tea-cups to serve as glasses.

"I know what you are," she'd hinted, picking up plates and leaving him to carry the rest.

"What? How . . ."

"I know things I can't explain." She'd walked past him into the other room.

HE'D STAYED WITH HER FOR three years. It was the longest time he had trusted anyone for centuries.

She'd never asked anything of him other than to sit for her, and that had been important to him, very important. So the one time she had asked a favor he'd complied without the slightest hesitation, despite the grandeur of the request. Her nephew, Alan, needed saving from the desolate apathy of a family that could not (would not) understand his ability to see the spirits of the not-really-dead ghosts that no one else saw, and who had had him psychoanalyzed and institutionalized from boyhood for what had been termed a reality dysfunction.

Raven had crossed the sea, taking the old bodhran and his stories, and had taught Alan as much as he could for as long as he could stand being around the people.

Alan had run off after the Sídhe had disappeared, and when Raven had eventually returned he'd had to search for the lad. Alan had had a profound stutter as a result of never having been allowed to speak his mind or be believed when he tried, and it had slowly gone away with the time the two had spent as friends. When he eventually found him the stutter had become pronounced again.

Raven introduced him to the Travelers because there was no going home to his dysfunctional, narrow-minded family, and he'd remained with them since.

He'd ignored the sexual desire that rose unbidden, not understanding for a long time that the attraction was mutual. Alan had loved the

Sídhe from the beginning and had been devastated when Raven had first gone away. He'd been young then. Not now. He was old enough to make his own decisions and to be clear about who he loved.

Raven reached out a hand toward the pentagram that hung from Kathryn's neck. She turned toward him, and he took hold of the small talisman, thinking.

"Hmm." He looked up into her face.

"What . . ."

"Did you have this on the other night?"

"Sure. Merrin gave it to me. She wears one as well."

He sat thinking and Kathryn could see the flutter of agitation from the shadows that attended him. The raven that perched nearby uttered a low rorl in its throat and flew off, joining his companions that lined the rooftops.

"I need to talk to the others. I think I know what's going on."

The Travelers sat around the studio aimlessly, talking quietly and listening to music. No one seemed to know what to do now that they were back, relying on Selkie Duffy's ranging sight to discover the whereabouts of Hunter and Brighid and the human warrior before deciding on a course of action. The problem was that Hunter had masked them in invisibility, and they remained unreachable.

"I know why." Raven avoided the jumble of bodies that littered the floor, on his way over to where Willie and Seamus sat at the coffee table sharpening the sgian dubh that Seamus had been gifted a thousand or so years ago when he lived amongst Highland warriors. He was meticulous with the ancient weapons and the whetstone.

"Did you hear what . . ." Raven began again, turning for a moment as Kathryn entered the room, forgetting himself.

"What've you worked out?" asked Willie.

"Oh, sure. It's the talismans. The ones the mortal girls wear."

"How do you figure that?"

"I figure that with what you've been talking about—the bombings and shite—that they followed you because of the talismans."

Kathryn joined them at the couch just as Merrin, Annis, and Rowan returned from shopping for additional supplies.

"They must have thought we were witches," Kathryn said, sitting.

"Aren't you?" Seamus seemed surprised.

"Merrin is. I don't quite know what I am." Both Willie and Matt laughed out loud, and Selkie rolled her eyes.

"What's so funny?" Kathryn wasn't offended, but she really hoped someone had an answer, not to the how—she'd been told that—but the what.

"Halfling, changeling. No difference really," offered Selkie from a distance. "You just got lost, is all."

"So I can think of myself in those terms?" Kathryn was quite pleased with the idea. "So Merrin's a witch, I'm a halfling, and you're all fairies?"

Willie roared with laughter.

Merrin came and plonked herself down on his lap. She plumped an ornately embroidered cushion that she'd picked up at a flea-market a month ago and threw it at her friend. "So you think it was us that caused the fuss?"

"If that's the case," said Seamus, "then what's the point of Hunter and Brighid doing what they're doing?"

"You don't travel with us," Willie snorted sarcastically. "There's nothin' that those two do that's a mistake—not like the rest of us. Not anymore, and never Hunter."

Chapter Twenty

Phillip Adler nearly wet himself when he saw them go past. As far as he was concerned they would not recognize him because he'd never actually attended the pagan gatherings up there on the far north coast while he was married to that sexy O'Neill bitch. But he'd seen. He'd always hidden out with his binoculars so that he'd be able to report everything that occurred. He had paid dearly for the sin, both of watching and for the sensations of lust and desire that his voyeurism had induced.

It had been the fires; the dancing, the sheer alienness. They'd put away barrel-loads of booze and not got drunk; they'd washed naked and unashamed down by the creek. The music that they played always stirred him badly, and the sight of the women—the visions they invoked in his mind—caused him painfully cruel erections, forcing him to relieve himself time and time again. And at night. That fucking big, dark-skinned bull of a guy with the dreds. Evoking strange gods, demons. The very devil himself as far as he knew.

And here he was again with that woman who used to be dressed up at the gatherings like she was some kind of queen. Well they wouldn't know him. Would they?

Fear. Crawling through his innards like a sickness. All he wanted to do was to go home, but that was impossible. Reverend Blacker had set *him* the task of the kill, but the bulge under his jacket still didn't stop the heebies from crawling everywhere under his skin, making him sweat.

He and the other men started off following. The two witches he'd been told had been with them were nowhere to be seen and neither was the rest of their brood, so this ought to be easy. It was just two weirdoes, wasn't it?

They kept a fair pace back, hugging the encroaching shadows sufficiently so that they were certain that they tracked undetected, in and out of the derelict ramble of lanes. Where the fuck were they going? At least twice Phillip was certain they passed the same crossroads—hard to be sure with fog closing everything in. He couldn't help himself though. He kept to the back of the bunch. He felt like such a coward, but surely that was not a sin?

For close on thirty minutes they kept pace with the two before they lost them. Just like that. One second they could still see them walking as casually as you please, the next they had vanished where the narrow street hit a T-junction.

"Shit," Ray Davis spat. He suffered no such fear and treated the whole thing like a sport, enjoying himself until now. "We've got to split up and find them. You lot ready?"

The others assented while Phillip merely mumbled something under his breath.

"Phil, you come with me. Tony, Jake, you and Rabbit meet us back at the club one way or another."

"When?" The lanky shaven-headed, buck-toothed man, aptly named Rabbit, scratched his armpit where the sweat dripped, despite the chill of the evening.

It was just past nine. "Give it an hour or so. We'll meet you at 10:15. Whichever of us gets 'em doesn't matter. Boss just wants 'em gone. If we're done doin' it earlier we'll head back and have us a beer while we wait for you."

Ray was sure that the kill was to be his. He thought secretly that every other man sent on this little tour was either a weasel or a wimp and he wondered why on earth Blacker would team him up like this, feeling slightly resentful at the insult.

"Yeah, if you get 'em first," Rabbit jibed. The other two men laughed.

"Fuck off, Rabbit. Just get going before I do you instead." Ray wasn't pretending to be nice anymore—he just wanted some action. He turned his back on the other four and strode down the way to the left with Phillip following after him.

They moved as quickly and as silently as they could. Ray was mumbling profanities under his breath, as much as he was praying to his god for guidance. He had a sure feeling in his gut, though, that their quarry had spotted the chase and had done a bolt.

The lane came to a dead-end except for a narrow track leading between two high warehouses that allowed them to proceed only in single file.

The night was black on dirty gray, and the last street light had been a block or so back the way they had come, so Ray had out his halogen torch and was shining the thin beam onto the rubble-strewn path. He lifted the light toward the end of the tunnel and it fell onto the silhouette of a small man, looking like he was dressed all in black with—shit! Was that a sword in his hand?

You stupid little bastard, he thought, moving the torch to his left hand, noting the abject stillness of the dupe up ahead. He moved his right hand under his jacket, unsnapping the holster.

A DEEP-THROATED GROWL FROM close behind him caused the hairs on his arms to rise and his mouth to go instantly dry.

"R . . . Ray?" Phil's voice at his back sounded like someone rubbing sandpaper together.

He didn't dare turn. He pulled his gun to shoot down the freak up ahead, but the man passed fluidly to his right and out of sight.

Ray spun around to see Phillip standing stock-still, sweat pouring from his face and the acrid scent of urine marking where his bladder had let go. He was hyperventilating.

"Get outa the way you stupid . . ." he yelled, leveling the gun at the creature right behind his companion. But it was too late. The biggest wolf that Ray had ever seen leaped straight at the back of Phillip's neck, crunching down sickeningly. As he squeezed the trigger something struck him a blow to his right shoulder and the shot went wide, taking off the side of his accomplice's face before his arm dropped paralyzed to his side, the gun clattering uselessly to the damp asphalt.

He dropped to his knees, a searing, white-hot pain roaring across his shoulder and into his neck. He lifted his left arm to touch what he was sure would be a mortal slash, expecting blood but finding nothing but a severe welt that swelled as he touched it. He was terrified. Before him the enormous pale wolf stood spread-legged over Phillip's obviously dead body, and from behind him stepped what appeared to be a half-caste black man with some Eastern blood thrown in, looking for all the world like some shaven Samurai. He had the sword in its sheath at his side, tucked into a wide cloth belt, but held a thin wooden pole in his hand. It was this that had done the damage.

Ray looked ahead, eyes fixed on nothing, shivering uncontrollably with fear. *I'm gonna die here*, he thought. He had no way of knowing whether the demon-beast would take him or the little man whose face remained expressionless.

"Well, who's a pretty boy then?" A woman's voice, like a shard of broken glass, hissed right up beside his ear. "Got your attention, have we? Found us, did you? Turn around and look at me—I want to see your eyes, mo chroí."

Ray didn't know what to do. There was no way he could have moved. He shut his eyes and began to pray.

"You can be such a scary bitch sometimes," said a deep, soft voice. Ray opened his eyes just long enough to realize that the wolf was nowhere to be seen and that the big, dark man that he and Phillip had been pursuing was now standing just behind his smaller companion.

"Get him up," ordered the woman.

Hunter squeezed past Vincent and lifted Ray to his feet, but his legs refused to support him.

"Tsk," Brighid exclaimed. "Are we going to have to drag you or can you perhaps summon up some of that cocky bloody attitude that pretends to be sooo in control?"

Ray figured that if they were going to kill him then he'd rather have some dignity left to him, so he forced his legs to move.

"It's a little chat we're after, mo chroí."

"What about Owen?" asked Hunter.

"Who . . ." Ray was suddenly confused.

"Leave him," Brighid said, ignoring their captive.

As they turned back the way they'd come the fog seemed to move with amorphous shapes and flutterings as hundreds upon hundreds of ragged blackbirds filled the air above and before them.

"Merrin's it is, then," Brighid replied, seeming to speak to them.

Chapter Twenty-one

"Are you going to tell us what this is all about?" Hunter was seated on the arm of the sofa where Ray had been deposited minutes before. He looked around himself at all the loopers filling the space.

"I . . . was just . . ." He was thinking as quickly as the pain in his arm, now tingling like lightning as the nerves recovered, would allow. He couldn't give the game up. If this lot didn't kill him then the Brotherhood would for sure.

Nobody spoke. They waited.

"We were just larking about," he said finally.

"You liar!" hissed the dark-haired woman whom the others called Brighid.

"We was just shit-stirring, honestly. We didn't intend for nobody to get hurt."

"What? With a gun under your coat?" Hunter responded, certainly not smiling. "Doesn't matter if you don't say anyway." He turned toward the others. "Where's Raven?"

"He said he needed to get some space," Willie informed him.

Everyone had been filled in on what had gone down. Kathryn had been horrified that someone had died, until Annis had told her about the fire at the Summer Gathering, and who had died.

She wanted to know what was to happen to their captive, but no one was sure what Hunter had decided.

Ray had already determined, having seen Merrin's pentagram, and then Kathryn's, that he was deep in the heart of some coven and that the wolf had to have been one of their familiars, though what all those ravens had been about he couldn't begin to understand. All he had to cling to was a religion he didn't really believe in, except that it gave him the excuses he needed to behave the way he did.

"Selkie?" Brighid queried the young-looking Seer with the white hair and the soft dark eyes.

"I was just about to," she replied, moving away from the group to sit in front of the hearth, where the glowing coals assisted her to concentrate her talent.

Merrin and Rowan were busy making a big pot of chili while Matt fixed everyone coffee. Another long night lay ahead, quiet enough in the cramped but cozy atmosphere of the bright, quirky studio, but devastating on the streets where the actions of the smug burned and hurt in their self-righteous zeal, all in the name of a god who didn't seem about to protest at the shame and defamation.

"Does he want a cup?" Matt yelled across the room. "Do you want some coffee?" Hunter asked Ray.

"Ah . . . I . . ."

"Yeah, make him a brew," called Brighid, "but don't anybody dare feed him that chilli 'cause he already smells bad to me." A few of the others snorted and chuckled.

"Found him," Selkie called out. Raven was only a little over a block away, and he looked like he was heading back. Alan was quietly relieved, never knowing when his friend was going to just take off again.

Raven came through the door only minutes later, dripping wet from the night. As he entered the room his whole body recoiled, slamming into the large wooden door as if struck, his hands reaching like talons to hold himself upright.

Several of the Travelers were shocked as he glared across the room at where Ray was sitting all scrunched up in the seat. He screeched an unearthly noise before charging through the room, almost falling over two still-seated Sídhe, intent on destroying the source of an overwhelming despair. Raven had immediately fallen into the depths of Ray's life and experiences, sensing the human man's cruelty and excuses for the excesses that had given him pleasure.

Both Hunter and Willie jumped on him, holding him back with obvious difficulty.

"Stop now. Stop!" Willie chanted softly. "S'all right man, stop it now, we got you. We got you."

To the telepath, the mind of the heavy-set, balding, pock-marked man was obvious, and it showed on his face and in the absolute absence of shine. The effect on Raven was like something toxic. Ray had turned a gray color under the scrutiny of the gentle-looking man because, despite what seemed to him, at first glance, to be just another queer, the eyes that looked into his own were downright demonic in their intensity.

Raven sucked his breath in through his teeth and looked momentarily toward Alan, seeking an anchor for his emotions; seeking calm. It was there. Brighid was holding the younger man's hand as though saying leave it alone for just a bit, don't react. He understood their ways sufficiently to allow his feelings to lie dormant.

"What do you hear; tell me what you hear?" Hunter was right up close to Raven's ear.

"I'm soft. It's okay. I'm soft." Raven's meaning was clear. *Let me go, I won't do harm.* The men let go of him, and Brighid's hand relaxed its grip on Alan just as Raven looked at his friend and winked in the way he used to, assuring him with a *Don't-let-it-get-to-you, Sunshine* message.

Raven moved the things on the coffee table to one side and sat down on it, staring at the cringing man. He attempted to bypass all the personal cruelties, apathies, and innuendoes. Behind—mixed in—secrets—the smooth, suave face of an abject predator.

"Who is Michael Blacker? Who is your master?"

Ray sniveled in terror. *What were these things? How? Say nothing,* he thought futilely. *Think nothing.* How did he do that? he pleaded.

"What's the *Eclipse* . . . the Brotherhood of the Eclipse? What's that?" Raven had the attention of everyone in the room.

"Father, son, and holy ghost? Got to be kidding me, yeah?" he growled, almost spitting into Ray's face, then grinning at the irony of the thought.

His moods changed continuously. Clouds on the water.

"Who do you kill? What is this evil you think about?" He sat bolt upright. "You cut those women, didn't you?"

He paused for a moment. Realization dawned as he contemplated the arrangements of mismatched thoughts.

"You think it's us, don't you?" That made him laugh aloud. He turned to Hunter.

"He thinks we're evil. So . . ." again he paused as though listening.

"The Reverend Michael James Blacker—there it is. Wipe out the magic, is it son?"

His eyes cleared and he took a steadying breath, and stood, and walked away, saying "Get him out of my face."

"Consider it done," replied Brighid.

HUNTER FOLDED HIS ARMS ACROSS his chest. "It's time for you to leave us," he said softly.

"Where . . . What are you going to do?" Hunter gestured for Matt, by far one of the tallest and strongest of the Sídhe present in the room. Ray went limp as he was dragged to his feet.

"Say goodbye, Sunshine," called Raven as Hunter led the way out the door and into the night, with Matt following, easily maneuvering their captive.

"Where are they taking him?" Kathryn asked Merrin, who had stood with her throughout the interrogation.

"I have no idea," she replied. "Willie?"

"They're takin' him to the Outside," he told them as though everyone should know that.

"Yeah, I can see that, but . . ."

He tugged at her plait teasingly, "No, *Outside*."

"Is that supposed to make sense?"

He rolled his eyes. *Mortals!* he thought. *You had to explain everything like they'd never heard the language spoken properly.*

"It's like the beyond; it's an Otherworld, but not like Tír na nOgh. There's lots of Outsides. There's no good could come of killing him when there's no battle you see, and there's no legal system here that's going to listen to the likes of us even if we did go to them, which would be just bloody hilarious."

Kathryn's brow scrunched. "Why not?"

"We've got no identification. No place in any of it," he smiled with charm. "And besides—are you lookin' at the way they'd look at us?"

Merrin took over. "The law'd end up making them out to be the bad guys because they've got no records—nada—think about it."

"Yeah, okay, I heard him the first time, Merrin," Kathryn said defensively. "I just want to know as much as I can as soon as I can."

"Oops. Sorry, Cat. I'm just wired is all." Merrin felt awful. She wasn't feeling calm, and she wasn't feeling peaceful. The whole situation was jangling her nerves. The idea of packs of what she termed *generic males* wandering around being all fundamentalist and charged on some sense of perverse purpose gave her the creeps. The laws against Witchcraft had been defunct for a long time now, but she knew that for a large proportion of the population she and her fellow witches were in league with the devil, which was ludicrous considering they didn't even credit it with an existence. But that didn't stop the fanatics from figuring all wrong.

Chapter Twenty-two

Shape-shifting was not a talent that all the Sídhe had been gifted with by the Mysteries.

Brighid was one who was. She was the only one among them all, in this land, so far as anyone knew of—not only being the greatest of the shape-shifters but insofar as she was also capable of being in more than one place at a time and to be in any of them in whatever form she chose.

She moved with the warrior clan, for sure, because Hunter had asked her to remain with him from the beginning, but her true nature was as a psychic: what the Dé Danann call a Dreamer.

She currently inhabited three places. She sat by the fire out back of Kathryn's house, enjoying the company, the music, the night. In New Rathmore she watched the whole episode unfold with the pasty man called Ray—her relief at his exodus being physical as well as psychic—and in the body known as C'av'arn she tutored a new generation of raven-people in the mystery of the Dream.

To do this it was necessary to teach them the art of stillness—not a simple thing for any corvid, let alone a raven—which allowed them to see through the landscape of familiarity to the starlight threads: the almost invisible ley lines that crisscrossed the earth, space, and time. Within the stillness they would be capable of sending out along these lines into either past or future, both being really the same thing seen from a different perspective, to recognize the patterns of both harmony and discord that existed within the environment of the landscape of familiarity.

Unfortunately, most of the discord occurred where there were large clusters of humans; in the worst places ugly, jagged, messy patterns splurged across the silver and gold leys, creating a painful configuration of sound and color that had the effect of seeming like a disease.

Among the forty that had fulfilled C'av'arn's demand for attendance, Beatha was the best of them—the quickest to learn, the cleverest to recall, a natural. She scanned with a precision unmatched by any other, especially by one so young, in C'av'arn's forever memory.

The two had traveled together, leaving all others to puzzle, and they returned to the landscape of familiarity, parched and hungry, with advice. They sent others winging across the city night to find T'arn, who arrived just after dawn with a full entourage.

The night had been filled with the uglies. All over the city the patterns of daily life were being destroyed. Great flashes, loud noise, burning things where burning things should not be. Dark-walking men pulling the silver from the leys and hurting it somehow. It made no sense. Brighid, in her Sídhe form, knew, but as C'av'arn she struggled in her attempt to explain complex concepts to Beatha and the others—concepts that had no relativity in their language. Ideas like bombs and murder did not have any validity because they were not raven-thinking things.

T'arn was told as much as was explicable, and ultimately, for the time being, all he could do was to warn the enclaves to keep the feeding away from human habitation as much as possible as it was only buildings and houses, and any gardens close to them, that were suffering, and not the parks and wild places, and none of the schools or rubbish dumps—so far.

BEFORE EVEN T'ARN AND THE visitors had left, both Beatha and C'av'-arn took flight to within the vision places, urgency, and a purpose clear—to find the one that the gray man had called the michael-blacker, to look for an ugly that could match the color that the two could only imagine.

They knew that they were traveling blind, but C'av'arn's gut instinct assured her that she would recognize what it was when they saw it. She was very old—and not merely of body but of awareness, especially so because of the human plague and how it had infected the mysteries—and so she was actually relieved to have the young Beatha with her, and considered that it might even be valid to let her know (at a more appropriate time) about the Otherworld and what could be done there. Perhaps it was time to train a successor? *Right about now,* she thought, *I feel the need for a holiday in a very warm place.*

She'd pretty much given up on the other thirty-nine volunteers. The time was too discordant; the others simply could not keep the silence. It was up to the two of them.

They ranged. They followed the spirit paths and avoided the ugly patterns, no matter how ugly, because they were known now. They sought the unknown, the unrecognized.

They went as wide and as deep as they safely could in that second journey. The silence of Beatha's dreaming-self was both impressive and beatific.

They saw it simultaneously. Tendrils like tentacles, each one a seeming whip of hopelessness; each of them a moment of trust broken. Tentacles as sharp as razors. A tumult of them, all radiating from a single point that . . . that was absolutely beautiful. A tightly swirling spiral or incandescence trapped at the epicenter of the storm of writhing danger-danger filaments. "Is it?" breathed Beatha softly, not losing the silence more than by just a whisper.

"Never seen such a thing, yah?" C'av'arn wanted to take a look into the landscape of familiarity from which this thing radiated and so she marked the place in her memory before recalling the two of them back to the safety of the Bentley Fort School.

She wanted to do this hunting without attracting undue attention, so only she, Beatha, and the elder warrior known as Nar'norl left the branches of their principal tree and headed in the general direction of the visioning.

THEY LANDED SOME TWENTY MINUTES later on the edge of a small satellite dish atop the roof of a very modern, but soulless, building.

To connect that strange and savage pattern with anything recognizable would take vast amounts of concentration, so in Merrin's studio Brighid seemed to doze but did not.

They were in it for the long haul. They were prepared to wait and to wait until such time as something—anything—reminded them of the tendril-thing that they had seen in the vision lands.

"This is the place is, is sure." Beatha's feathers felt like they needed to be pulled out, or rained on or something. She breathed in the tarnished smells of aftershave and soap and cheap cosmetics that so often attended this kind of architecture. She figured humans needed the smell ritual to be allowed to attend certain places, either not realizing or not caring how horrid it made the air.

"Is sure. We wait for the whatever," replied C'av'arn.

The local enclave kept their distance from the three. Everyone knew the Dreamer, and no one would dare to enter her presence without permission, let alone challenge her right to bring the two strangers with her. But they congregated in vast numbers down by the front of the building, along the wires and on the adjacent rooftops, occupying any available outcropping and anticipating news.

Michael Blacker exited the rear of the building into a dawn that was turning to drizzle, ending a long run of pristine weather, and Beatha instantly recognized him as the predator in the window of the tower near the park. She rorl'd this information to C'av'arn.

Down on the path leading to his waiting cab, Michael sensed them. Damned birds, he thought. He'd been aware of their presence as being different to that of the ordinary flocks that frequented the public places. He'd been unnerved by them ever since the scene he'd witnessed from the hotel window. He felt like he was being spied on, unnatural, Satan's minions.

The ravens flew to the back of the building from where the man had come and watched the locked door until someone else came or went. They waited for a long time. Finally, a hard-looking older man with a military-cut flat-top haircut and a face like a pocked rock exited and left the same way as the michaelblacker.

Before the door closed automatically behind him, C'av'arn noted the harsh interior, all steel and reinforced plastic, complete with multiple PCs, a wall chart of the city and surroundings on the far wall, and a network of phones and intercom devices.

Hmmf, she thought as Brighid, opened her eyes in the studio.

THAT SAME NIGHT THE TRAVELERS and all their companions headed across town on the underground rail to Mary Flannery's Tavern on Yeats, picking up Dimity along the way.

The place was packed with patrons, but Dooly managed to evict the pair who had taken up the big table near the stage, hogging it all to themselves, offering them free drinks if they'd find some other seating. No problem.

Wendy Wu let Merrin and Willie behind the bar and into the back room, where she kept her small TV set. The night was full of news. No one knew quite what was happening, but New Rathmore had never known such violence. The media were talking terrorist cells. The local police had been joined by several regional squads, and the city council was seriously considering invoking an 11 PM curfew. The problem was that the attacks were all over the place, not localized to any one area, making monitoring of events impossible, if not ludicrous.

It had been an easy strategy for the Brotherhood to include both Jewish and Catholic establishments with known occult groups and outlets, seeming moral-majority targets like abortion clinics, another gay bar, and a large Westside sex shop.

The media were speculating militant extremists, probably Islamic fundamentalists, which was just what Blacker had said they would do.

Back in the solitude of his apartment he was smiling and making long-range plans for several weeks hence, humming happily to himself as he did so, but in the tavern, among the gathering, seemingly absorbed in the music of the local band, called Tor, the silence was a studied exercise in contemplation.

More than an hour passed before Willie and Merrin rejoined the others. Willie was looking pale and Brighid was concerned to recognize the minute but obvious crease to the left of his mouth that had not been there earlier. To her sight, even that tiny age line was symbolic of the kind of ugliness and cruelty that was the only thing that could truly take a toll on the Sídhe, other than downright murder. They may be long-lived but none of them were immortal, although she wasn't sure about Hunter.

The ancient queen of fire decided then and there that despite every ounce of argument they would return to Kathryn's demesne and stay there until this carnage had run its course. Their hunt had, after all, been only about finding Owen and, in this, justice had been served and the Wild Hunt was fulfilled, and it was not their way, no matter what, to interfere with events unless they found themselves in the thick of a thing, unable to withdraw, or were invited.

"This is absolutely crazy," said Merrin, sitting down with Willie after picking up a pint of Guinness from Wendy on the way back to the table.

"It's like this place has gone off the deep end," Willie began. "The whole thing's just getting worse out there."

"Yeah," Merrin interrupted, "the cops don't know who's responsible. The media's talking up hysteria with the terrorist cell thing, but there's too many white boys on the streets, apparently, for that to make sense."

"And that Owen and his little friend Ray were up to their necks in it," added Brighid, "but that doesn't make it our business."

Matt's jaw dropped in disbelief. "You're kidding us!"

Annis agreed with him. "You've got to be joking. If it had nothing to do with us then Owen wouldn't have been part of that crew. For all we know he could have been sent up to the Summer Gathering place for them . . . What are they?"

"Eclipse," said Raven, suddenly very tired.

"Yeah, the Eclipse Brothers."

"Listen to yourselves," Brighid hissed. "It's already turning your light down. And no, I'm not kidding." She turned toward Kathryn, where she sat close to Vincent, who was feeling very protective toward her. She was obviously still slightly disoriented from whatever visionary experience the Folk had generated.

"How much can we receive?" she asked.

"Pardon? I don't understand." Kathryn was confused by the terminology.

"Do you ask us to leave your life?"

Merrin almost stopped breathing. She knew what this meant. If Kathryn said yes, it's too much, or gave any hint at all that she couldn't deal with this new situation then the Travelers would leave. She'd have to make a choice or—well—there might not even be one. *Be careful*, she thought, keeping her eyes on her glass, not wanting to betray the depth of emotion she was experiencing (no panacea yet from Hunter, who could block her mind from what would surely be regret).

Kathryn watched the play of light and shadow, color and texture that the bird and animal forms around the Sídhe exhibited, becoming deeply aware of their mind touch. They waited. She laughed lightly, which relieved Vincent and triggered an immediate wave of bliss from the ecosystem with which he dwelt.

"Now you *are* kidding!" she grinned. She looked from one face to another. "Is this what love feels like, I wonder." She leaned into Vincent. He was disturbed by the gesture but not unpleasantly. He smelled her hair—it smelled of the forest near her home and the woodsmoke from the fire, and the creatures around him had their ears pricked up out of curiosity because it'd been a while.

"So why did you ask me that, and what did you mean when you asked about receiving because all I've got to offer is my place, and if that's it then it's freely given."

Hunter looked at Brighid, startled. How could this woman know so much? She even spoke the language that was thought lost to the world.

"Freely given is freely received," said Hunter softly. "Where'd you learn to know to say that?"

She briefly told of her nanny and the stories she'd heard of the Fair Folk when she was young and how you didn't receive anything from them unless it was freely given.

"They still tell the children," smiled the Rowan.

"They're mostly thought just harmless stories though," Jack admitted. It was the first time he'd said anything for hours.

"Then there's hope," Brighid sighed.

"Here we go again with the hope . . ." Annis reached across the table for the jug of beer.

"Shut up, you!" Brighid snarled.

"Well you keep on about it while the world keeps goin' to shite, that's all," she retaliated.

"What do you know, yer so bloody young!"

"Give it a rest, the pair of you," Hunter warned. "It's Kate we're facing, remember?"

Brighid sat straighter in her chair and turned her body pointedly away from Annis, in Kathryn's direction.

"We only ever in this land had one place outside of the tunnel that we'd thought safe—and it's been troubled of late."

"Owen." It wasn't a question. Kathryn had the full story.

"Owen. Which means that this Michael Blacker, and whoever else is connected to him, has probably got the gatherings marked. If he thinks to wipe us out that's where he'll try it."

"But I thought you were all immortal?" Kathryn kept being certain she'd worked it all out and continued to prove limited in all the facts.

"We *can* live for a very long time, and it could seem like forever except I don't know what that is . . . but it doesn't mean we can't die." She let her eyes brush past both Willie and Raven to let them know she was aware of their stress.

"I'm immortal," said Hunter gently.

"Well that's good to know," and Brighid flicked him the look that pretended rancor. He smiled at her with conciliatory humor.

"We might need to." She ignored Hunter, directing her words toward Kathryn.

"Use it," Kathryn answered the obscure statement.

Brighid turned her entire body in her chair to face Dimity.

"We're going to try to get the bus out . . ."

"But you've got my van if you need it," Dimity finished.

"You want to join us?" Hunter invited.

"No. I've got what I want here in town, love," she replied with certainty.

"Does this mean we're leaving again?" Annis huffed.

"Until our natural time to return to the city," said Hunter.

"Winter," added Rowan, remembering when they'd found him.

"There's too many of us out there at Kathryn's place though." Hunter looked at Selkie and Seamus. "We'll have to decide who stays and who goes."

"Why can't we all stay?" asked Selkie. She'd loved Kathryn's big, deep garden.

"The village folk. There's always plain old me. And Rowan and Jack look pretty average." Kathryn looked to the two men, who nodded before she continued. "We can do the shopping and stuff. Merrin, what about you though?"

"I can stay with Merrin 'cause she already thinks I'm fabulous, doncha Merrin?" Willie grinned.

"Ooh! Bloody cheek!" But she agreed.

Dimity interjected. "If you need to be with the others at the farm, Merrin, I can keep things going at your place," said Dimity.

"What do you really want to do, Willie?" Merrin asked.

"Truth?"

"Truth."

"For a wee while some private time with you would suit me fine without all this lot." The others responded with whoops and jibes, but Merrin merely settled more deeply into her foxy man's arms, satisfied.

Everyone ordered another round except for Vincent, who was very quiet, thinking. He didn't feel necessary to any of this. Experience had taught him, also, about the way things went for him with women, and it wasn't that he was afraid of going some kind of distance with Kathryn, but he knew himself well enough to know that sooner or later it was bound to fall through. So was there even a point to his staying? He'd have to think about everything a bit more than he'd had time to so far. Plus there was Mariani to consider, and the few things, including his instruments, that he'd left behind at his site.

He was still very much a loner, although he felt affectionate toward this whole bunch, especially Kathryn.

The Quickening

Part Two

Chapter Twenty-three

The Children of the Dreaming Lands

Puck never missed Hunter when he was gone. She loved him simply, without question, without demand. How else do you love a god?

She had dreamed him ever since she'd been a child, just like she had dreamed Brighid and others who had come and gone, known to those with whom she traveled but not met for forever, it sometimes seemed. She also dreamed of those she had yet to meet. But she would. She always did.

Puck had been raised by her great aunts, Sylvia and Emily Drake, who'd lived at the Wellhead Abbey, an old stone monolith of a structure, once home to the monks of a Cistercian order who had left or died out long ago, leaving the draughty halls to the owls and the rats.

Sylvia and Emily had a substantial inheritance left to them when their father had passed away, being two of his three surviving heirs. Their estranged brother, Joseph, lived three counties away—as far, in fact, as he could arrange when he had left home after completing his degree. The three had never gotten along. He had abhorred his sisters' eccentricities and had determined to be Mr. Business Man. He'd died of a heart attack at forty-nine, not long after his wife had left him and disappeared with another man. He'd had one son, whom the sisters had never been allowed to meet, and therefore knew nothing about—not even his name.

They'd attended Joseph's funeral. Sad. No one else came, not even his son.

Because of their peculiarities, neither woman had done more than take lovers as they chose. They traveled extensively during the first four years after receiving their trust, from Cairo to the Arctic wilderness of Alaska, from Uluru to Samoa to Machu Picchu and Angkor Wat, carefully purchasing their collection of beautiful artifacts and having them stored in a private warehouse in New Rathmore until such time as they finally settled somewhere.

Sylvia and Emily Drake were witches. They were also unbelievably attuned psychically to each other, so much so that they seemed to have one mind between them that shut people out who could not see the world as they did.

In each of the lands where they traveled they learned the language. They symbiotically merged with whichever indigenous culture they visited and were always recognized by whatever wise or holy man or woman who officiated among them. The sisters learned and they shared. They were completely uninhibited, and to the ignorant they could even have been perceived as amoral, but that was almost a blasphemous idea to the two because whatever they did they considered sacred.

They happened upon the abbey circumstantially. They'd been invited to Alessandra Dardier's country estate by an art dealer in Bromford who'd known of the Dardier collection of rare ancient glass. The sisters had decided that their newest venture was to be the creation of perfumes from wild ingredients: certain recipes being passed on to them on their journeys, along with a deep knowledge of herbal lore and wildcrafting that had been taught to them by both their maternal grandmother and several of the witches that they'd met in tribal cultures over the years.

Perfumes and exotic intoxicants.

The idea of purchasing the collection of bottles, jars, philters and vials was simply the desire to store their ingredients in containers of beauty.

They passed the high lichen drystone wall, which enclosed their future home for what seemed like miles, before they thought to ask what was beyond it. When the driver informed them that it was an abandoned hermitage they had insisted on going in. Consequently they had been three hours late for their meeting with Alessandra, who still sold them the collection and, shocked, prepared to welcome the sisters as neighbors.

THE ABBEY INCLUDED SEVERAL ACRES of dense woodland, with what had once been extensive gardens and orchards that stood overgrown and fallow, but with herbs and vegetables growing delightfully wild, much to the sisters' joy.

It had taken two years for local tradesmen to restore the majority of the buildings and to have modernizations like electricity, telephone, and plumbing installed, and to have the contents of the warehouse storage trucked in—from several dozen Persian carpets to the rarest of orchids and all manner of furnishings, artworks, and artifacts from many lands and many cultures.

They were both in their early fifties when a welfare worker had brought to them a small girl. Joseph's son and his wife had been killed in an auto accident, leaving Pamela Therese Drake with no other living family. She was three years old.

No problem. It was love at first sight, and an inheritance of complete freedom and absolute devotion by the women that had no chance of spoiling the little girl who, it turned out, was as fey as them anyway. They hadn't liked the name Pamela so had called her Puck.

The sisters had decided that traditional education was not what they wanted for their charge. For everyday learning of the basics like reading, math, and science, they hired young, vital tutors from all over the region, paying them well and offering free accommodation if they chose.

As for history, languages, art, literature, mythology, folklore, music, and all the many skills of herb-lore and more and more and more, the sisters taught Puck personally—a task at which they were adept.

By the time she was nine years old she could speak five living languages, other than English, and two revived languages—Gaelige and Cymraeg. She could read Latin but was lousy at speaking it, basically because it bored her. She'd learned history from the unbiased vantage point of both the conquerors and the people who had been conquered and, in most cases, suppressed. This was her favorite subject, other than music and folklore. She was taught piano from the age of four, and her aunts had tempted her with several other instruments until she'd discovered the guitar, which became her specialty even though she continued to explore other media. The sisters went silly on a sound system that cost many thousands of dollars, and which allowed Puck to gain the greatest appreciation of everything from classics, through blues, jazz, and rock (her favorite being a style of music called Gypsy Ska), and many varieties of traditional folk music.

She was never lonely, even though her company, until her eleventh year, was among adults, because the sisters never aged in their hearts or their spirits. Both had an extreme wit and an abundance of energy for everything she wanted to do.

They had had five horses that roamed the seven acres of wild land just beyond the drystone walls that bordered the orchard and gardens, four dogs of unknown pedigrees—all of which were refugees from the local pound—and five black cats that were ratters of the highest order.

Gavin and Sheena Pilley were eighteen and twenty years old—brother and sister—who came to the abbey every morning just at 6 AM to help Puck catch the horses, groom and dress them, and go riding with her. This was her joy, her experiential opus. She *could* ride with saddle and tack, but she preferred not to, exhilarating in the wild freedom of the open countryside and the deep forests of spruce and rowan and birch and oak, every inch known and every cave explored for treasure.

The only thing that Gavin and Sheena refused to do was to enter that forest, claiming it was the haunt of pagan gods and the Fair Folk, and admonishing the sisters politely for not preventing Puck from entering its ancient depths—not that they could, or would.

They were right, in some ways, about the place being haunted. The forest was alive with ancient mysteries and did not welcome those of the new god. But Puck? She was a wonder to them, all fey and bright, riding Chaucer, her high-stepping Appalachian, along forest tracks that most humans wouldn't even see; playing the tin whistle down by the pool; stripping and swimming even as late as autumn.

Chapter Twenty-four

The first time Puck dreamed what she came to call her *Doorway Dreams* she was down by that pool, lying on the warmth of a flat rock beneath a dapple of gold and green.

She dreamed she woke up to see a giant gray wolf watching her warily from where he drank at the pool. She would have thought she'd be afraid but she wasn't. Around him were foxes and their kits, heron and crows, a whole lot more hares than ought to be around in full daylight, what looked to be a couple of either weasels or ermine—Puck couldn't tell the difference—and a white doe with her young.

Well, this was all very weird, she thought to herself. She sat up on the rock slowly, figuring that except for the wolf the others might be skittish at her presence although, for the life of her, she couldn't work out why they weren't afraid around the predator.

He lifted his head, and Puck could have sworn he smiled at her.

I'm just dreaming, she thought, believing that that would make sense of all this.

This is not the place of "just dreaming," she heard, only there was no one to speak it.

"Then I'm not dreaming?"

Sure you are, said the deep male voice.

"Riddles, is it? I love riddles."

No riddle. This is the dreaming place, sure, but there's no "just dreaming" about it.

"I don't get it." She was certain the wolf was thinking at her and that it was him she could hear.

When you say, "I'm just dreaming," you make it sound like it's not real or something.

"Yeah, so?"

So the dreaming place is as real as you are.

"But I'm only dreaming I'm awake. The real me is asleep."

Tsk, said another voice. A big raven with pale eyes landed beside her on the rock, close enough to touch.

"Is that you?" Puck asked, looking at the ragged bird.

Is that how I look to you? That's rude. Yes, it was the raven talking.

"What?"

I'm not ragged, I'm hot! it said, taking offense even at Puck's thought.

This is very cool, she thought. *I wonder what'll happen if I reach out to touch you.*

I'll peck your bloody hand, girl.

"Hey, this is my dream. You're not allowed to be nasty if it's my dream."

The raven wanted to tell her she was being naïve, but Hunter shot her a warning glance telling her to behave.

Don't you sass me just because you're a god!

That's it. Just give it away, why don't you? Can't you let her simply have a pleasant time here?

Not when she goes insulting the wildlife, no.

You can be such a bitch Brighid, said the wolf, rising from his haunches and padding toward the flat stone.

I want to wake up now, thought Puck. She had been okay so long as the wolf stayed at a distance.

I wouldn't harm you if my life depended on it, she heard.

Yeah, well, that's easy for you to say, the raven huffed.

Oh shut up, bird.

The raven promptly hopped off the rock and seemed to stroll right past the approaching wolf, purposely avoiding him.

The wolf came up to Puck and sat beside her, his tongue lolling from the side of his huge jaws, looking for all the world like he was grinning.

"What'll you do if I touch you?" she queried.

Depends if it's behind the ears.

She reached over and scratched behind one ear, causing him to lean heavily into her one hand until she used the other to attack his other ear.

Within no time at all Hunter was playing with her like he was a pup, and Puck realized that she could rough and tumble with the wolf and that even though he was enjoying the game immensely he remained gentle. So gentle.

A COLD BREEZE BLEW OVER her body as she lay upon the rock, and she woke to find the sun slanting heavily to the west. She sighed. Just a dream after all.

She told her aunts about it. They'd finished dinner and were sitting by the huge fireplace in the library. The big room—wall-to-wall books, large tables that had once seated monks engaged in the translations of ancient texts, deep, overstuffed, mismatched armchairs purchased at an auction simply for their comfort, and a touch of lace and velvet—was where the three did most of their talking and all of Puck's tutoring. The smells of wood and beeswax, leather bindings, and old paper hinted at another century, encouraging the exploration of its memories.

The two sisters looked at each other but said nothing.

Before her bedtime, Sylvia had taken Puck aside and casually suggested she let her know if she had any more dreams like it. "Why?" she'd asked. Those woods, Sylvia had replied, are a world away from where most people like to go.

Puck didn't get it, but Sylvia wouldn't be drawn out on the subject as she didn't make up her mind lightly on matters pertaining to things like magic.

BEFORE SLEEP PUCK ALWAYS OPENED her windows wide, except for in the middle of winter, because she loved the way the night smells lulled her.

She looked out across the lawn to where the light from an almost full moon turned everything in the garden to silver and shadows, and she saw him. Over by the fragrant garden. The distinct shape of the wolf from her dream. His face was turned toward her window. She went to call out to him, but he turned and padded out of sight.

THE DOORWAY DREAMS CAME MORE regularly as she approached puberty. She began to be aware that there was seepage; that many of the creatures and animals that she encountered in the dreaming place were finding their way into her normal daily life. Sometimes they were mixtures of human and animal or animal and bird and person.

Sylvia and Emily got used to them easily. It's in the genes, they'd agreed, almost flippantly.

The house and grounds became a haven to all manner of exotic shape-shifters that Puck had dreamed through. The sisters needed to warn them off when Gavin and Sheena or the tutors were due. They didn't at all bother the dogs, which Emily thought quite strange, as any usual critter straying into the gardens was always a trigger for raucous barking.

Puck moved downstairs to the back of the abbey. What had once been the abbess' quarters, which opened out onto an enclosed courtyard surrounded by high briar rose hedges, complete with the remains of a well that had been created to catch the water that trickled continuously from the spring emerging from a tumble of moss-covered round stones, became her sanctuary, and home to her unusual children. The sisters had the plumbers and the builders in. They created a lavish stone and tile bathroom, well-lit and able to be heated in the cooler months.

After a time the numbers of the dreamed leveled out. Most would confine themselves to Puck's quarters, the untamed and jumbled scented garden just beyond, or the woodlands through which they originally emerged from the dreamscape. The wolf came occasionally, so Puck knew he still cared for her.

One night in the winter of Puck's fourteenth year, after Emily had finished reading Sylvia's book on the history and persecution of the Rom, they had made an almost throwaway decision to paint a *patrin* on the main gate, thereby alerting any who passed the abbey of a safe place to camp.

The traveling people, including the Sídhe, began turning up the following spring, setting up camps on the edge of the acreage where the Ardrigh River divided the Drake property from the Dardier estate.

Chapter Twenty-five

Puck began her teenage social years in the Travelers' company, enjoying the music, the dancing, the stories, and, especially, the boys.

When she first met Hunter in human form she knew him. The eyes.

He'd always felt he was a guardian to her absolute feyness and didn't deal very well with the intense animal sexuality that she emitted when in his company. Human women were not his thing, and he'd certainly never met one that he'd choose to hang out with through forever by way of the Quicken brew.

But, although he'd known her for years, it had been as a wolf and not as a man.

This was many years ago and Wellhead Abbey had been merely a stopping point for the Sídhe on their way back from their cottage at the top of Razorback Mountain, where they stayed for the season of Meán Fómhair (the Autumn Equinox). Many times they had passed down the narrow, heavily treed lane and had recognized that the mysteries were dense in the area. In the years just after Puck's arrival Hunter would travel the dreamscape often just to enjoy what she was doing in the summonings that her ability brought into the world.

Now this.

The first time she approached him—brazen, exuding the smells of a wild female animal, completely lacking in guile—he ignored her. He was not at all himself, not at all honest. He also realized that Puck was not fooled and neither were her great aunts and neither were the Sídhe nor any of Hunter's companions. Even he was not aware of where the chemistry would eventually lead.

She actually confused him. Brighid thought it was very funny and Black Annis considered it hilarious, but kept her throwaway comments confined to Brighid, knowing just what Hunter was capable of effecting should he, for even a moment, become angry.

When they'd left, Puck had been devastated. She had no idea he was a god, not that it would have made a difference. She hadn't been raised to be in awe of any one thing over and above any other, and the aunts' teachings in matters of the sacred mysteries had instilled in her love rather than worship. It had been Emily and Sylvia who told her that he was the forest lord and that in the legends he was known as Herne. They were as fey as fey could be, those two. To them the whole gathering had wafted magic, and they felt as though some life's mission had been fulfilled.

THAT WINTER EMILY DIED IN her sleep. Then everything just kind of fell to pieces.

The Dardiers must have known that the sisters' strength had been in their twinship. The following spring, when the first of the Rom came through, someone set the police onto them. They'd been told that a break-in and theft had occurred coinciding with the arrival of the group. Sylvia and Puck had both come to the defense of their visitors, but it had been of little use. There had been no arrests, but a search warrant had allowed the police to thoroughly disrupt the group, and Yolo, the head man, had everyone pack up in the night and by morning they were gone, painting over the patrin on the gate to let others know that Wellhead was no longer safe.

Sylvia followed her sister to the grave that same month, suffering a massive cerebral hemorrhage, and Puck was left alone to deal with everything.

The estate was in the hands of a trustee law firm, which proceeded to abuse the accounts in its own favor. Because Puck was not yet seventeen years old the courts ruled her a ward of the state and ordered her to the care of the Blakemore Welfare Facility, a soulless and dangerous institution housing the innocent among the hard-core.

She packed her few belongings under the supervision of a woman she didn't know and the police officer who attended her. She was terrified. All the changelings and shape-shifters were in hiding, either within the secret labyrinthine passageways that snaked their way beneath the ancient buildings, or beyond the abbey grounds where the word spread through the forests and the dreaming lands like a brushfire.

Hunter heard the news from the wind. He was outraged.

Puck shuffled through the dark oak gate, which was the only entrance in or out of the grounds that had cloistered the abbey, in the blackest mood she had ever known, unable to cry, thinking as hard as she could how she was going to get out of this situation. She had the unsmiling guardian on one side of her and the policeman on the other, and she carried all that remained of her whole life in one small suitcase, which was all she had been allowed.

As the three walked the remainder of the way to the waiting car, Hunter tore from the forest at full run, silent and deadly. He leaped the police officer, knocking him to the ground. The court-appointed official from Blakemore stood screaming as the wolf hovered right over the jugular of the cop, his fangs bared, his eyes glowing.

Puck hugged her case to her chest and ran for the forest.

Later the officer would have had to explain how a huge wolf had felled him, removed his gun from his belt with his teeth, looked at him with the eyes of a man, and left both him and the woman unharmed as he followed after the girl. Although the Blakemore woman had been in shock for several hours, she had eventually corroborated his statement, and so a search was mounted to find the girl, which proved futile, as Hunter had removed her, and all the shape-shifters, bodily into the dreaming lands. All chose to remain there until such time as they could be with their "mother," when she had a place for them.

Puck had been moved through where time and space warped, to find herself in the company of the Sídhe in the city encampment. There Hunter had held her and held her while she cried out her grief at the loss of the splendor that had been her life. In the end he had kissed away her tears, and she had turned that gentle thing to a passion that Hunter chose not to refuse. And the forest god fell into love beyond anything he had known.

The Rowan hadn't come to be with them at that time, so they had no idea what had befallen the estate that rightfully should have belonged to Puck according to the last will and testament of both sisters, and it would be years before they discovered that it had been sold off on the presumption of her death. Still, her life was with Hunter now and only sometimes, when she lifted the stone that she'd laid over the hole in which she had stored her sorrow, would she allow herself to mourn.

She no longer called anything through her Dreaming door for fear that they would have no home, but she had learned well the ways to enter into the dreaming lands where she would often spend days in the company of her children, many of whom had learned new shapes with which to impress her. All of them were content though, for the dreaming lands fit the way of the dreamer and so they were beautiful.

Puck had not yet taken the Quicken brew, made from the sacred berries of the Tree (an ancient rowan that had stood—huge and mighty—as a symbol of the truce between the Tuatha Dé Danann and the Gaels—but which had been brutally cut down by a savage and mindless invader).

She was nineteen years old when she found that she was pregnant, and she was ecstatic.

Hunter and the Sídhe were floored. He didn't know how to respond as this had not happened in over a thousand years (to his knowledge) and that line had been wiped out by the Normans.

When his dismay turned to delight, the winter sun shone like spring, and trees budded and flowers bloomed well before their time. Out in the rural region of the country the farmers exalted in the rich planting season and the gentle weather.

The heart of the city, however, could no god touch with splendor, and on the night of the winter solstice, freezing and bitter, with the Rowan dragged, most unwillingly, from the 4 AM streets to bear witness to the event as the only other human representative, the child of a mortal woman and the forest lord was born. They named him Robin and her other children, the shape-shifters she had awoken as a girl, spread the news through the Dreaming lands and rejoiced.

Puck had taken the Quicken brew the following summer, when the O'Neill tragedy had occurred, and passed the visionary experience and the borders of life and death with ease. Her choice. She was now virtually immortal.

Chapter Twenty-six

The Quickening

It was a random twist that changed everything. Two days after the Travelers had arrived at Falconstowe, Puck had decided to walk to the village so that Robin could get a feel for his new surroundings, because once the child experienced the ley of the land, he was permitted to go wherever he chose, the crossing of the human blood with that of the land itself giving him an unbelievable canniness ensuring that he could never get lost.

Things just seemed to slide one thing into another. Once they reached the village they experienced hostile glances from the local women because of Puck's ethereal beauty, which caused them to feel ineffectual and dowdy by comparison—and greedy, hungry looks from the men. Puck and Robin kept on walking. Robin was aware of his mother's tension and a ferociously protective instinct surged in the small boy, but he knew, like second-nature, that he had yet to come into his true power. Instead he kept close beside her, willing their invisibility.

They walked until they arrived at the rail. Puck didn't even think about it. She bought a ticket to New Rathmore Central—she was uncomfortable without Hunter's proximity.

Both mother and son breathed more easily once within the carriage of the train. Robin knew her intention without words and so settled down for the hour's journey.

They reached the city at 4:12 in the afternoon and walked in the direction leading to the Travelers' subway camp, unaware that the others were at Merrin's studio packing their gear and awaiting Dimity, who was bringing the van.

They rounded the corner into George Street, where Puck knew they could catch a bus for the remainder of the journey. The air was filled with ravens, and they were calling, calling, crying out, *Go back, go back!*

Robin, who communicated mainly through telepathy rather than his voice, tried to get his mother to listen, to stop and listen.

Puck slowed, looking up, looking worried.

"Go back, is," Robin finally said.

"Not this way?" Her brow furrowed as she ranged around herself, sensing for danger.

There was nothing she could see but there was no way she was going to ignore either her son or the ravens, so the two turned back the way they had come, Puck determining to find another route to the winter home.

Too late. Far too late. Three of the men who had originally tracked the group from the parking station stood on the opposite side of the road. They rushed Puck and Robin in broad daylight, knocking her to the ground, one man laying his boot into her prone body, taking her in the ribs and cracking two in the process. The other two grabbed a kicking, biting Robin and ran, with him growling and snarling like a wild animal.

It took all their might to hold him, but they determined to get him back to headquarters, knowing how pleased the Reverend Blacker would be at this turn of fate. Their friend's body had been found in an alley, his throat torn out and his eyes wide open in terror. Demons, Michael Blacker had informed all concerned. Satan and his minions were fighting back.

Now they had two of them. Now they had a pawn. This would flush them out.

The afternoon crowds that had witnessed the event merely walked around Puck's semiconscious body—they had lives to live, things to do; one didn't get involved.

The three men half-carried, half-dragged the ball of fighting child into the nearest side street, where Jake hit him so hard he knocked him out.

"Crazy little fuck," he said to his companions, one of whom had had his hand bitten badly.

"You better see to that," he indicated to the injured man with his head. "Little bastard could be rabid." Rabbit stopped sucking the wound immediately.

They ran the two blocks to where they'd left their car and bundled the little boy into the back seat, where the third man straddled him in case he woke up.

Rabbit drove after wrapping his handkerchief around the wound, while Jake phoned ahead to let the Brotherhood know they had a little surprise.

They drove at the speed limit to avoid being stopped by the highway patrol. If they'd been traveling any faster they might have missed the slight tremor as a small quake shuddered way down deep in the heart of the earth beneath them.

"You feel that?" asked Rabbit.

"It was nothing. Don't get spooked by nothing," answered Jake, a tingle in his groin passing as quickly as it came.

HUNTER HAD FELT THE BLOWS, first to Puck and soon after to Robin, as though they had struck him personally. The rage that exploded from his son had been palpable.

He let out a roar that shook the earth momentarily, until Brighid, responding reflexively, slammed her hand over his mouth, saying *Not now*, as clearly as she could.

He instantly shut down and regained his control before moving between the worlds and manifesting on the street beside Puck, careless of any onlookers. He knew the mind-blind well enough to know that they'd tell themselves they'd seen nothing unusual.

He knelt beside her, gently probing around the epicenter of heat where the damage had been done, merging with the bone of her rib, healing. Puck groaned and opened her eyes, which flared bright as the realization of Robin's absence hit her.

"Robin!" she screamed, looking about herself, attempting to gain her feet and even pushing at Hunter in her effort to rise and run she knew not where. He held her.

"Wait. Not here," he demanded softly.

He moved them through time and space to Merrin's place before she could protest, to where Brighid sat looking remote. Hunter realized she was already out among the ravens searching.

THE BLOW TO THE SIDE of Robin's face had been cruel, splitting the skin above his left eye and causing the cheek to swell with bruising, but it had almost healed, much to his captors' dismay, by the time they reached the Brotherhood's headquarters at the Church of the Penitents of the True Faith.

The men had bound his arms and legs while he was still unconscious and had needed to throw a jacket over his head when he awoke fully to prevent him from spitting and trying to bite.

Jake had suggested that. He'd said the kid was likely able to let the others of his kind know where he was if he could see. Good thinking, they'd praised.

They deposited the squirming, terrified child on the floor when they entered the secure room.

Michael was already there. Quiet, dangerous. Smiling in such a way as to unnerve the other inhabitants. The few men present who might have objected to the abuse of a child kept to themselves.

"They'll be looking for him by now," he said to no one in particular. "Take him downstairs and shut him in."

Downstairs was a steel-reinforced concrete bunker that ran the length of the entire building. Michael had had it built into the original plan. "For the Apocalypse," he'd said, when in actual fact it was there in case there was ever a need to disappear for a while. It was a fully stocked arsenal and contained enough supplies for a dozen or so people for several months. It had its own water and power sources that were independent of the main grid. It had an eighteen-inch-thick steel door only accessible by a high-tech security software system, which was doubled with a two-man key entry device. It was easy to get out of if you knew the correct number sequence, but impossible to access without authority.

They locked Robin, still bound, in a holding cell, kept for just such a purpose should it be necessary. Jake took back his jacket, which meant the child could see and speak—but there was nothing to see and no one else there, and he was left in the dark.

Robin's wrists throbbed where the binding bit cruelly. He had to work very hard not to cry while he waited for his mother and father to find him. His stomach was knotted with hunger, and he wished someone would at least feed him. He knew he could range if he was stronger. His automatic system closed down. There was nothing he could do.

Chapter Twenty-seven

Michael put Brendon and Rabbit in charge of playing nursemaid to the child while he figured out how to go about keeping the advantage while drawing the pack of devil worshippers, or whatever they were, into some kind of net. He was not pleased.

As far as he was concerned this changed the momentum of his plans in too random a fashion. Up until this point everything had been planned and executed with the kind of military precision that left no room for conjecture. Stupid bastards. Why did they have to go thinking? Stupid, stupid bastards. The last thing he wanted was some crazed, angry loopers hunting him or his crew. He couldn't afford to have the kid harmed. He *could* just have him taken down a street somewhere and dumped. That could work. He would get found and there'd be no trace, no connection. Or should he just kill him and dump the body? That way the cops, or whoever, would think it had been some pervert or whacko, and what with the news being all over about whackos, it would just be one more unsolvable crime.

But he couldn't help himself. He wanted to have a look. He wanted to feel whether this was a normal kid or something supernatural.

Rabbit came back from outside with pizzas and cokes for everyone and put some aside for the kid. Michael ordered Brendon to hang loose while he and Rabbit went downstairs.

He pulled aside the peep-hole that looked into the cell without opening the door. It was black in there. He shone a torch beam into the room just as Robin opened his eyes to look toward the light.

Michael almost dropped the torch. The eyes that looked toward him were glowing just like the eyes of the quarry that he and his father would trap in the floodlights of the four-wheel drive when they'd go out at night to hunt—the eyes of a beast trapped by the light.

"Please can I go home," a small voice pleaded from the darkness.

Michael said nothing. He slid the metal plate that covered the peep-hole.

"Don't open that fucking door." His hands were shaking, but he would not lose face in front of his subordinate. "Just slide the stuff through the feeder."

"But he's tied," said Rabbit.

Shit, Michael hissed under his breath.

"Just leave him the way he is," and he turned to go.

"But . . ."

"Leave . . . it!" he snarled through gritted teeth. "Let's get out of here. You boys have brought me a problem I don't need."

Rabbit was momentarily confused. One of their men was dead, and Ray had disappeared to God knew where and was probably also dead. An eye-for-an-eye—that's what they had all been taught was the way of the Bible. At least they hadn't killed the kid.

Blacker exited through the massive door, letting the other man pass before slamming it shut behind him. He walked silently up the staircase and into the main room. He sat down at one of the PCs and stared at it. Rabbit didn't know what to do. He had the uncomfortable feeling he was in big trouble.

"Where have Jake and Tony gone?" Michael asked of no one in particular.

"I think they went home . . ." Rabbit replied, grabbing at what was left of the pizza.

"Get 'em back here. The three of you have suffered the sin of fucking pride!"

Rabbit began to stutter out a justification, but Michael turned toward him and glared. Instead he cringed, the food forgotten, and reached for his cell phone to call the others.

Chapter Twenty-eight

As night fell, so also did a mist like a thin silken curtain. The Sídhe and their company of fey mortals and immortals arrived back in the city. The seers of the Owl clan led them all the way to Merrin's now crowded lodgings, just as Puck's other children, fully alert to their mother's distress and the disappearance of their boy-brother, began dropping into the everyday from the Dreaming lands like pebbles into a pool.

They didn't go to her. That was not their purpose, and she had not called them. They moved now, through the streets and alleyways of New Rathmore, just like Michael Blacker's Soldiers of God—in packs—from the epicenter of Robin-brother's abduction. Scenting, scenting.

But Nav'norl had seen. As the mist had thickened he had almost lost his bearings as he winged his way across unknown territories in the deepening blackness, seeking the enclave at the Bentley Fort School. Once or twice he thought his heart would give out. He was desperate, but he was also a warrior.

At the perimeter of the school's territory he was attacked by sentinels. Night raiding was banned in every enclave known.

"C'av'arn!" he screamed, as four warriors dove in his direction. "C'av'arn now! C'av . . ." He was knocked into a downward spiral. No. He would not be stopped.

"C'av'arn . . ." he screeched, pulling up and soaring for the closest sentry, driving a near-lethal beak into the meat of the other bird's underbelly.

Beatha heard the distant call before C'av'arn, who seemed to sleep but didn't. She took off at full speed from the roost, recognizing the call of Nav'norl, crying "Let be, let be!" all the way across the football field. She almost had to savage one of her own before they fell away to allow her to reach the warrior. They swooped to the ground.

She waited until the older bird regained his dignity.

"Is the Traveler baby," he said finally, his breath calming and his heart rate slowing.

"Is sure?" Beatha should have known not to question, but Nav'-norl let it go. She might be bright, he thought, but she was young enough for him to forgive for the insult.

Beatha sucked in her breath. "Orl . . ." She dragged out in apology.

"Is," he continued, "and he is scared."

Chapter Twenty-nine

Rain lashed the coastal city with a fury, and high winds downed power lines in the suburbs, putting out the electricity in over twenty thousand houses and businesses.

The crusade that the Brotherhood of the Eclipse had mounted was stymied for the first time since the campaign had begun, and Mariani Bizango sat at the window of the Societé house listening to Vincent's story.

He had come to the temporary hounfor by train and by bus at Annis' suggestion. Hunter had been moving in and out of time and space for hours, searching for a way to access the prison in which his son was being held, and the weather had worsened as his frustration had mounted.

The streets of New Rathmore were deserted of people, but alive with mystery. As Mariani looked from the sitting room window, out across the harbor, she could see faces in the wind and swift-moving amorphous forms, each so elemental as to be almost frightening.

"You go back and give them some advice from your Mariani now," she said, wiping the pane of the window as condensation reformed.

"They know what they are doing," Vincent assured her. He knew she was worried for his peace even more so than for his body. This was all very unbelievable, except that he had never lied to her.

"I think they need people in this matter," she continued. "And other gods."

"What makes you say so?"

"Because they are used to themselves and sure, by what you have told me that is a potent magic, but if all that you have told me is connected . . ."

"The bombings and the murders?"

"Oui. If all this is one thing then you are up against a lot of people."

"Hunter said the Lady told him it was one man."

"One man cannot do all of this."

"D'accord," he agreed.

"You tell them that we are not fools, oui? And you tell them that many people are real with the Mysteré and her companions." She took up a thin cigar and lit it, blowing the scented blue smoke toward the ceiling, delicate hands tapping ash from the tip before it had a chance to even form.

"You advise them from me that there are other gods and that finding the people—what are they now? Bruja? Brujo? Les sorceriers? They will not be all dibblers."

"Dabblers," he corrected.

"Whatever. People are not all one thing or the other, comprende?"

"What do you mean?"

"Blind-fey, fey-blind. Not everything is so clear cut. Do you wish for me to come with you? I would like to meet them. The mother of the child—I would like to meet her."

"Oui, Maman, it is up to you, but they are not very sociable right now. There is great distress."

"So. That is a good reason for me to come."

She stood, took another drag of her cigar, and left it to burn itself out on an ornate silver dish. There was no arguing with her when she had decided on something.

They took Mariani's friend's car and parked it a block away from Merrin's place. The two-year-old Mercedes would have been extremely conspicuous if noticed, perhaps drawing unwanted attention to the area.

When they entered the courtyard it was like entering a carnival. The exotic, unusual gathering caused Mariani to breathe deeply of their mystery. Several of the company waved and greeted Vincent on his return, staring, openly curious, at the tall, stately black woman dressed entirely in white, her hair hidden within an intricately bound red and white head scarf.

"Where is the mother?" she asked Vincent, who pointed at the studio. She brushed him aside and strode purposefully toward the door.

She entered the room and scanned its occupants, easily recognizing the distraught woman, who was surrounded by a bizarre assortment of very tribal, exotic individuals.

Puck looked up as the older woman entered and could not have explained the sense of relief that flooded through her at the other's approach. It felt to her as though her own mother had arrived. Her chin quaked as she fought off a fresh wave of despair, but she stood up and moved through the press of others just as Mariani opened her arms. Even Brighid had not been able to console her, no matter her healing abilities. Puck was engulfed by the big woman's embrace, held without words.

Vincent entered the room, looking for Kathryn, who was standing in the kitchen with Merrin, Willie, and Annis, a coffee cup in her hands.

He walked over to her and touched her face gently. She leaned in to him. "Nothing yet," she said. "We know where he is, but the place is like Fort Knox."

"Why can't Hunter get in?"

"Don't know. It makes no sense."

"I told you," Willie piped up, "they've worked out a way to shield."

"What's the alternative?" This debate had been going on for quite a while, and Kathryn was feeling way out of her depths. The kami—she'd started using Vincent's word for the mysteries, as it explained them so simply—were as agitated as the people.

"If I could know that I could find a solution," Brighid commented, going past them to rinse her cup.

Willie squatted down and took a pouch of tobacco from his vest pocket and rolled himself and Merrin a thin cigarette each. She leaned over for him to light hers once he'd handed it to her.

As she stood she flashed on an idea. 'What about witches?" she suggested.

"What're you talking about, girl?" Brighid replied, leaning against the shelf, her arms crossing her lean body.

"I think she's thinkin' about huffin' and puffin' and blowing the bloody place down," Willie smiled.

"Well . . . yeah, I guess so," said Merrin.

"You think mortals can do what we can't?" Brighid's eyes widened. She was ready to laugh at the joke.

"Shit," Merrin couldn't help but be on the defensive around her lookalike. "Do you always have to do the putdown?" Brighid's eyes widened even more so, "Because it's getting to be a real fucking drag."

"I don't . . ." Brighid started, but Merrin had had enough.

"Oh, whatever!" she huffed and walked off, needing to get outside and find a place to be by herself for a while.

"Well, what was *that* all about," Brighid said, completely bemused.

"You've gotten to be a right bitch lately is what," Willie replied in Merrin's defense. "She's turned her place over to us willingly; she's *not* one of the Lost, but she's as fey as they come; she takes her love of the Craft really seriously and she's still got faith in people. Is that too hard for you to get your immortal bloody head around?"

Brighid's jaw dropped.

Hunter had returned again and was getting acquainted with Mariani, who was very matter-of-factly taking hold of Puck's fear and anguish, saying *trust, trust,* and caressing her gently, knowing full well how a mother needs another mother in times such as these, to gain some sense of empathy.

She sat Hunter down and hushed him, like he was a boy and not a god, and began to acquaint him with the possibility of drawing others of like spirit into the situation. Hunter and several of the Sídhe listened attentively. Everything about the queen of Vodoun commanded respect, and her opinions were being taken very seriously.

Brighid regained her composure and went to the deep place in herself where she sought her own wisest counsel. She had a short but brutal conversation with herself.

Hmph, she thought, turning to the stove and putting on the kettle for what must have been its hundredth boil of the day. She absently wondered how long the gas would last at this rate as she took two cups and spooned instant coffee and sugar into both. When the water had boiled she poured it calmly into the cups, leaving them black the way both she and Merrin liked it, and strode across the room with them, heading for the door, avoiding the many bodies that sat around the studio.

Once outside she looked for Merrin. She found her sitting on the paving stones, squeezed between the bathtub full of fish and plants and the concrete wall that divided her place from next door. She had her knees up, her arms hugging them, and her head resting to one side. She was looking distant and sad.

Brighid sat down beside her and held out the coffee. Merrin sat up straighter and took the proffered offering.

"I'm sorry."

Merrin took a long sip of the coffee before raising her eyes to the Sídhe woman. "I'm sorry I lost my temper but not for what I said." She was feeling very much an outsider and useless for all that except for helping with her home.

The two sat in silence for several long minutes.

"Can I show you something?" asked Brighid softly.

Merrin nodded.

"Can I put my hands on your ears?"

Merrin put her cup down beside her, expecting anything. "Sure," she shrugged, "do your damndest."

"Will you shut your eyes and not be angry for a while?"

Merrin closed her eyes and felt Brighid's hands, soft and warm, cup themselves over her ears. The tension that she hadn't realized was bunching the muscles around her shoulders poured away like water, and she was left in a still place.

Images, clear as day, formed in her mind's eye. Forests.

First there were the forests and the lakes. The untouched shore-lines lush and rocky. She felt herself moving into the depths of the wooded landscape and observed the profusion of wildlife that inhabited it. Things moved. Time moved.

Merrin saw Brighid appearing to be much younger. She looked so like her it was disturbing. She was in the company of at least two hundred other Sídhe. She looked so vital, so happy. The music of fifty or more musicians rang out across the landscape. Dancers leaped and twirled around a great central fire.

Merrin saw Brighid fall into the arms of a wildly handsome man with firelight in his hair and his dark features glowing like amber. She saw them kiss and watched as passion rose to a frenzy—unin-hibited and raw—and the name Leoghaire (which sounded like Leery) flashed into her mind.

Time sped on. The landscape changed and within what seemed like minutes, centuries—millennia—passed. Merrin saw the forests destroyed, the fields carved and fenced, the cities spring like cancers to blight the earth. She saw the factories, the destruction of habitats; she saw war. And more war. And more war.

She saw the Quicken Tree cut down and recognized the spite of greedy men. Occasionally she would see gatherings of the Sídhe, their numbers dwindling as the ugliness and despair took their toll. She saw Brighid with them always, but she never again saw the beau-tiful man who had been with her that first time. No. Always she was with others but always alone.

She witnessed many races of humans, but only one aggressor that raped and destroyed and warped the patterns of the more peaceful ones—or wiped them out.

She realized that the Lost and the fey were those born of cross-mating with the destructive race, usually through force, where bloodlines eventually, over generations, released them from their genetic prisons.

She saw Hunter. And always he walked the earth trying to protect it whilst seeking others—Sídhe, shamans, witches, fey, the Lost—needing their help as equally as they needed his continued existence.

She saw him link up with the band of Travelers with whom Brighid and Willie had aligned themselves.

She witnessed what people had done and was devastated.

And always Brighid was alone. Trying.

She realized that once upon a time the ancestors knew her because she was so gifted, so inspired. She taught many the arts of writing and creating and healing. They thought her a goddess. And perhaps they had the right of it after all.

Merrin realized with horror that the new religion killed her name, turning her into an effigy of sterile holiness. Pretended to the people that she was mortal, dead.

Alone.

Merrin broke from Brighid's "gift," thrusting her hands from her ears and staring at the other woman, who sat silently, her face giving nothing away.

Merrin took one of Brighid's hands in her own and raised it to her lips, gently kissing the fingers.

"So forgive me if I seem bitter," the older woman admitted finally, "but sometimes, when I look at you, I see myself before the whole thing went to shite," she chuckled. "And sometimes when I see you with our wild fox boy I get plain fuckin' jealous."

"Wow," Merrin exclaimed. "I can't imagine what it would be like to live that long," and she shook her head in wonder.

"But you might, the way things're going . . ." She shouldn't have said that. It kind of slipped out.

"What do you mean?"

"Nothin' now. Forget I said anything."

"I never forget stuff," Merrin assured her.

"Well, then leave it, will you? Now's not the time to turn from the immediate problems we face."

"Agreed on that. I'll take you up on it when everything settles down though."

"It will though, won't it?"

Merrin didn't know if she was supposed to provide an insight.

"Rhetorical," Brighid grinned. That was better.

Kathryn observed them through the window above Merrin's altar. They were so alike as to create the illusion of twins at a distance.

She and Vincent sat to the side of the delegation that was gathered around Puck, Mariani, and Hunter.

"What do you think?" Mariani concluded.

"I don't know your gods." Hunter listened, fully attuned to the shine that this woman emitted, aware that she was as capable of connecting with the gods of her ancestors as she claimed.

"No, but I do," she admitted, "and for many of them interference is their business. The Loa are abundant. They are concerned with the doings of people. And the Mysteré is the same everywhere, I believe."

"We do not name her," said Hunter.

"No, neither do we," and Mariani hugged Puck, enfolding her.

Brighid and Merrin walked in. Willie looked worried, but Merrin had obviously shaken off her earlier mood.

"Call them, Hunter." Brighid's face was calm, if solemn. He looked at her and raised his eyebrows.

"Can't hurt," he said softly, as he moved beyond them all, through a fold in time and space, and entered the Dreaming lands.

Chapter Thirty

Unseasonable cold held the city in a frozen fist, but the Southside seemed unaffected, causing intense speculation by the meteorological department.

Michael sat in his apartment on the top floor of the Halloran Regent, facing the television, watching a third news broadcast in a row.

He was angry. He had arranged for the 5th Eclipse to go ahead as planned despite protest from many of the soldiers who would have preferred to wait until the sleet-biting cold snap had passed. Roaming the streets looking for trouble seemed stupid under the current circumstances.

The Brotherhood itself backed him all the way, but had needed to pay incentives to the faction heads as well as supply equipment. This bit deeply into reserve funds. Seemed like everyone got greedy when their comfort was threatened.

He fell asleep on the couch with the television on and was awakened by the dream of the dog again at 3:31 in the morning. His neck was stiff and his arm was dead from where his head had cut off the blood supply as he'd slept. He groaned as he clicked off the set with the remote.

He was walking toward his bed, stripping off his clothes as he went, when the blackout hit. Submerged in total darkness Michael felt instantly claustrophobic, and wondered if he'd been struck blind.

He felt his way back into the living room, stumbling over his briefcase and almost falling. He maneuvered across the room toward the plate-glass sliding doors that accessed his balcony.

He could see the night. Wild winds and driving rain had knocked over some of the seating outside, and as he put his hands on the glass and looked out he realized that the power was down across the whole of the city, and as far as the eye could see.

Michael was stunned at the alien-ness of the landscape. Nothing clicked. This had never happened since he'd lived here. Nothing was familiar, and he knew a moment's panic as he realized he was trapped unless he took the stairs.

He felt his way to the table where he'd dropped his cell phone earlier and dialed Richard Dobbs' mobile at headquarters. The phone was answered immediately.

"What's the situation?" he asked, keeping his tone level.

"We're fuckin' stuck in here is the situation, sir."

Shit, thought Michael. "Any call-ins from anyone else?"

"It's the same everywhere, but we can't get hold of the news or anything. Seems like it's knocked the land lines out as well."

"The boy?"

"We can't get to him."

"How long since anyone checked on him?"

"About half an hour before this hit."

"And . . . ?"

"He was singing."

"What?" Michael found this very disturbing and couldn't fathom why.

"Yeah, singing like a lark in some other freakin' language. Shit . . . wait—no, look, I gotta go, I'm almost outa battery here. Call me on Rabbit's phone."

"No, I'm done. I'm sure it can't last. I'll get back later."

"Yeah, that's what I . . ." but the connection was severed.

MARIANI HAD HAD TIME TO make it home and to gather the Societé together.

AT FALCONSTOWE THE SÍDHE AND all their companions and all the half-seen shapes of bird and beast had heard the sound of singing and wondered at its purity.

BETWEEN THE WORLDS HUNTER STOPPED weaving the Summons he had been creating, and listened. His son. His son was quickening.

ALL ACROSS THE CITY AND within a hundred-square-kilometer radius, natural-born witches awakened from their sleep—those that *did* sleep—with a sense of foreboding and exaltation all mixed together.

The power was out everywhere, but, witches being witches, the flames of a thousand candles burned away the darkness in several dozen homes and apartments at exactly 3:33 AM. With no logic, but without question, each of them gathered together the basic stuff of ritual, stored it into backpacks and shopping bags, and headed for car, motorbike, or bicycle with no other thought in mind than a clear destination—the cliffs overlooking Smuggler's Cove.

From a cruel and unseasonable wildness to an absolute calm. As the hundred and twelve witches readied themselves for the journey to the headland, the night fell silent.

Darcy Rawlins had just woken her boyfriend David to ask him to look out for the kids while she was gone, worrying him, calming him, telling him she'd explain later, wondering how she'd get to where she knew she'd been called on her battered old bike. She was in the middle of donning her all-weather gear when the rain stopped and the wind died. She merely smiled.

"I'm on my way," she whispered to whoever or whatever had called her.

Over the landscape the last of the tattered cloud scudded across a bright and waning moon, showing glimpses of starlight. And deep beyond it all the Great Mystery would have smiled with delight, if she could have been bothered with a face, as Hunter completed his Summons and as the god-child sang, shutting down a city.

PUCK HADN'T BEEN ABLE TO sleep. The soft glow from the many candles in the room kept her anxiety at bay as she sat her vigil, trusting in all of those who sought her child, frustrated because she was unable to do anything.

She was as surprised as the others who were still awake at the sudden silence outside.

Brighid stirred from where she'd lain seemingly unconscious for hours.

"That was weird," she commented, stretching like a cat as she moved over to where Puck sat.

"What? The weather?"

"No—can't you hear it?"

Puck strained against the white noise affecting her ears. She shook her head.

"I can't hear anything."

"I keep getting snippets of someone singing in the old tongue." She walked to the window and opened it from a slit to wide.

She shook her head. "No, it's gone now."

As she spoke the first of the sirens began in the distance. Ambulance, fire, she wasn't sure, but within minutes the night was filled with their alarms.

Willie awoke from where he lay amidst cushions, all tangled up with Merrin, who groaned and rolled onto her other side. "What's up?" he queried. Others were stirring also, awakened by the intensity several streets or more from the almost uninhabited dock area.

"I'm going to check it out," he said. Matt and Annis and several of the others were also into it.

"What if you're gone and Hunter comes back with a way to get Robin out? How can you just leave?" Puck was angry. Now was not the time for them to be spontaneous.

"Oh calm down," Annis responded in her flippant, acerbic manner. "We'll just be gone for a bit. We'd know if he was dead, yeah? Selkie, you comin'? You can keep your ears up for what's happening here, surely."

"No, I don't want to go with you," the seer replied, moving over from the hearth where she'd been only half-asleep anyway, and coming to stand beside Puck.

"Okay, Plan B, 'cause listen to that," and Willie indicated toward the window where the noises in the night had intensified to include car horns.

Raven and Alan joined the group, readying themselves to walk into the city. "Selkie," said the pale, dark-haired Sídhe, "keep your mind's eye on me, Sunshine. If we're needed I'll hear you."

Selkie shrugged. It was as good an idea as any.

Puck was in a state of agitation as the others bundled out the door, with Merrin and Kathryn hurrying into jackets to keep up and Vincent following calmly at the rear of the procession.

Once beyond the back alley they discovered the blackout, but it wasn't until they got closer to the city that they recognized the extent of the impact of what could only be described as a disaster.

New Rathmore never really slept, with tourists arriving early this season due to what had been a gentle spring. Just before 3 AM was probably the quietest time of the day, and yet the traffic in the inner city was locked into tight chaos. Traffic lights were down, and people who had still been awake had emerged from their apartments and homes seeking answers they could not get.

Police and emergency services seemed to be everywhere, and looting had already begun.

All radio and television networks were off air and telecommunications and land phones had ceased to operate.

People were sitting or standing around aimlessly and as the fey walked the streets, block after block, all they heard was, "It won't last. Don't worry."

The lights from occasional torches and the on-road vehicles were the only lights anywhere. In side streets or where there was little congestion the Sídhe could see flitting movements and hear strange callings, as though all the little mysteries and hidden wild things had come out to play in the dark.

Chapter Thirty-one

Hunter dwelt between the worlds, down by Forgotten Lake. The bracken all around him rustled occasionally with the passing of creatures; the soft mists evoked by the evening rolled toward the shore and up onto the land. Eerie, the way it moved. Slow upon the ground, all wraith-like and silent, wrapping itself around the trunks of living trees further up the bank, more like smoke than anything.

Eagles called out to one another from high above, whistling messages across the sky, specks in the fading light.

He made his way around the water's edge until he reached a patch of boulder-strewn beach, where the last of the sun touched the ground.

She was already waiting for him. This time she wore the body of a young girl, looking no more than six or seven years old in human-gauging years, all dressed up in scarlet and green leathers, and seated upon what could have been a war-horse: high and fierce, with the motley colors of lichen-covered stone. She held the reins of a night-black mare, who stood pawing at the ground in anticipation, sending sparks from the stone that shattered beneath her hooves.

"You wanna ride with me?" The goddess grinned, exposing a gap where a tooth had not yet grown.

"This is new," Hunter replied, taking the unnecessary reins into his own hands.

"Yeah, well . . ." A russet- and black-plumed hawk shifted, from the heavy leather gauntlet that she wore on her left forearm, protecting it from the cruel talons, to the board at the front of the saddle, riffling its wings into a more comfortable fit.

"I'd rather sit and talk about a problem."

"Nothing to talk about, Hunter."

He shrugged and leaped onto the black mare's back.

"Where do you want to ride to?"

"To the battle, silly," she laughed.

"Whose war?"

She looked at him, nothing remotely human in the gaze. Hunter was a god and yet still she could make the hair stand up on his arms and the skin prickle all down his back.

The horses moved, slowly at first, high-stepping over the tumbles of rock, but gathering pace as they entered the bracken and the knee-high mist that moved across the land. By the time they broached the ancient primordial, mistletoe-hung forest they rode at a death-defying gallop. They headed through time and space with the tawny hawk winging before them, screeching out a challenge to the unwary.

"Uh, oh," whispered Brighid. It was quiet, even peaceful, with the others gone. She had heard the call of the hunting bird somewhere off in the 'tween worlds—a sound she hadn't heard for longer than she could remember.

"Sometimes I feel like I don't belong," said Puck, knowing that Brighid sensed what she did not.

The Dé Danann chuckled. "Yeah, well, I figure that's annoying, but I don't think now's the time to be feeling all fragile-like."

Selkie had taken over the couch where she was stretched out, part dozing and part listening. The others were in varying states of relaxation around the room, while Brighid and Puck took up most of the space before the fire. Puck snaked across the floor, resting her head in Brighid's curled lap.

"So, what's going on? You know something and you're not telling."

Brighid reached an idle hand to stroke back the hair from Puck's forehead.

"I think the shit's about to hit the fan, mo chroí."

"I thought it already had," said Puck, raising herself up onto one elbow.

"Well, it seems to me that the Mystery is getting involved this time."

"But she doesn't . . ."

"Yeah, I know—she doesn't interfere." Brighid's brow furrowed as she sought to understand.

"Perhaps there's more at stake than what we think?" Puck put it as a question, fishing. Brighid looked at her, her eyes dancing.

"Perhaps you've got the right of it."

"I THINK OUR SIGHTSEEING'S ABOUT done," Raven announced. They stood around in a tight group watching the chaos across the road, where the traffic had come to a standstill and frustrated drivers yelled at the cops on horseback, a pot about to boil over, tired and angry and scared. The air was filled with it, and much more.

The night was thick with wakefulness, and the blackness seemed to laugh at the idea of near-dawn.

If the electricity didn't come back on soon, and the services weren't restored, the city would become a very dangerous place very quickly. The envisioned scenario was lost on no one. It was time for the Travelers to get off the streets and out of sight.

They'd walked only half a block when Merrin was called or summoned—and a clear destination sprang into her awareness. She was sure it was Hunter that she heard. None of the others seemed to notice. She stopped dead, causing Willie to stumble as she clutched at him. He watched the fierce concentration play across her face, oblivious of its cause.

"What . . ."

"Hush a minute, Willie." They were soon left behind as the others continued on ahead.

'You can't hear it, can you?' she asked eventually.

"I don't . . . ah, I don't think I know what I'm supposed to be listenin' to, mo chroí."

"You up for an adventure?" Merrin suggested, eyebrows raised.

Willie grinned at that.

Chapter Thirty-two

The Dúile: Nine Smooth Stones

The high beam of the Custom XVS650 Yamaha that Willie had "borrowed" arced across the backs of several people, many who turned in anticipation of new arrivals. The Dé Danann pulled in among the already parked vehicles and cut the engine with seeming regret. Merrin swung her leg over the bike and jumped to avoid the exhaust pipe burning her. She removed her helmet, shaking out her plait, while Willie slung his fiddle, in its old leather case, onto his shoulder.

This made a hundred and thirteen people gathered at Smugglers Cove on this unusual night, and a hundred and twelve of them were witches—Willie being the exception.

Some of the people walked toward the newcomers.

"What're you all doing here?" Merrin called to the group.

"We could ask you the same thing and hope you knew," one of the men replied with attitude.

"I . . ."

"I figure you were summoned," he finished for her. "We all were."

"Yeah, whatever . . ." She was a bit peeved by the guy's arrogant tone, and she turned her back on him pointedly, pulling a face and mimicking what he'd said. Willie chuckled as he sashayed from the bike and removed his own helmet, leaving it dangling from one of the handlebars. He looked ready for trouble, but with his fiddle case on his back he didn't quite achieve the glamour he was attempting, and Merrin rolled her eyes at the ragged, wind-tousled figure he presented.

The other man, realizing he'd virtually been dismissed by the Goth girl, merely shrugged and wandered back toward the rest of the gathering, scuffing at sand with his sneakered feet and mumbling under his breath, his hands shoved deep into the pockets of his baggy cargo pants, looking thoroughly out of place in contrast to most of the others. He stood an impressive six-foot-six-inches tall, but was lean and geekish, with close-cropped ginger hair, a face awash with freckles, pale hazel eyes that turned down slightly at the corners giving him a somewhat melancholy and lazy look despite his intelligence, which leaned precipitously toward genius and had spearheaded him into the forefront of computer technology when he was younger.

He changed his mind, mid-stride, and turned. He walked back, purposefully, until he stood directly in front of Merrin.

"Hi, my name's Dog," he offered, holding out a hand for her to shake, "and none of us have any fucking idea what we're doing here."

Merrin relaxed at the change to the tone of his voice. "How'd you get a name like that?" she asked him.

"Long story . . ." and the corners of his mouth tilted with irony.

She shrugged. "Some other time," and she took his outstretched hand and shook it vigorously, and the three of them moved quickly to join the others over by the fire, out of the relentless onshore wind.

After several minutes of excited small-talk Merrin determined that she wasn't interested in merely hanging around until someone maybe broached the subject of why, perhaps, they *had* been summoned here in the heart of such a miserable night.

"I'm here because I'm a witch and the gods are bloody loud tonight," she exclaimed to anyone and everyone.

"You're a witch?" This came from a lion-maned, gamin-looking young woman who had wandered over to stand beside Dog and who later introduced herself as Celeste, his sister (equally as tall as her sibling, but without the self-consciousness he exhibited but of which he was decidedly unaware). She looked from Merrin to Willie, and her eyes crinkled with a smile as she let her gaze wander over his decided strangeness.

Dog turned to the others, who had been listening intently. "So'm I, I suppose," he mumbled, figuring it was only a small lie.

It was all hubble-bubble after that. It seemed like no one had wanted to say the words while they remained unsure of each other; seemed like most of them knew themselves to be witches in one way or another.

Everybody got acquainted as they huddled around the slow-burning, smoky fire that had been hastily slung together by the first few to arrive. *Bloody city witches*, Willie thought disgustedly, kneeling upwind and whispering encouragement to the sparky little mysteries when he thought no one was looking.

Several discussions broke out among the curious that ended up being irrelevant. None had had a choice, and if they'd felt like maybe they did it was moot anyway—they were here, after all. They'd come.

For a few this was a real revelation. For others it was a relief. For the majority? Precious and special it was, for sure. It made for good company.

Merrin relaxed easily into conversation with Dog and Celeste and the others, but Willie was guarded, not wanting to be questioned when the strangers turned their attention in his direction—pretending to be antisocial because what he wasn't was a witch, and they might wonder at his being there. Merrin explained that they had heard the call while they'd been out exploring the mess in the city-center with their friends. Willie couldn't help himself though, and proudly explained that it had been the first time ever that he'd hot-wired a motor-bike.

The wind kept up as the witches settled into each others' presence, but eventually blew itself to bearable as the last of the rain passed away from the coast—the ragged cloud thinning to feathers just before dawn.

The group instinctively made its way down the dangerous, rocky cliffside as the first hint of rose smudged the horizon. The tide was out. Seaweed, shale, and small shells formed most of a beach that would be almost nonexistent at flow. The rich smell of the ocean's detritus caused most among them a heady ecstasy.

"Can we form a circle and see if we can make contact?" Merrin was the first to voice the need to actively respond to the calling that had brought them together.

There was no pomp, and no fuss.

Several people had brought their personal objects of power with them, and Merrin drew her athame from its scabbard at her belt.

"Oh my—weapons, is it?" Willie mocked, but a smoldering look from Merrin silenced any further insolence.

One by one the others who had ritual daggers hidden about their clothing or buried in bags and backpacks did likewise, discarding whatever was unnecessary as they walked closer to the shoreline.

Celeste was the only one of the hundred and twelve witches to brandish a staff—a simple, dead-straight piece of hazel carved with spiral motifs around one end. She laughed a little, in seeming awkwardness, as she began casting a wide circle around all present.

Merrin and Dog moved with her while others busied themselves calling on the blessings of the four directions, the ancestors, and the elements of life, while Willie struck up a haunting air on his fiddle. All spoke or hummed in whispers, giving an enchantment to the morning that would have evaporated with a raised voice.

Without conferring with each other—unnecessary—they wove a spell of seeking using their hands and bodies to move the air into patterns that they knew would be pleasing to the mysteries. Willie was fascinated and deeply moved by their brightness.

Ah, fey, he thought. It was like a beacon, he was to recall later when he told it to the others.

HUNTER AND THE GREAT MYSTERY were drawn by the improvised ritual as they thundered from between the worlds, coming onto the shingled beach where the large coven danced their magic, surprising everyone with their sudden appearance.

As one, the group turned as the riders approached from the north.

An almost palpable sense of calm alarm shivered through the gathered witches at the sight of the two as their horses' powerful legs ate the distance between them—Hunter because of his enormity and "otherness," and because of the illusive, wavering form that refused to settle into a recognizable anything, that rode a sand- and russet-colored horse beside the dark man's night-black mare.

Hunter stayed astride his mount, as the Entity emitted waves of sensation toward the group, overwhelming many with awe and turning the legs of some to jelly with a fear that was not equated with malevolence but was rather like the sensation one would suffer looking down into a volcano from its lip.

She dismounted and approached the circle, moving directly across the barrier meant to keep the magic strong within and the attention of that which was unwelcome without, parting the people effortlessly as she billowed to its center.

In a dance of grace her movement inscribed the wet sand with a pattern, both offensive and beautiful—nonsense to the logical eye, obvious in its meaning to the instinctual.

The witches understood, and Willie fell to his knees.

Do I have your permission to ask you all to interfere with one of your own?

Merrin heard this as surely as if the words had been spoken even through the turning of the tide.

"You need our permission?" she asked.

You must all either agree or disagree. Surely I'm intelligible.

Merrin repeated the request loudly for the benefit of those who were having difficulty hearing over the sounds of the ocean and the pull of the wind. Many looked confused, and Willie thought it was all very funny and grinned like a lopsided canid.

"She won't interfere unless there's an agreement," called Hunter.

Make up your minds, hissed the wind.

"Uh . . . I agree," said Merrin without hesitation, looking toward Celeste.

"Who gets hurt?" asked the latter, to mumbled agreement from many others.

"What bullshit," Merrin huffed, flouncing to the ground beside Willie.

People are already hurting, replied the voice to more than one mind.

"Glad we clarified that," Celeste mumbled, ignoring Merrin's jibe, directing her attention, instead, toward the impish, but unnervingly attractive Sídhe. *I'll have him*, she growled softly to herself, the fleeting sensation of lust quite overshadowing the circumstances (but not before Willie had read the narrowed eyes, leaving him wondering at the implication).

"I'm in," she concluded, gripping the staff with a white-knuckled hand.

Dog and the others agreed to the request, until no one except Willie was left silent.

"What about you?" Dog asked him.

"I don't count." He squirmed under the others' scrutiny.

"Of course he agrees," said Merrin, giving him a pleading look. "Just say yes, Willie."

"Tsk! Pressure!" He looked across the boundary of the circle to where Hunter raised his eyebrows, sending a blatant message.

"Yeah, I'll agree to anything, me." Merrin visibly relaxed. *Now is not the time*, she reprimanded him with her mind. He merely grinned and looked interested.

THERE WAS NO MORE HESITATION. All knew that this was a deep mystery, and the understanding of the necessity for an agreement reinforced its purpose.

Then look upon the pattern in the sand and convince him to free the boy, or millions will die instead of hundreds.

"Who is he?" asked Celeste.

The boy or the pattern?

"Well, both."

The pattern is the many, dying without any let-up, trapped within a beloved who has become my enemy. The boy is the world's bane unless he is freed.

"He is my son," said Hunter.

"And who are you?" called a woman standing close to the seaward edge of the circle.

He didn't answer but turned his face in her direction until she could see his eyes. She broke into a sweat as comprehension dawned.

"Oh my god," she said softly.

The whirling, shifting force sounded like she chuckled.

Now get busy. And thank you.

The Great Mystery withdrew from the group, seeming to draw form around her previous amorphousness as she moved back to where Hunter waited.

Clothed now, in a body, she mounted in one fluid movement.

THE HORSES TURNED AND CANTERED back the way they had come: the big man on one and a girl in scarlet and green leathers with a hawk upon an outstretched, gauntleted arm, upon the other.

It took a moment for the Gathering to realize that the girl riding away beside the huge man, with dreds flying, had been the Presence in the circle, and that something bright and incredible had gone from them, but they had the markings in the sand to show that she'd been real.

They had each other. They had work to do. Merrin grinned at Willie.

Chapter Thirty-three

Michael Blacker made his way slowly. It was pitch black. Others were coming down the stairs also, and they moved silently, alert for the unknown, using feel. Blind.

The experience unnerved even him. It was like the world had stopped, or they had all died and didn't know that the stairwell was the journey down that led, eventually, to hell. Not that Blacker believed that. He used the fable to scare the gullible, sure, but he was far too learned to buy into the children's story.

Time had ceased. He constantly depressed the pin that illuminated his watch to reassure himself that reality dwelt mere metres beyond the thick fire-proof walls of the emergency exit.

Floor after floor. He counted each landing fanatically, fearful of missing the lobby exit and ending up in the tri-level underground parking ramp. It had heavily barred security doors that were accessible only to residents with key cards between midnight and 5 AM. He'd get lost down there, for sure—waste too much time.

It took him just under an hour to reach the lobby. Someone had lit a candelabra, and the warm glow was an intense relief after the interminable blackness. Michael unclenched his teeth.

The guest lounge was crowded, and the staff mingled among them reassuringly.

Michael strode up to the group of concierge congregating beside the sealed entrance, smoking cigarettes and playing cards.

"What's going on here?" he demanded.

One of the scarlet-clad men looked up from the game, adjusting his tie as he assumed a professional air that seemed ridiculous under the circumstances.

"Sir, we assure you . . ."

"Crap, man. Open the fucking doors."

"Sir, the doors are electronically . . ."

Michael ignored him, turning instead to where the bank of ornate brass luggage trolleys stood beside an exit marked Private.

He grabbed one and rammed it into the wide glass entrance doors. They were reinforced and barely cracked.

"Somebody help me here," he yelled.

Three of the concierge jumped up, eager to participate, heedless of consequences when the initiative had already been taken.

Others from among the guests responded, picking up whatever heavy object was to hand. They slammed repeatedly at the glass, weakening it until one entire panel collapsed, cobwebbed but whole, onto the steps of the outer entrance.

En masse the trapped people launched themselves out into the street to . . . nothing. No lights, no vehicles, only the distant sounds of sirens, the acrid smell of burning—a false sunrise to the north indicating extensive fires somewhere out toward the airport—and the keening wind.

Shit, thought Michael. He was determined to get across town to the church and to somehow access the lower levels of the Brotherhood's headquarters, an obsessive desire to see the feral child foremost in mind.

He began walking, moving off the main city arterials, searching for an abandoned vehicle.

People milled in hushed clusters, many still in pajamas, with overcoats donned hastily against the raging winds. Most remained close to wherever they had been staying prior to the blackout. An illogical fear wafted like an animal around everyone.

Michael knew that most of the city still slept, oblivious. The real impact of the power outage would not be felt until the morning. Unless the problem was discovered and corrected quickly things were likely to become really messy. People were used to turning on the television and being updated on these kinds of events. What would happen if no one knew what was going on?

Four blocks from the hotel Michael saw a newspaper delivery van with the driver-side door open, the headlights illuminating the road ahead. He walked past it, looking within to see if the driver was perhaps merely sitting inside, but it had been abandoned with the keys still dangling from the ignition. He climbed into the seat, killing the lights to save whatever juice was left in the battery.

He was sweating despite the frigid wind. He'd never stolen anything in his life. He felt exhilarated.

The engine turned over first go, and he gunned it before switching on the lights. Whoever had deserted the van had not been gone long and could come back, so Michael drove away quickly.

The darkness closed the headlights in. Beyond and beside them the movements of unnatural things flitted and lurked. There were so many of them, so many more than he had experienced in the past. Moving night—alive with evil. He was glad he was no longer on foot. Every now and then eyes would shine in the headlights—there and gone. Michael sensed that they were aware of him, hated him.

The circuit around St. Brendan's Park was the most bizarre. The park was the equivalent of several acres, housing the war memorial, a myriad of pathways through a tame forest, and many fountains that were all fed from the man-made lake at its heart. It was guarded by ten-foot-high stone walls, gated periodically with heavy, pike-tipped wrought-iron, which were traditionally locked between sunset and sunrise.

All along the walls were unearthly creatures. All were watching Michael's passing. He became more and more agitated by the second, thinking that whatever tests of faith these visions were supposed to evoke from him were a waste, were puerile. Some puerile god's spite.

Agitation mounted to anger, anger to rage. His route took him toward the main gates of the park, where hordes of the flitterings were gathered around two shadowy figures mounted on light and dark horses.

He slammed on the brakes, whipping the keys from the ignition, leaving the headlights to play on the mêlée up ahead. He ripped open the door of the van, screaming, *I banish you in the name of our lord Jesus, I banish you in the name of our lord Jesus*, over and over like some insane chant. He strode toward the riders. The predawn wind tore at his clothes and bit into his flesh.

He laughed, pausing in his exorcism.

"Is this the fucking best you can do?" he spat, before beginning his litany again.

The horses pawed the ground, the sound ringing out into the night like hammer on anvil.

He recognized Hunter from the many descriptions he had been given, but the hooded woman astride the pale horse could not be seen except for the blazing red of her hair that billowed around the cowl of her cloak like a living thing.

Michael strode up to them, the words dying in his throat. The creatures were stillness itself.

The dark man gazed into Michael's eyes, and Michael was transfixed, pinned. He felt like a rabbit frozen in the stare of a tiger. He could hear a distant warning from somewhere deep within saying, *Don't look at him; don't look at him.* He felt his bladder release and a flare of warmth fill his groin before trickling in rivulets down his legs.

"What have you done, Michael Blacker?" Hunter's voice was difficult to hear over the screaming of the wind, but the question had bypassed Blacker's ears and razored to within his brain. He could not answer. He was unable.

Beyond the Pale, he heard, like a hiss.

He was released from the dark man's gaze, his head doing a slow, uncontrolled journey to the figure seated beside him. His horror increased and his throat constricted as he realized that what he had thought was hair was not. Bees. No face—just bees.

This ought to be fun, Michael, my son. Why aren't you laughing? The voice was in the air around him; the wind spoke; the bees.

Michael's legs gave way beneath him and he landed on the concrete, skinning his hand in a vain attempt to prevent himself from being injured.

"Release my son."

From the depths of self-disgust, Michael clawed a response. "Get fucked," he spat before passing out.

Hunter looked toward the goddess. "Why do you stay my hand?"

You know why.

He knew well enough not to bother questioning. She never elaborated anyway.

MICHAEL REGAINED CONSCIOUSNESS UNDER THE glare of a torch. He raised his arm to shield his vision and enable himself to see who stood above him, just as the beam was deflected to the ground beside him.

Two uniformed police stood watching him.

"Can you get up?" asked one.

Michael's knee had twisted in the fall, and his left hand throbbed where the skin had ruptured on the rough ground. He grimaced as he stood.

"What's your name?"

He looked at the cop asking the question as though the man was an idiot.

"Can you show me some I.D. please?"

"What's wrong with you two? Can't you see I'm hurt? Get me to somewhere that I can clean up."

"Show me your I.D. please, sir."

Michael scowled, looking around himself to see if the nightmare creatures and demons were still apparent, while reaching toward his jacket pocket to retrieve his wallet.

The cop to the left of him pulled his pistol.

"You do that slowly with your left hand," he demanded.

"What the . . ." But the two officers were deadly serious. Michael slowly lifted his right hand and used his left to reach into his inside pocket, exposing the loaded shoulder holster more in the process.

Both men responded instantly, the other also drawing his weapon.

"Put your hands behind your head. Now!"

"I can explain . . ." Michael began as he lifted his arms.

The first man moved in and took the gun from its holster. "You have the right to remain silent . . ."

"Hang on a minute . . ."

"Anything you do say . . ."

"You've got no right . . ." But the police officer merely spoke over the top of him as the other jerked Michael's arms behind his back and snapped on handcuffs, ignoring the pungent odor of urine that was still wet upon Michael Blacker's body.

They bundled him unceremoniously into the squad car, saying nothing, turning on the siren and lighting up the night with the flashing colors of the blue and red warning lights.

Police and emergency services were stretched to breaking point. Robert Straun and Senior Constable Peter Ames had been patrolling for looters when they had seen Michael exit the van, scream at nothing, and behave in a psychotic manner. They'd meant to take him to psych, over at St. Vincent's Hospital, to get him out of harm's way, until they'd realized that he was armed. Both knew that the arrest wasn't valid as he'd committed no crime that they were aware of, but just too damn much had been out of control for the past week to leave him on the streets, even if he *had* been unarmed. It was not an option. The man presented a clear and present danger, either to himself or somebody else.

Michael's person and belongings were searched upon reaching the precinct headquarters, and it just happened that two detectives, a man and a woman from Special Branch, were there when Michael was at the charge desk being written up as being under arrest for disorderly behavior and possession of a suspect fire-arm. Michael insisted he had a license for the weapon, but as all systems were down there was no way to check. He also insisted that they had no right to hold him, and he further refused to speak without legal counsel being present, which was, under the circumstances, impossible.

The woman detective recognized him as he argued with the desk sergeant. He'd been under investigation for several months—the religious head of a right-wing, maybe-political, Christian cult that the branch had had complaints about. They'd been reported as a fascist organization, and scrutiny had picked up during the past week alone. She spoke to the arresting officers, taking note of the details for future reference.

The night was far too busy to devote more than a momentary interest in him, but release was refused due to the erratic behavior he had displayed at the park. A change of clothing was provided from lost property and he was interred in a holding cell along with ten other men.

MICHAEL SAT ON ONE OF the benches beside a sleeping giant who snored, oblivious of his surroundings. He was stunned at the turn of events and was desperate to remain calm, feeling altogether powerless for the first time in almost three decades.

AT SMUGGLERS COVE THE WITCHES packed up their belongings as the wind swept away the talisman that the goddess had carved in the sand and the tide rose to reclaim its realm upon the land.

"Do you think anything happened?" Celeste asked Merrin, who simply shrugged, understanding the irony of spellcrafting—that you knew but didn't, at the same time.

"Do you and Willie maybe want to come back to our place before you go home?" Dog asked. "We're just down the road a bit and we're on gas, so coffee's as good as made."

It sure seemed a good idea, what with fingers and toes turning blue from the cold, damp sand.

WILLIE HAD LAGGED BEHIND THE farewells. He had found several smooth, round stones that had lain where the sigil had been drawn, unnoticed by the others. Each was black, without flaw, and each of them was engraved with a symbol. There were nine of them.

Dúile stones? he wondered.

He ran across the moving sand, followed by the incoming tide, and caught up with Merrin, holding his prize out for her attention.

"What have you got there?" Merrin asked, fingering the stones and feeling uncomfortable at their touch.

"They're Dúile. We've got somebody's soul here."

"And where did you get them, and can you please explain what you're talking about?"

"Oh, they were left where the pattern was. I just grabbed 'em up before the sea took 'em, is all. You know the ancients from the old land, like . . ." His brow furrowed as he attempted to remember the lore surrounding this mystery. He hadn't thought, much less talked about, this arcane understanding for several centuries.

"Well they thought of things as comprised of nine elements: the bones, the flesh, the hair, the blood, the breath, ah . . . the mind . . . oh, yeah—the face and the brain and the head. That was for people— it was different for everything else, but everything else consisted of nine things, in one way or another.

"See, three is a potent number that's all creative-like . . ."

"I knew that," interrupted Merrin.

"Yeah but three lots of three is *really* potent, so spells were sometimes made up of nine things if they were meant to represent someone or something complete."

"What do the little marks mean?" she asked, gesturing to the intricate designs carved on each stone.

"No bleedin' idea, mo chroí. I'll have to ask the others when we get 'em home."

Willie was about to pocket the Dúile when Dog slid down the sandy face of the dune that led up to the parked cars, losing his footing on the way down and stumbling between them and grabbing at Merrin's coat to break his fall.

"You comin'?" he began, dusting sand from his windbreaker. Then his eyes dropped to Willie's hands, still holding his treasure.

"What . . ." He reached out and touched the almost-perfect egg-shaped mounds too quickly for Willie to retract them and was struck with the same jag of weirdness that had affected Merrin.

"Ah . . ." Willie hesitated, not at all sure that this was something he wanted to discuss with mere humans.

"C'mon man! What have you got?"

"Can we maybe talk about it over that coffee you mentioned?" Merrin asked carefully.

"Yeah . . . Sure." Dog's gaze lingered as Willie stowed the stones deep into the pockets of his coat. Then he turned and using his hands for purchase stumbled back up the shifting slope to where Celeste stood with her hands on her hips, looking impatient but disinclined to join her brother in getting all sandy.

"Willie, do you think we should tell the others before they all leave? Considering we were all part of this thing tonight?" Merrin whispered.

"No!" he replied sharply.

Then taking a deep breath and letting it out abruptly, he softened his tone.

"Nah, me duck, though I can't explain what I mean. I'd rather just keep this for Brighid to fathom." He didn't want to mention the uneasy sensation that had left a smudge of darkness upon him from the wily look that had come from Celeste earlier. He also didn't want to voice his fear that she and her brother were frauds who'd had no right to be at the Gathering because that was the vibe that they both emanated—although, if that were the case, then why had they been called?

MERRIN SQUATTED ON THE GROUND beside the motor cycle and took her tobacco from her pocket, rolling herself a thin cigarette before passing the pouch to Willie, listening all the while to the muffled, incomprehensible argument taking place behind the closed windows of Dog's pick-up truck.

Now why do I not feel pleased with this whole bloody situation? Willie thought to himself.

They left the cove along a ragged dirt track, following in the shallow wake of dust raised by Dog's vehicle. Willie uttered a continuous stream of profanities under his breath.

Chapter Thirty-four

Robin slept, which was just as well for the city. He was fitful though—his small body cold so he wasn't quite in one world or another.

Puck also slept, and dwelt within the Dreaming lands where she hadn't been for years. Brighid had laid her hands upon her and spun a spell of quiet—to attain a little peace for herself, truth be told. For the ancient Sídhe this was all too much drama. She sensed, as though through a mist of confusion, that nothing about the unfolding events was random, and she needed to concentrate without interference. With Puck asleep, the agitated awareness in the studio all but disappeared. Selkie smiled to herself as she sensed the glow brighten about the other Dé Danann, but paid no mind otherwise.

Now what's missing in this whole messy picture? thought Brighid, listing off the recent events, one after the other. She was fully aware of how interesting things had quite suddenly become as she thought about Kathryn and Vincent turning up, the action that the Brotherhood and that creep, Michael Blacker, had stirred up, the involvement of several hundred mortals who hadn't been involved a week ago, the interest in the whole thing that the Great Mystery displayed when she was usually preoccupied with whatever goddesses were preoccupied with. Robin's little antic caused chaos on a grand scale—and how aware was he of what he had done anyway? Hunter pretending to be helpless.

Us. It's us. She couldn't work it out at first.

Then the light bulb came on.

The Sídhe weren't really involved in any of it, weren't doing anything, were just moving around from place to place, collecting Lost and fey, playing music and otherwise having a fine time. But no magic. Not for a long time.

She proceeded to argue with herself that there'd been no need, nothing pressing. *Just the world going to shite all around us,* she huffed. Still, that was old news.

So they'd found Blacker—so what? Any good psychic could have done as much, and Beatha had been as responsible as she for doing so.

It felt like a spell of *same* had been laid upon them. Idle Sídhe—not a calming thought.

From somewhere deeply deep within the Otherworld she heard a snigger and her ears pricked up.

Now what was that? She was alarmed.

She left her material body without thought, as quick as light, and bolted after the sound. Selkie followed right behind her.

THE DARKEST HOUR BEFORE DAWN is always such a busy time in the Dreaming lands, and Puck searched among the flotsam of people's images as they passed back and forth through all the possibilities, on the chance that Robin was there somewhere. The trouble was she had no idea where to look.

He found her. His body had let go enough for him to rove and he saw her, oh, such a seeming long way off that he wondered if he had the strength of will to cross the gulf. But he did.

Puck felt him rather than saw him. The signature of her son's dreaming body wrapped itself around her with a strength she didn't know that he possessed, and she stifled down the instinctive fear that pulsed through her. This was her son, but something of him had changed and had become potent.

She opened her eyes, unaware that her body was no longer by the fire at Merrin's place. She was in pitch blackness. It was like being blind. Wherever she was, it was ice-cold, and her body temperature began to decline dramatically.

Eyes turned in her direction—feral and green—whilst the thought *Mother?* was thrust at her. She reached out in the darkness and felt Robin's cold, cold body as it sagged into her arms.

"Oh, Robin." She didn't know what to say after that. What now?

Trapped are we, he thought to her.

"Can you get us out, Rob?"

Where is father is?

"Somewhere."

"Hmm," he said aloud.

Chapter Thirty-five

Hunter knew that he could get Robin out, but to do so would call destruction down on the city. All he had to do was to raise his voice. The earth would shudder. Would this crack the walls of his son's prison? He had ranged around the building, sensing the reinforced steel and concrete solid enough to hold against a missile strike.

He also knew that there was something else going on. There were wards upon the place, a potent magic deflecting his entry.

His rage was at a point of overflowing, and he worked very hard to withhold it. When he had faced Michael Blacker at St. Brendan's Park he had seen, other than the man, the pattern that Beatha and C'av'arn had also seen. And it was most disturbing. The tentacles were vast. The network of discord around him was not caused by the man himself, but was an alien thing—no pattern that he had ever seen upon the earth. It had exuded a horror, a malignancy.

When Blacker had fainted Hunter had wanted to trample him to death beneath the ready hooves of the black mare. He had wanted to morph and rip his throat out with his own teeth.

Do that and we lose the outcome, the goddess had said.

"Explain this to me," he snarled.

She looked at him with eyes that warned him not to dare that tone of voice, no matter what.

She was tempted toward compassion because she loved him so, and nothing he ever did could damage that. And she knew he loved her utterly. But now was not the time. Too much hung in the balance for her to take away his anguish.

Her cruelty was a matter of survival—and not hers, as nothing could defeat her sovereignty—but of magic and wonder, the soul of beauty. It had its own existence, a separate thing to her, created for the sheer delight of it. She had let it go its own way an eternity ago, and it had thrived on its own independence.

Now it was being emptied. Something was siphoning it, and whatever it was could hide well. The Unseelie human was its plaything, and that pissed her off because he'd been her child once. Fey. She didn't know if she could undo the ugly from him, unless she found its core, as it was not her way to interfere with what had been created as, live or die, it was all the same to her, and all of it was wonderful.

But this?

Keep Hunter calm. He was the soul of the forest and the one who reminded the wild things that they were ever-important, including the human ones (despite the rest of them that she'd just as rather turn to compost—except that somehow, in the long run, they were part of the pattern-that-moves).

Keep Hunter calm. Wake the Sídhe up, somehow, from their doldrums, as they were becoming a bore and forgetting to do special things.

She was rather certain that she had it all as planned as it could be.

And it had been wonderful, had it not, to expose herself to the mortals on the beach? She knew she wouldn't do so again for a thousand years or more because it would become repetitive, consequently dull—there was enough of that already, what with seeds and stars and babies and such.

Oops! From within her reverie she heard Hunter once again.

"Are you going to tell me what's going on, Lady?"

No. She kept to herself.

The Unseelie man is caught, she replied. *The child is with his mother. And Brighid, oh my fair Brighid, is looking for her lover in the pit.*

"You said we rode to war." He was not yet prepared to let the man before him live.

No, you said that. I merely said, "To the battle, silly."

"Is it not with him?"

Find him, I said. Found him we have.

"Then whose battle?"

Theirs. She raised her arm and pointed out across the city, taking in the shapeshifters and the multitude of gently morphing creatures that thronged before them.

"The city is no place for them." Hunter's brow furrowed, and he shifted to a more comfortable position.

You tell me?

"I love you, but I also love them. Too much bloody harm here."

Robin's such a clever little god, and you're too worried for your own good.

"You know something I don't, yeah?"

Comes with the job. She tossed her head and grinned at him, exposing sharp, white teeth.

They rode away, leaving Michael guarded by creatures that despised him, just as the patrol car doors opened and the officers who'd watched, and seen nothing but a crazy, turned a torch upon the prone body as they walked across the dark street.

Chapter Thirty-six

Dog and Celeste took turns talking about themselves as they settled their guests and put a pot of coffee on the stove.

Seems Dog had been a computer whiz-kid, making a small fortune hacking into the security systems of developing software for companies that hired him for just such a purpose, while Celeste had studied for a fine-arts degree during the day and DJ'd at the Maximum Stack dance club most nights.

Their mother and father had helped with the deposit on the house, where the brother and sister now lived, which had seemed to be a good investment despite its having no modern conveniences. It had been rented out as a summer holiday accommodation for several years, at huge and exorbitant cost, due to its close proximity to both the beaches and the city. The brother and sister had easily paid back what they'd owed.

They'd continued to live with their parents until the latter had decided to sell up and buy a yacht, fulfilling a desire to just sail from port to port, island to island, indefinitely. Dog explained that their folks had been initiated into a coven before either he or Celeste had been born, and had never hidden their practices of the Craft from them.

He was in the kitchen, humming away to himself as he poured the brewed coffee.

He put the full mugs, together with a carton of milk, a jar of sugar, and a couple of spoons, onto an old round tray which he carried into the living room, plonking it onto the coffee table between his guests and suggesting they help themselves.

He sat down, taking one of the cups for himself and spooning liberal amounts of sugar into the soupy brew.

"It all fitted together like a plan." He stirred his coffee, tinkling the spoon three times on the rim of the mug just for luck. "Celeste wanted to move here so that she could sculpt for an exhibition . . ."

"I'd had a constant flow of visitors," she interrupted, "who didn't seem to understand what either 'work' or 'no' meant, when I was ever-so busy."

She leaned back into the snugness of the couch, pulling her knees up in front of her. Willie was beside her, and she tilted her body sideways until she was leaning up against him before resting her steaming mug on her knees. He was uncomfortable with the overt gesture, but realized that she would have fallen had he moved—though, by the gods, he was silently tempted—so he just stayed very still, putting his hand on Merrin's thigh where she sat—oblivious?—on his other side.

Dog went on and on about how the house had started out as a stone stable, complete with shingle roof and loft. They'd put in some false walls so that they could ignore each other when they wanted to, a slow-combustion heater for the winter, a state-of-the-art generator for Dog's computer, a phone, and a kiln.

The plumbing had remained antiquated, but neither of them really cared, and most of the money had run out anyway.

Willie didn't mention the stones again, not at all sure they ought to be public knowledge, and hoping against hope that Dog had forgotten. Merrin didn't question him; she'd picked up on his reticence as soon as they'd arrived at the house.

"We ought to be going," the Sídhe announced finally when the conversation died.

"The stones, chook," Celeste responded, clicking her fingers. Obviously Dog had told her about them in the truck, and she wasn't about to be left out after all that had happened.

"Ah . . ."

"No way are you going without show and tell," she smiled, all charm, but with an underlying something in her voice. "After all, you can't really claim them just for yourself after what went down."

Dog sat on an ornately carved, high-back chair opposite the others and carefully cleared the table between them of the assorted jumble that littered its surface.

Willie's senses were awry. Why was he feeling the heebies when no one else was? But he was, and the sooner he could get himself and Merrin out of there without a fuss the happier he'd be.

"You know, I'm willing to lay odds on that these stones are the ones I used for a spell I buried out on the shore three years gone this Beltean," said Celeste with an air of mild disinterest.

"Are you now?" piped Willie, playing along for the moment. "And what kind of spell takes nine smooth stones, all carved like?"

"The ones I placed there. Made by me—a talisman to bring a lover to my house." She paused, looking like she was trying to remember. Her face brightened.

"If I'm correct . . ."

"You figure they're yours," finished Willie, poker-faced.

"Well, let's have a look, then." Celeste settled back into the comfort of the couch, seemingly content.

Willie took the eerie artifacts, one by one, and placed them on the table. As he did so Celeste snuggled into him, and for the first time Merrin's hackles rose.

Willie didn't let on he'd noticed. The stones affected him with sadness.

"Well, well," she crooned. "They *are* mine. Fancy that!"

She turned her face up to look at Willie. "Does that make you the respondent then?"

Merrin pretended to ignore her, looking instead across at Dog, noticing the gleam of sweat that had broken out on his forehead and the glassy look in his eyes as he stared down at the Dúile. What did he see? What was going on?

She had the silly thought that they were in some kind of game and this was stalemate, but she hadn't counted on Willie.

The stones arranged on the table seemed to brighten rapidly. Just as suddenly they vanished.

And Celeste responded with a roar of rage.

"What just happened?" Dog spluttered, standing and pushing back his chair, staring down at Willie, who sat nonplussed, grinning at the empty table.

"They're gone." The look he passed from one to the other was one of sheer innocence. "What just happened?"

Celeste flat-lined into a black mood, and Dog sat back down, obviously confused.

Merrin wasn't about to let it end there. She stood and grabbed her jacket from the back of the couch.

"What's with you two?" She swung her attention toward Celeste. "And you! You're so full of shit. That was a lie and we know it."

"Do you know what just happened?" Celeste asked, her voice like a razor-blade.

"As if I'd tell you? What kinda witches are you two anyway? You're twisted. You wanted those stones for yourselves, and you didn't care how you got them. We going?"

She went to pull Willie from the couch, but he refused to budge.

"All that stuff you told us about yourselves—was it true?" the Sídhe asked (looking thoughtful, distracted).

"Just because we wanted the magic doesn't make us liars," Dog defended.

"She is!" Merrin hissed. "All that rubbish about spells . . ."

No one spoke. The wood settled in the fire and the indecisive on-shore wind outside the house died down. The sound of the ocean could be heard in the distance.

Celeste shifted on the couch, pulling her legs up and wrapping her arms around them. She looked ready to bite someone's face off.

Dog sighed, seeming to collapse in on himself.

"What?" Willie asked.

"We always thought it was crap. The whole 'witch' thing, our parents. Neither of us believed any of it. Then last night . . ."

"What about the staff? The circle-casting?" Merrin gestured toward Dog with a tilt of her head, "Mister Spokesperson?"

"The staff was our mom's. It's not as though we didn't know all the lingo. Shit, we lived with them; they often included us in their rituals. 'It's all real, yeah?'" The rhetorical question was directed toward his sister. "There's magic; those stones were magic."

"You're both such babies!" Merrin was unimpressed. Celeste had still lied; she had still tried it out on Willie. They'd been ready to steal the Dúile, hadn't they?

"So you worked on security systems?" Willie slid the question in Dog's direction, straight out of left field.

Where'd that come from? thought Merrin.

"Ah . . . yeah. For years," the other man replied, looking even more mystified.

"And you were good?"

Merrin stared at Willie. Why was he changing the subject?

Then it dawned on her.

"Who's up for one more coffee?" she suggested.

"Can I have one of those?" Dog indicated Merrin's tobacco pouch jutting from the top pocket of her jacket. She handed it across.

"I gave up," he announced, grinning and shaking his head at the same time.

"I'm going to bed," announced Celeste, shooting her brother a brutal look. "Make sure you show them the door before I get up."

She flounced up from the couch, giving Merrin a thin-lipped excuse for a smile—meant to antagonize rather than appease—and stormed from the room, slamming a door behind her.

"Ouch." Willie glanced at the traces of the field of fury she'd left around the exit.

"Look, I'm sorry, okay?" Dog's shine had visibly brightened at his sister's departure.

"So what kind of security stuff did you hack?" Willie asked, as he wondered, fleetingly, who held the reins in this family.

"What's this all about?" It was obvious that Dog was completely taken aback by the turn of conversation.

"Can we borrow your generator?"

"Wh . . . ?"

"Will you help us with something?"

"Does it have anything to do with magic?"

Merrin and Willie exchanged glances. "Yes and no," replied the Sídhe, grinning.

"What's going on?"

"I don't know if I trust you yet, mo chroí. I'm askin' though."

Dog was still tense. "Is this some kinda trick?"

"Sweetheart," Willie smiled, "gettin' the stones to vanish was the trick."

Dog looked disbelieving. "You mean you did that?"

"Aye."

"But how . . ."

"Fuck it, Dog, you in or not?"

"Absolutely!" He beamed for the first time. "What do I do?"

"Bring whatever you need to do computer stuff with. Where's the genny? We're going to need that too, by the look of things."

He didn't let on to either of them just how pleased he was with himself. It had been such an easy thing to do—the magic, working the mystery.

I've been around humans too bloody long, he thought, smiling on the inside, not wanting to give the sensation away—just really aware of how little time he'd given to being Sídhe for the last thousand years or so, give or take.

Now I've just got to figure out how to find those stones in the Otherworld . . .

He let the thought go unfinished. One thing at a time.

Chapter Thirty-seven

9:15 AM, Mornington Military Academy, 157 miles south of New Rathmore.

"No, we've had surveillance confirmed. It's looking like we've got a full-scale crisis on our hands unless the boys from TransEn can find the problem as soon as yesterday."

General Peter Stanwick spoke to the bureaucrat on the other end of the line as though he was talking to his nine-year-old son, Nick. He detested politicians almost as much as he detested the media. They never actually did anything except hold things up and cause more red tape than he was ever prepared to do.

"No, nothing. No, no way in by land—all exit and entry points are already jammed up tight. We've got men in the air, and they'll be all over the place by oh-ten-hundred." He looked at his watch and listened impatiently as the other man's voice whined on about a national emergency and the need to call a press conference and would he be available to meet later on in the morning to raise a public response? As if.

"Sir, I'll put you through to Lieutenant Rivers and she can make those arrangements for you. If you don't mind."

The other man interrupted, going on about public confidence, and Peter Stanwick was tempted to hang up. He was due at a meeting in two minutes.

"Yes. Yes, we'll keep you fully informed. No. In about an hour. Yes sir, I will," and he thrust the receiver back into its cradle like a vile thing.

He pressed the intercom connecting him to his personal assistant.

"Keep the bastards off me, will you *please*, Barbara?" he implored.

Rivers laughed and disconnected. She'd been with the general for four years, in both combat and noncombat situations, and she knew she was indispensable. She'd passed over a promotion just last May because of him.

Stanwick was a brilliant man, and she'd learned more from him during the first six months under his command than in all the years at the Lucas Downs Academy. Her passion and expertise lay in the fields of special weapons, strategy, and tactics, and Stanwick was a master at each, but never neglected to ask the opinions of those closest to his work, realizing that valuable insights were not his private domain.

She phoned through to Communications, ordering that all calls for the boss be monitored for *Stickys*—nonmilitary must-speak politicos—informing them that they'd be at an Intel meeting for at least an hour. Any important calls were to get to her first if they came through from Mains.

Stanwick bowled out of his office just as she completed stowing all the relevant information documents into a portfolio.

"Party time," he grinned, opening the door to the hall.

The day was already looking like getting crazy.

EMERGENCY PERSONNEL HAD DRIVEN OUT of New Rathmore, headed for Mornington, Smith Airforce Base, and Carrington Bay, the head office of TransEn, the energy giant, well before the rush.

Crews had also been sent to regional grid facilities and emergency headquarters, attempting to be as unobtrusive as possible, and the news was relayed through to official sources as high up along the chain of authority as was possible.

But press leaks occurred even before 6:30 AM. The entire country was aware that New Rathmore was in the grip of a crisis as televisions were turned on and radios blared with the 7 o'clock breakfast news.

New Rathmore was finding out for itself.

Between dawn and 9 AM a crescendo of panic had gripped the inner city. The suburbs remained fairly calm as most people had no idea of the extent of the outage and were merely annoyed that there was no hot water or that the food in their fridges and freezers could spoil. The phone lines were also down, so no one could find out how long they would be inconvenienced. People dressed and organized their kids for school and prepared to go to work, getting in cars that weren't stuck in electronically controlled garages, or walking the blocks thinking to catch public transport that didn't come.

By 9 AM the air was filled with the thucker of military transport helicopters and the distant sounds of sirens.

People just didn't think. The main arterials leading both into and out of the city center were at a dead standstill and yet still the drivers leaned on their horns, taking out their impatience on nothing. Or each other.

As commuters took risks—or opportunists took chances—the accident rate rose. Fights broke out, women yelled, and gunshots could be heard as looters from inner-city enclaves sought to take advantage of the situation while they could.

General Stanwick ordered ground transports to locate as close as was feasible to the incoming accesses, and fully-laden Medivacs, and troop and equipment helicopters, to strategic landings throughout the city, close to main hospitals and services.

Troops had been prepared for civilian distress and emergencies, but instead they encountered unrest unprecedented this early into a disaster situation.

At the main power facilities there was a great deal of head-scratching, even embarrassment, as technicians endeavored frantically to find the reason for the outage. Nothing was registering. According to all available data, everything at New Rathmore was normal; according to all available data, the grid was still active and behaving as it should. How did a problem get fixed when to all intents and purposes it didn't even exist?

Chapter Thirty-eight

Robin sat awake in the blackness, held tightly in Puck's arms to help conserve his body heat. He sang softly, both to assuage his anxiety and to keep himself amused while he waited. It was in a language long-forgotten that even he did not understand, except for its comfort.

Puck smiled despite their situation. She waited calmly, also, loving the sounds her son made—aware of their impact; unsure if he was—and proud of his courage.

THE SÍDHE AND THEIR COMPANIONS remaining behind at Falconstowe . . . well . . . mostly they partied, but they also set to digging up most of the lawn in the backyard, in the clearing away from the trees, figuring to balance out the honor debt of Kathryn's hospitality by planting her a decent-sized vegetable and herb garden.

The first two times they'd swooped into the town was to buy up tools and seedlings and other supplies, initially shocking and disturbing the small rural community with their appearance and otherness. The Dé Danann turned on the charm in a major way, with a fair dose of glamouring thrown in, and by the end of their second visit not one of the people they had met wanted them to go home.

The word soon spread, as gossip will in a small town, that the new people were a little weird but very friendly, and don't you think we should give them a fair go?

On their third trip they brought the music with them. They set up in the main park, between the only outdoor café in the town and the railway station, drawing a crowd within minutes. They played for most of the afternoon, stopping for breaks occasionally, having coffees and cakes provided for them free of charge by the woman who ran the café. Fingal announced to the gathering that they were throwing a barbecue out at Kathryn Shilton's place to celebrate all the planting they'd done and that there'd be music and beer; that anyone who wanted to come was welcome, and bring your own instruments if you've got 'em and we can have a jam.

They were shocked at how many actually came. Most brought food and drink to share, and the group were showered with house-warming gifts as though they'd just moved in and Kathryn didn't even exist. A bonfire was set to blazing as the sun went down, and the rain and wind that affected other places remained absent.

Several of the Sídhe were so ancient that their knowledge of the land and its productivity was vast. Still they asked advice of the older men of the village, adding tips of their own but not too many, talking growing techniques, livestock, and the weather, and drinking pints, until well past midnight.

The younger people, and most of the women, danced, and were seduced utterly by the charm and wit of the Travelers, while children slept all huddled amongst blankets and pillows, out of the way of the revelers but near enough to the fire to be warm and observable.

All the while the music played. During the evening bonds of friendship formed that none had anticipated. No one at the party realized that the lights had gone out everywhere.

BRIGHID HURTLED THROUGH ALL THE worlds, following the threads that the snigger had left—daemon-bright—the same pattern as the tentacles that had amassed around Michael Blacker. Selkie swooped behind her, silent and swallow-bright.

THE GROUP IN THE CITY, and their new companions, Kathryn and Vincent, returned to Merrin's place to find it empty, the embers cold in the hearth. The place felt disturbed somehow.

The group was divided as to what to do next. Raven, Matt, and Seamus figured they'd be better off out on the streets as they'd had enough of sitting around, and altogether too much was happening out there for them to wait patiently for some sign. Jack, Rowan, and Annis also refused to stay behind, but Alan opted to remain—trouble wasn't something he was good at and daylight was wreaking havoc on New Rathmore.

Kathryn said she was staying. Someone should be at the studio just in case the others returned. She was missing Merrin's company and thought it was spooky that both Puck and Brighid had vanished without leaving word. Not okay. Definitely not at all okay.

"I will stay with you," Vincent decided, unasked.

WILLIE, MERRIN, AND DOG LOADED the compact generator, the computer, and other necessary bits and pieces into Dog's pickup truck. They drove as far as they could before being blocked by traffic snarls. The two men waited by the equipment while Merrin scouted an alternative route. She returned fifteen minutes later fighting with two supermarket carts.

"Is that it? How far is it, anyway, to where we're going?" Dog was frustrated and tired.

"A fair way still," Willie admitted. "Should be easy to find a car when we get across town—the place we're going is in the 'burbs.'"

Hunter, he thought to himself, shrugging, and trying very hard to keep his sense of humor, *where are you when we need you, man?* But there was no answer.

LIEUTENANT BARBARA RIVERS TOOK THE call from TransEn informing command that they couldn't find a problem with New Rathmore's power supply and that even with every man at their disposal, tracing a phantom glitch would take an indefinite period of time—unless they got lucky.

She relayed the information to Peter Stanwick, who sat very still, wondering how on earth a city of more than two million people could survive something of this magnitude, thinking as quickly as he could but seeing no immediate solution. This was not the third world; this was an entire population unprepared for this kind of disaster.

He wondered how long before martial law became necessary. What kind of idiots were in charge out there?

MICHAEL JAMES BLACKER DOZED FITFULLY—upright and as far away from the other men as he could get. He passed in and out of nightmare, coming to almost-consciousness once at the sound of the metal door to the holding cell sliding open. In that moment he wondered if he'd ever been anyone other than who his father had said he was, and he wished he was dead. Then he dropped back into the dream again.

He finally came to full wakefulness when the guards brought a cold breakfast to the inmates. He tried to recall something of importance that had occurred during his brief sleep but couldn't for the life of him remember what it had been.

AND THE RAVENS DID WHAT ravens always do.

Is glad is I that not I human be. The fleeting thought crossed Beatha's mind. She'd been pondering the past few days as she'd savored the after-taste of the bug she'd just consumed. *Is way too much trouble.*

HUNTER WAS AWARE OF IT all. He sat on the sand at the edge of Forgotten Lake with only a mole for company.

He liked moles; they never had much to say, and this one was quieter than most—an appreciation not lost on his companion.

He was content to be there, between the worlds, for just a while. For the serenity. Unlike the world where the mortals live.

The Great Mystery had sure stirred up the pot. And now she'd up and gone again, but not before she'd shown him the pattern. Yes—let them be afraid if it changed the way they did things. A little fear was a healthy thing—it let your instincts out of the false box; it would remind them of the truth of things, of their mortality; that they couldn't make it go away no matter how much glitz they invented as a pretense.

"Here I am!" the neon and the lighted windows shrieked in defiance of the night. "Here I am!" the interminable clogging of the air with jaggle and babble claimed, like it was something worth paying attention to.

"Here I am!" the cars and trucks and buses and trains and planes and ships and rockets and guns and bombs and smoke-stacks and drilling and voices on the radio and voices on the television and microwave ovens and people talking on cell phones, and telephones with their ceaseless ring, ring, and fridges that go brrr all night and dishwashers and air conditioners, and just how many machines does one species need anyway?

And quiet?

Quiet sufficient to hear?

Well, Hunter soaked up the silence and breathed the sense of it to deep within himself. Then he let himself weep. The mole moved closer to his side but did not interfere.

Chapter Thirty-nine

Unseelie—

Alexander Shilton sat behind an exquisite hand-crafted mahogany desk, an unstoppered crystal decanter the only object upon it. He swirled the amber contents of his snifter lazily, patiently.

It wasn't his real name. There was no one left alive in the world who knew his real name. No. He'd hidden that—in the long, extravagant depths of what seemed like forever ago—he'd buried it beneath a resentment that had been born of a shattered fantasy.

His real name was Aengus an Tríbhís Mór, for his mother, spun from the dream of more ancient ages past, had wanted great things for this son—this one child that she was ever able to bear (for the Sídhe do not conceive easily nor often). She had been one of the oldest of the old race, and she would fascinate Aengus with tales of the Otherworlds and when the gods of land and sea and sky walked, seen and heard, among both mortal and Sídhe alike. She was fickle though, and could turn from grace to gloom, to downright apathy for the least thing, in the turning of a breath.

They'd traveled with the first band to leave Tir na n'Ogh and step onto the shores of Connachta, where they were assailed by fierce resistance from the Firbolg—the earlier inhabitants. This had so annoyed his mother that she'd returned to the Otherworld in disgust, leaving Aengus to pursue his life without her (and he'd never seen her since).

He'd loved his mother—maybe too much for what she was capable of giving—and an emptiness had engulfed him as a result of her abandonment that had aged him terribly. He'd changed from the appearance of a boy to the appearance of a fully grown man in the cycle of less than one moon. It had disturbed his sense of what was real.

All that seemed to change when he first saw Brighid.

Blind, unreasonable infatuation.

He'd crossed paths with the band with whom she traveled and had seen her dancing, fair and dark, in the light of a blazing fire, to the chant of many drums and the drone of many pipers. He became increasingly besotted with her as days passed, but she never seemed to notice him at all, except in passing once or twice when she met his eyes and smiled briefly, because of the Dé Danann with whom she kept company—Leoghaire ó naSìogaì—a wild-eyed, autumn-haired seannachai of the Madadh Rua Clan: named for the fox.

Well, it should not be so. She was destined, in his mind, to be his beloved. He couldn't conceive of things being any other way. So when he'd finally summoned up the courage to tell her how he felt, at the gathering of Meán Earraigh (Spring Equinox), and she'd laughed gaily, saying, *In your dreams, whatever you said your name was*, before dancing off to rejoin Leoghaire over by the music, he'd called on all the gods his mother had taught him and cursed the two lovers with the curse of an Thríbhís Mór (for which he was named): *May the sea rise to drown you, the earth open to swallow you, the sky fall to crush you!* because her rejection was impossible, unbelievable.

The problem was that the curse did not work. They went along as merrily as before. Aengus would have to take matters into further consideration.

And so he changed . . . and Leoghaire became his principal hatred—his first revenge—and he determined to learn of spells that no Seelie Sídhe had any right learning.

The Quickening

THE SOFT GLOW OF SEVERAL lamps fed the vast room with buttery warmth while subtle wall lighting accentuated his collection of artifacts once gathered lovingly by the Drake sisters on their travels around the world and procured for him by his law firm at the time of the disappearance of the deceased women's grand-niece, the only surviving heir. Several priceless masterpieces graced the walls of the vast chamber that he called an office, and the dusky gray kid-leather couches, peppered with cushions, did nothing to hide the grandeur of the hand-loomed Persian carpets that would have paid for a modest uptown apartment.

Alexander was obscenely wealthy and was now faced with losing everything, and he couldn't care less.

His fun had basically turned to rubble around him, and it was definitely advantageous to bail as the ship sank, but not before he had one last taste of pleasure. He had to show his face before he left it all behind him. His pride demanded that much—after all, who else could have pulled it off?

He wasn't at all upset at how things had turned out. No. He was very pleased with himself—it had actually ended up being more entertaining than he had intended.

He had planned for almost everything. It was amazing what money could buy in the mortal world. There was the marriage to Patricia Mansfield, who was all too willing to allow him to be a father to Martin, then only fifteen months old. The boy had been putty, raised to greed as he was, used to always getting his own way. Dad's eventual choice of a wife was neither here nor there.

There was Kathryn's abduction; her feigned adoption by Henry and Loretta Bolton after Henry had been offered the CEO position at Schlesinger-Shilton. His wife's agreement not to conceive children of her own was easy—she hadn't wanted them anyway; she was much too vain. The choice of the nanny and the introduction to the legends, the isolation? Easy.

Like mutual moths to the flame he knew that Kathryn and the Tuatha Dé Danann would somehow find each other, that it would be her shine, eventually, that would draw so many of them to the city at one time.

Dimity's rape and abuse all those years ago had triggered her need to settle down—and the opportunity of the bookshop, at a remarkably cheap price, had been, for her, too good to be true, especially with its unique stock of myths and legends thrown in as part of the deal. The café had actually been her incentive, which had surprised him. What a twist.

Michael Blacker had been tricky for a while. He'd been a natural-born fey and Shilton had almost lost him once or twice, despite the boy's father's enthusiasm to make men of his sons by way of his own standards, until he'd decided to implement the Dúile—binding all those innocent, dying eyes to the boy's spirit.

And the Brotherhood—all that power—such ugliness!

And just like he knew they would, the Sídhe had come to the party.

He'd been *that* close to really, really disrupting them.

That's all I've ended up wanting, he thought, pouting. *Just a bit of fun, really.*

Then some stupid white boy had taken it on himself to be spontaneous. To snatch the Hunter's son.

He'd set up seals and wards around that dungeon the Brotherhood had thrown the child into so bloody fast that his own mother would have been proud of him—if she'd stayed. It had upped the taste of pleasure until the little bastard had hummed. Who'd have thought he'd quicken for another thousand years?

Okay. So he could keep the power flowing around his office long enough to have this final bit of juice before he returned to his Court between the worlds.

Brighid.

He'd loved her once in a moment of weakness. But no. She'd gone off with the red-haired, pretty-boy Sídhe story-teller.

Alexander Shilton had used up several thousand years of power trapping him and had only recovered fully just over eighty years ago by human standards of time. Long enough to set this lot up.

A soft whine escaped the wooden crate on the floor beside him. He kicked it hard, chuckling. The russet and white shape of the fully-grown fox cringed against the bars of the box furthest away from his enemy, eyeing his captor with both terror and futility.

"*Show and tell*, Leoghaire me ol' mate," he savored. "Show . . . and . . . bloody . . . tell!" and he sank back into the luxury of his chair, putting his feet up on the desk, taking a deep swallow of the vintage cognac.

BRIGHID PULLED UP SHORT AS she realized that somehow all the traveling between the worlds had landed her on the roof of a skyscraper in the heart of the blackened city.

What is this? she thought, confused.

But there was light spilling from a door that someone had left ajar to her left. Electric light. She moved toward it guardedly. This felt all awry.

Selkie stopped just the other side of the veil—Brighid's apprehension warning her to keep away—and she concentrated her Sight on what had led them here.

She saw the man behind the desk, a slight smile curving the corners of his mouth. He had an unnatural shine. He was Sídhe. But his shine was all wrong, was painful—dreadfully painful.

She shot a message to Brighid telling her, *Get out; get out!* but there was no way the Dé Danann was going to change her intention to get to the bottom of this.

Selkie was deeply afraid. She didn't know what was going on, but she sure was going to get Hunter; she didn't care what was keeping him wherever it was he had gone.

Brighid exited the stairwell door, cautiously moving onto the plush carpet of the penthouse foyer, noting that there was only an elevator, one main set of high, wide doors of solid wood, and two auxiliary doors to their right. The hall was well-lit, defying the crisis everywhere else.

Every hair on her body stood erect, warning her to be elsewhere, but there was something undeniable pulling her, some smell that didn't have anything to do with her nose. Something painfully, poignantly familiar.

She pulled open the polished wood doors and entered the vast palatial room.

It took her a moment to realize who it was sitting so smugly behind the ostentatious desk.

"You?" she hissed. "What . . . ?"

This was too confusing. She knew she'd met him—knew he was Sídhe—but she couldn't remember his name or the circumstances around the meeting. His hair was short; he wore an expensive tailored suit; he was much older than the last time she'd seen him, but she knew she'd met him once or twice . . . somewhere, sometime in the long ago.

He flopped his feet to the floor and stood, walking around the desk in her direction, his arms spread in welcome.

"Brighid! How you've aged!" He sounded thrilled. He was beaming with delight as he strode across the floor in her direction.

"Where . . . ?" She couldn't finish. Disgust rolled over her in livid waves. He was Unseelie. Something had caused him to become Unseelie—as Unseelie as a Sídhe could get. Her gut twisted as he radiated an unseen ugliness that struck her like a fist.

"Piss off, you," she spat, as he sought her unwilling embrace.

"Well," he chirped, hugging her tightly with his hatred, "nice to know some things never change."

She pulled from his grip, ageing burning through her veins like poison.

"Doesn't matter where I've been, mo chroí." His voice cut through her with an edge of madness. "Doesn't matter where I'm going either, but . . ." and he smiled and pointed, gesturing toward the desk.

". . . I've got a present for you! Wait, though," he put a finger to his lips, "Don't get too excited now, banríon. It's not for you to keep, like, but it's *such* a favorite thing of mine . . . and sharing can be fun, huh?"

He pranced back toward the desk, gesturing with an elegantly manicured hand to something down on the floor, out of sight.

Brighid heard a sound like a growl, and Shilton placed his hands on his hips, looking offended.

"Hush now," he scolded. "Behave yourself for the guests!"

Brighid moved cautiously across the room toward the unseen object.

"De da!" he exclaimed in sheer delight as it registered on her what was in the wooden cage.

Then she saw the eyes.

She staggered and gripped the edge of the desk to stop herself from falling.

"What have you done?" She almost choked as she forced out the words. Her throat constricted, and she fought back bile. She knew who it was, trapped in the fox's shape.

"What have I done? What have *I* done!" His lips quivered as though he would laugh, but his eyes bore into her with fury.

"'This is all your fault. Your fault, your fault, your fault!" He walked to the decanter and poured himself another drink. "Please forgive my lack of hospitality, chook, but just the one glass, you see."

Brighid knelt softly beside the cage.

"Leoghaire?"

"Now, now, enough!" and Shilton slammed his hand down on the table, shattering the glass beneath the blow, oblivious to the blood that poured from his cut hand.

"He's mine, my love," he cooed. His moods changed so quickly that Brighid was certain of his insanity. He sniggered, putting a hand over his mouth, as though embarrassed by his previous outburst.

"Anyway," he smiled sweetly, "that's all there is. Game over. Time to go."

"Change him back," Brighid said coldly, darkness building within her—an unlovely thing that she fought—affecting her shine in just the way he had planned.

"You can come too, you silly girl," he offered. "You might as well— I can't really let you leave me again."

"I was never *with* you," she screamed at him.

"We all remember things so differently, don't we, given enough time? Anyway, the little lad here could use a bit of company. No choice really, pet."

"Are you threatening me, you foul son of rotten spew, you seething mass . . ."

Shilton smiled. The room began to darken and shift before Brighid had a chance to complete the insult.

"Gotcha!" he snapped, as the room tilted sickeningly.

Chapter Forty

Willie and Dog had drawn the longest matches and were therefore grudgingly pushing the carts full of equipment while Merrin checked vehicles for theft-availability.

The streets were either crowded or eerily silent.

They avoided the main roads, after two near encounters with people curious to know what was under the jackets in the baskets. The first two guys had wanted whatever it was, while a second close encounter had been a patrol car checking for looters. The three had ducked into a side alley just in time to avoid being seen.

They skirted the crowd down by St. Martin's Square and had just turned into Atherton when Willie saw the other Travelers a block ahead of them, attempting to dodge a military presence working with emergency services to untangle what looked like a devastating pile-up of several vehicles.

He called out for Merrin to guard his trolley and raced off to get them.

On the way back he briefed them about the night before, and who Dog was and why he was with them, and he was informed, in turn, about the disappearance of the others who had remained at Merrin's, and how unnerving it had seemed.

They met up with the other two and moved into the shadow of the arched post office entrance, out of sight of anyone who might just consider the large gathering of unusual-looking people worth investigating.

Everyone threw around ideas as to how they were to get out of the city and into the suburbs where Robin was being held, but it was Seamus who came up with the first possible solution.

"Let's steal a bus," he chirped.

All right, Dog sighed with relief, his arms aching.

There were other options discussed before they eventually agreed to go with Seamus' suggestion.

THEY HAD TO BACKTRACK FOR several blocks with everybody taking turns pushing the equipment.

"So why are you called Dog?" Annis was walking with him and Rowan, trailing the others because both the computer guy's heels had blistered and he'd stopped to take his boots off.

"It's short for my last name."

"What's that?"

"Dogget."

"Well that makes sense then," she grinned. "What's your first name really?"

He didn't answer, looking at her with *don't ask eyes.*

"Just making conversation," she shrugged.

"I'm sorry if I'm not much company," he responded. "I've been up all night, and there's some very strange things going on . . . and you are all very strange people."

"Are you one of those witches?"

"Apparently. Ow!" He stepped on a sharp piece of rubble.

And we're not people, Annis muttered under her breath.

THEY APPROACHED THE MIDTOWN BUS terminal, which was crowded with frustrated commuters. Most were sitting or standing around waiting for something to change so they could get where they need-ed to be.

The terminal doors were closed and locked, the place deserted. Despite that, caution seemed a good idea.

They crossed the road and entered the *Do not Enter* lane that ran down beside the administration building. There were large, heavily barred steel gates halfway down, a chain padlocking them closed.

Annis walked to the head of the group and flourished a bow before pulling an assortment of file-like metal objects from one of the abundant pockets of her army surplus khakis and kneeling before the gate. She picked the lock within half a minute and pushed open the gates as the others hurried past her toward the Transac buses that were parked in unguarded lines.

"Why don't you just vanish the lot of us to where we want to go?" Dog asked Willie.

"Uh . . ."

"What? Can't you do it again?"

"Dunno. Didn't remember I could do it at all till I did it with the stones."

"Well? Why don't you try then?"

"Are you sure this is the time, sweetheart?" he grinned. Dog didn't answer, so Willie flicked his plaits back over his shoulders and squeezed his eyes shut tight, theatrically.

"Oh, stop it Willie!" Merrin slapped him on the shoulder, and the Sídhe opened his eyes, pretending to be offended.

"I don't understand," Dog looked disappointed, but at that moment the bus closest to them revved into life with Seamus behind the wheel, his fists bunched in the air in triumph.

Everyone piled in, carrying whatever equipment had been in the carts. Willie took a window seat and Merrin sat beside him on the opposite side of the aisle to Dog, telling him she'd explain when she had the chance.

Seamus launched the bus out onto the street and past the dumbfounded and outraged crowd hanging around the front of the building.

He powered it along the backroads heading north toward the outer suburbs, taking detour after detour until they finally left the city behind.

By avoiding the main arterials they made good time and had to backtrack only three times due to abandoned vehicles gridlocked at intersections.

This far into the blackout most people had given up on getting anywhere until the situation was resolved. Merrin watched the passing blur of houses over Willie's shoulder, thinking about him. She loved him dearly but he could be thoughtless with people's feelings sometimes, treating them like they were fools. It came with having lived so long and seeing so many mistakes she supposed, remembering back to what Brighid had shown her.

Once they had passed into the relative quiet of the suburbs she turned her attention toward Dog, who sat in frustrated silence.

"Hey Dog? You okay?"

He looked at her with tired, red-rimmed eyes, and she wondered how any of them were holding out after such a week.

"I just don't exactly know what's going on here."

"It's a long story."

"Well, try me. I feel like a jerk here."

"'Have you ever heard of the Tuatha Dé Danann?"

"Yeah sure. A long time ago my folks tried telling me and Celeste about those myths and stuff. Irish gods, weren't they? But what . . . ?"

"Not gods. They're a different race to us, that's all. The Sídhe. The Fair Folk."

"She?"

"Well that's how it's pronounced," and she spelled the word for him.

"Okay. But so what? What's that got to do with what's going on?"

"See him?" She pointed toward Willie.

"Yeah . . ."

"And him? And her? And him . . ." She pointed to most of them in the bus.

"What are you saying?"

"They're all Sídhe. They're not like us—well not exactly like us." She frowned, attempting to formulate what she knew, which was very complicated.

"Basically . . ." she took a deep breath, composing her thoughts. "Basically they've been around since the earth became the earth, without ever having died."

"They're natural, you understand," she added as he stared at her without any intention of interrupting, "like wind and mountains and all, but they're a race of people." She paused, gauging his reaction.

"I'm listening. I don't get it yet, but go on."

"But they're not human like we are. And they are magical. Not like most people understand it, but in their mystery—like shape-shifting, and how they can fool people into believing what isn't real, or even show them exactly what is real, and it's all too wonderful for most of us to trust so we tell ourselves it is an illusion.

"There's lots of human people that are connected to them though. The Dé Danann call them the Lost, and their quest is to find them and show them who they are, same as for the fey—the people without the blindness for the mysteries. They get found, and if they choose, they get to come on the travels."

Willie chuckled for no accountable reason.

"Do you want me to tell him or not," she defended.

"You're doing a good job, mo chroí," he replied resting his chin on her shoulder and kissing her on the neck.

She carried on, explaining as much as she could remember until the bus rounded the corner of Armidale Road forty-five minutes later.

"Anyway," Merrin figured it was time to stop talking, "the bottom line, Dog, is that they're fairies," she smiled, drawing growls and snarls from the others who were listening in on the conversation, and an amused snort from Willie.

"THERE," RAVEN POINTED AHEAD TO an angular building of blonde brick with all the architectural finesse of a sore tooth.

Seamus snail-paced the bus to a standstill a couple of houses ahead of the church. They had no idea if the place was guarded, but Raven said he doubted they would have just up and left.

"You got your wat-sits?" Willie asked Annis.

"Huh?" she queried.

"I think you'll find that they have a more sophisticated security system than lock-picking can handle," Rowan added, drawing grins all around.

They left Jack and Dog behind to guard the bus and the equipment until they'd actually breached the building. They moved silently down the walkway toward the back entrance, after first ascertaining that the front door was locked and that, having peeked through the only window looking into the interior, no one was inside.

The rooftops and adjacent fence were lined with ravens shuffling and making soft, rowly sounds in as close an approximation of quiet as they were capable.

Beatha had brought them. The Mórrígan, and pick-at-bodies-on-the-field-of-the-slain, and all that special stuff, being sufficient an incentive to encourage thousands to rally.

Raven sent out a telepathic message to her asking the *conspiracy* to watch his back, much to Beatha's delight. Several of the black shapes took note of the communion and notched the young female up a few points in the pecking order.

Just around the corner was a narrow concrete box, open to the sky, with a solid reinforced door that exhibited a card-access and security code touch-pad.

"Shit!" Seamus whispered. "Somebody go back and get the Dog—we're never gonna get in here without him."

"He's no good here," Rowan replied. "The generator's sure to make enough noise to alert anyone inside."

"You're all idiots," Annis whispered, gleefully moving to the fore of the group and knocking hard on the door.

"Tsk." She shook her head as she moved to one side.

There was the sound of a latch being disengaged from within, and the door opened with an audible sucking sound.

Brendon opened the door a crack but saw who was outside and immediately attempted to slam it again. He wasn't quick enough.

He shouted, "Shoot them!" over his shoulder as the Sídhe, and Merrin and Rowan, barreled past him, launching themselves at whichever man was closest before the Brotherhood even had a chance to draw their weapons.

Merrin got her one chance to launch a perfect turning side kick straight at Brendon's kidneys before the whole thing was virtually over.

The men in the church's headquarters did not know what had happened. One minute they were on their feet ready for a fight, and the next they were floored—sat upon—the unearthly strength of their attackers defying their size and appearance.

Merrin took their weapons from them gingerly and stowed them in a hastily opened drawer before sitting herself on the metal bench above it.

The Sídhe, one by one, smiled at their adversaries and, one by one, assisted them to their feet.

"You can go now," chirped Annis.

"What . . .what do you mean?" said one of the men guardedly.

"I mean you can go now," she repeated.

"Off you trot, have a nice life and all that, me ducks," said Willie, pushing his prisoner toward the door.

The men were disoriented. They'd stayed after their cell phones had run down. They'd waited, cooped up in there, waiting until someone fixed the power. And now this? Were these people as dumb as they acted? Didn't they realize that they'd return with reinforcements and enough fire-power to nuke them?

They left.

Stupid Brendon even said thanks as he walked out the door.

"I'll go get Dog," said Seamus.

"Not without me, you don't." Annis moved them both back outside as the raucous cawing, and the screams and yells began just ahead of them around the corner, as the ravens exacted justice.

They headed down the side of the building toward the bus. Two men were on the ground, covered in a seething mass of glossy black, and the other three had fled, pursued.

Beatha sat serenely on the wall as the Sídhe walked past.

What about you? Annis sent.

Not my destiny so, yah?

So?

Is Dreamer, me.

Ah! Is beannacht is, mo chroí, Annis blessed.

BEATHA TOOK TO THE SKY, gracefully and languidly winging her way back toward the Bentley Fort High School to take her place as the new White Eyes.

It took Dog all of nineteen minutes to hitch the generator up to the Brotherhood's computer system and hack into their security network, and only a further three minutes to override it, triggering the opening of the basement vault.

Both Puck and Robin squinted as the door to the cell was flung open and the light invaded.

Robin stopped singing and stood, taking Puck by the hand, dragging her toward the entrance quickly in case something happened and the door closed on them again.

They were both deathly cold, so the others led them straight outside into the sunlight.

The Dé Danann were silent as Puck hugged Robin to her tightly. The ordeal had aged him. He looked to be in his mid-teens.

Chapter Forty-one

Hunter realized that the wards and seals that had bound him from accessing his son's prison had broken when the Unseelie traitor had confronted Brighid, and he laughed aloud as he understood the limitations of the ugly Sídhe's magic.

When his family had been freed it had been like a mountain lifting from him. He felt the whip of Brighid's sending message, requiring his intervention, just beforehand.

He moved through the Dreaming lands, outside of all context of time, manifesting in the courtyard outside of the studio off Napier Lane. He knocked on the door out of consideration for the privacy of the two within and paused long enough for them to dress.

Kathryn opened the door, tousled and embarrassed.

"I've got a bit of an emergency," Hunter said, walking into the room. "Are you both up for a journey?"

The question was rhetorical, and in truth the couple were both more than willing to do whatever was necessary.

"Grab your sword, masurao," he gestured to Vincent's small bundle of possessions. "We have a situation."

THE THREE OF THEM BURST through the fabric of space into the room where Brighid stood locked in a battle of wills with Shilton. The room bucked and twisted in a sickening torment as the two fought to gain the upper hand.

"What did you say your name was?" she goaded, through bared teeth, sensing the others' arrival behind her.

She almost lost her edge in the attempt to stop the laughter that bubbled within her at the sight of her adversary's face as the question registered. He lost his hold momentarily, as fury replaced force.

The office ceased its pitching as Hunter walked slowly, gracefully, to stand beside Brighid.

"Fire queen?" he acknowledged with a raise of his brows. "Anything you can't handle?"

She did not take her eyes from Shilton, so was unaware of Kathryn's confusion. What were they doing here? What did Martin's father have to do with anything?

Vincent was curious but very calm, reading the situation at the same time as hearing Hunter's soft voice within his mind. He stood quietly beside Kathryn, waiting.

"He's not Martin's father, mo chroí," Hunter said gently, as Kathryn sought to understand what was happening.

The truth of everything was leaking out of the Unseelie Sídhe in a lazy, dirty unfolding, but it hadn't reached her yet, or else she couldn't comprehend its full meaning.

"Yes he is. He . . ." She shifted from one foot to the other uncomfortably. "Who is he then?" And she moved toward him.

Aengus an Thríbhís Mór composed himself, ready, playing Alexander Shilton—concerned father-in-law—to the hilt.

"I don't know who your friends are, Kathryn, and I'm a little confused about what's going on here. Are these the people that Martin . . ."

"Shut up, you . . ." Brighid warned.

"Well I've got all the time in the world," said Hunter.

Brighid shot him a look, and he raised his hands as though to ward off a blow.

"Brighid, where's your sense of the absurd, love?"

Very slowly the tension in her face relaxed. Of course. He was beaten, wasn't he? But no. The Unseelie's game was a cruel one.

Kathryn didn't deserve to be infected with his ugliness.

"End it, Hunter."

"No matter where I send him he could eventually find his way back, you realize?"

"What is *happening?*" demanded Kathryn.

"You've got a problem with these people," said Shilton, smiling. "Look, I can understand about you and Martin. I know what he can be like . . ."

"Stop it! Now!" Brighid snarled.

She turned to Kathryn and took her hands, ready to heal. "Mo chroí, he's responsible for all of it. If I don't tell you, he will. He's as Sídhe as I am, but he's Unseelie."

"I don't understand the word."

"Unclean, gone rotten without—not like dirt and fruit, but in an unnatural way."

"Who's unnatural?" interrupted Shilton.

It took Hunter all of just over a minute to explain the basics, and Kathryn turned paler and paler as the knowledge of how the man who sat on the edge of his desk, grinning like a fool and nodding as his exploits were counted off, had played her from birth.

Before anyone could anticipate she launched herself across the room, her hands reaching for his eyes. At the same moment he leaped toward her with unnatural speed and clutched her to him.

"Stalemate!" he crowed. "Stalemate, stalemate, stalemate, Brighid! I'll have this one then, shall I? Hmm?"

But no matter how he deluded himself he was not a god and could not move a mortal to the Otherworld.

Hunter and Brighid watched him try, morphing and shifting while maintaining a vice-like grip on Kathryn, who kicked out with her legs and bit deeply into his hand.

Still only seconds had passed.

Vincent moved with the deadly fluidity of a cat, and with one movement had drawn his katana from its saya and sliced Alexander Shilton across the arm that held Kathryn around the throat, opening the flesh to the bone from elbow to wrist—a mortal wound.

He shrieked, releasing Kathryn, who backed up into Vincent's body, and grasped hopelessly at his forearm, bleeding through his fingers onto Sylvia and Emily Drake's magnificent carpet.

"What have you done!" the Unseelie shrieked, dropping to his knees.

"You've been gone too long, *Aengus,*" said Hunter calmly, knowing that to name a thing truly was to sum up its essence. "The rest of the Fair Folk have learned to cope with cold steel."

Long ago iron (and all variations) was like poison to the Sídhe because it was so cruelly used upon the land, destroying more than any other metal possibly could, and because the older race was so intricately connected to the natural world. It had become a matter of necessity to develop an immunity—a thing that the Aengus an Thríbhís Mór had been too preoccupied to realize.

Hunter turned to Brighid and patted her on the head.

"Did you know this was going to happen?" she whispered out of the corner of her mouth so that only he could hear. "I'll get you for this."

"He wasn't the only one with a plan, no—if that's what you mean," he smiled, showing all his strong white teeth, with just a hint of canine incisors.

"Am I dying?" the Unseelie whispered, strangely amused at the thought, before doing just that.

"What was your name again?" Brighid replied offhandedly, as she walked past his fading body to the cage behind the desk.

She undid the latch and took the fox into her arms. "Is there anything you can do about this?" she implored Hunter.

"Bring him with us while I think about it."

He shifted them out of there, and into Merrin's studio, just as the others arrived back.

Chapter Forty-two

Willie took Hunter outside. He was ragged and tired; one of his braids was coming undone from its leather thonging and his jacket hung open, exposing his sweat-stained shirt. The revelry among the others crowded into Merrin's place, telling taller and taller tales of each others' exploits, made it very difficult to be heard, and he needed to face the consequences of the disappearance of the Lady's gift.

He had no idea where the stones were.

The two of them stood by the fishpond, Hunter calm and still, Willie shuffling uncomfortably. He explained how he'd felt unnerved by the strange way that Dog and Celeste had been behaving; that he hadn't thought it through but had reacted instinctively; that he'd simply thrust the Dúile beyond possible harm because they were too precious to maybe lose to people whose intentions were unclear.

"Have you ever done it before?" asked Hunter.

"What?"

"The Otherworld thing—on your own, I mean."

"No, but wow—what a buzz!"

"Well, it'll come in handy some time or other if you get around to learning to do it right, me ol' son."

Hunter was attempting to take Willie seriously, but the enthusiasm and embarrassment of the usually laconic enfant terrible of the Fiach Dubh clan was really very funny.

"If you think, then maybe it'll come to you," the huge god grinned, flicking his feather-heavy dreds back over his shoulder.

"What's so funny? Think about what?"

Hunter shrugged.

"Oh. Just think, right? That's it?" Willie asked, confused.

"Aye."

"Okay. I can do that," and his shoulders slumped in seeming defeat.

Hunter patted him on the shoulder and left him to work it out, tears of mirth escaping from the corners of his eyes.

Sídhe! he thought as he headed back to his family and the party.

Think about it, Willie mused.

He sat with his back against the warm brick of the façade of the studio, in the softness of the spring sun, trying to force his concentration to focus on bringing back the stones, but ending up thinking about Merrin and how she felt when he held her and about how good it was when they lay together.

After a while so many thoughts and memories crowded his mind that he gave up, opened his eyes and sighed, pulling his leather tobacco pouch from his jeans pocket.

Some fuckin' fairy you are, Will o' Wisp, me boy! he thought to himself, disgusted.

Kathryn came outside on orders from Merrin to pick a handful of basil so she could make up some pesto. The gas had run out but the fire was being put to good use boiling up pots of water for enough pasta to feed everyone.

She saw Willie's shape-shifting creatures before she saw him. They all seemed excited and playful, attempting to get his attention, but he was all fallen in on himself.

"Willie?" She went to him and sat cross-legged on the ground beside him.

"Hmm?"

"What's wrong?"

"Well I lost something important, mo chroí, and Hunter told me how I can find it, but I'm all over the place, like."

"What'd he say?"

"To think."

"Think what?"

"He didn't say."

"Well . . . do you think he meant to think about where you lost what you lost?"

"I suppose so."

"Look at them," she remarked as the shiftings—mostly dog and fox, or mixes of both—worked at piquing his attention.

"Do you figure they know something I don't?" he asked, scuffing his boots on the stone flagging.

"Probably. Look, I don't want to pry but . . ."

"I lost some poor sod's soul is what I lost," he finished for her.

Kathryn blinked. What was he on about? Willie groaned helplessly.

He turned to fully face her. "Did Merrin or the Dog man tell you what happened out at the cove?"

"There hasn't been time for any real talk yet."

"Well there was this bunch of witches, and Hunter and the goddess came, and there were these sigils in the sand like, and then it was all over and there were these nine smooth stones left behind.

"And they were Dúile—all the elements that make something or someone what it is—and it was somebody's soul even though that's not always what the Dúile is, and I pocketed 'em. Then things got all weird like and I sent them into the Otherworld, but I didn't look to where they went and so now I've lost 'em, and they were from the Great Mystery so this is a real shite-type balls-up."

He took a deep breath and let it out, shaking his head as he rolled his cigarette.

"Y'see?" he said hopelessly.

"Okay . . ." She took a second to digest all of what he said. "Well, how did you send them to the Otherworld?"

Willie stared at her, his face expressionless, until what she'd asked registered. His face lit up as the simplicity of what Hunter had said came home to him.

"Ah, I just thought them there," he grinned. "Like I'm thinkin' them into my pockets right now."

He shoved his hands into the pockets of his jacket and drew out one hand with four stones in it and the other, slowly, theatrically, with the other five.

Kathryn got to her feet, brushing the dirt from her kilt and looking like butter wouldn't melt in her mouth.

"I'll just get the basil then, shall I?" she remarked, reaching among the creatures that were silently rolling in the dirt with pleasure, and rubbing a couple of insubstantially furry backs as she passed to the herb pots.

"But now what do I do with 'em?" he asked after her, his hands held out before him . . . Then he remembered he was supposed to give them to Brighid.

The beautiful, elemental Sídhe woman sat hunched up in a corner of the couch with Leoghaire, fox that was once lover, in her lap, looking tragic.

Her multitude of black, beaded braids fell like a curtain over both of them as she gently stroked her beloved from the long ago. They behaved as though there was no one else in the room. The others kept as much distance as they could, leaving her to come to terms with everything that had happened.

Willie didn't think he'd ever seen her look this sad as he moved to sit beside her.

"Bridey," he said softly, using the term of endearment that she usually snapped at. She took no notice of him.

"Bridey, I found them."

She looked at him, initially not seeing him, but seeing Leoghaire when he had been her man. Then her vision cleared as she realized it was only Willie. Leoghaire thumped his tail against her leg.

"Ah . . . Oh. Oh, okay. Well break them, then," and she went back to stroking the fox.

What? Willie looked confused again. *Break them—yeah like that makes ever so much sense.*

Raven read his thoughts from where he was forking spaghetti into a strainer.

"Break the stones—free the bind. Here," he called to Matt, "finish this for me will you, Sunshine?"

Matt was sitting tuning the chanter to the drones of his uilleann pipes, and he growled a warning in Raven's direction without looking up.

"I'll do it," Seamus responded grudgingly. He hadn't been doing anything anyway.

"Who wants to come see what we've got?' Willie asked everyone.

Matt wouldn't budge and Brighid was distracted, and Seamus, Jack, and Selkie were too busy with the food preparations to stop for anything—even this—but everyone else followed him out into the courtyard.

He'd thought they would be hard as he struck the first one with a half-brick that served as a hammer, but it shattered like porcelain.

It was filled with dust and he realized that someone had made them—they weren't natural at all. They were like eggs.

"What is it?" he asked around him.

"The bastard stopped a thing from dying properly," Hunter replied. "Bet it wasn't dust until you broke it."

"It was a dog." Kathryn saw the vague shape before it vanished like smoke, just as Willie struck the second stone.

MICHAEL BLACKER HADN'T BEEN ABLE to eat the food that the guards had brought. He was nauseous from the stink of the other men around him, nauseous and bored and exhausted beyond belief. He'd had little more than a couple of hours sleep in the last forty-eight. That must be it. And they had been filled with the horror dreams.

He had to get out. He didn't belong in a prison, he thought, and he had a headache screaming up the back of his neck so bad he couldn't move his eyes any more. It felt like something was crawling in his skull.

Every thought was confused. He tried to concentrate on coming up with a reason to be released that he could offer the cops, but nothing would stay in his mind. No thought seemed to have a point, or to hold still for long enough to make sense.

It's all so fragile, he realized, brutally aware of his predicament and how everything had gone to shit when the lights had gone out.

He even tried to capture the sense of the purpose that had driven him for so long, and had given him what he thought was his life's mission, but it all seemed like something he'd read in a book somewhere.

Later in the day sandwiches were brought in, all wrapped up in plastic, informing the men that it must be lunchtime. The smell of the cold meat filling made Michael retch, and he curled up in a ball on his corner of the bench and tried to sleep reality away.

YOU'RE ALL RIGHT GIRL, HE dreamed, taking the cruel chain from around the dog's neck where it bit into the tender flesh. *S'okay girl, shh, you're all right, I'm gonna take you home.*

The dog moved up close to where he sat, afraid of spooking her any more than she already was.

I'll read the rest of The Farthest Shore *next week,* he thought, as she nuzzled his hand.

He awoke, pain crashing through his head in waves, fighting back tears, knowing that that would just make his head hurt more, and also not wanting the men around him to notice him any more than they already had.

THE DOOR TO THE HOLDING cell slid open and two uniformed police officers stood together, along with a man in plain clothes.

"We're letting you all go for the moment," one of them announced. "There's still no breakthrough in the current situation so we advise you all to go straight to your places of residence and remain there. We have your details so don't anticipate going too far. We'll be in touch as soon as everything dies down."

"What about my friend Sam Nowles?" asked a thin, reedy man closest to the door, as the others readied themselves to leave.

"Are you kidding?" the plain-clothes cop snorted. "S'far as we know you lot didn't hurt anybody. That's the only reason you're getting outa here so easy. We can change our minds . . . "

"No-no, it's cool—just askin'."

The men moved past him as the reedy man collected his jacket and Michael rose painfully from the bench.

One of the two uniformed officers put his arm across the door. "Stop at the front desk on your way out. You'll have to sign a release form and pick up your stuff. Anything even remotely like a weapon will not be returned to you."

There were a few mumbles about personal property as he removed his arm to allow the men to file past, but no one was about to argue.

The desk sergeant handed Michael a large Manila envelope containing his possessions. He looped his belt back onto his trousers and removed his jacket to buckle on the shoulder holster, empty of its gun, and pocketed everything else except his watch, which he checked for the time automatically before slipping it onto his wrist.

He walked across to the front doors and down the wide steps into the sunshine. He had to reach out and clutch the metal banister before he even got to the street, he was in so much agony. He turned around to go back inside to see if maybe someone had something they could give him but couldn't bring himself to do it.

Fuck it. Go home, he told himself. Then he flashed onto all those stairs and the empty apartment and the isolation of the whole of his private life, and just started walking instead.

He walked all that day. The further he walked, the clearer his head became.

By sunset he had left the suburbs behind and everything became quieter. He stopped to drink from a tap at a deserted truck stop. It never occurred to him to just walk into the shop adjoining it and take something he might need later.

He was walking past the residence next door when he was confronted by a pair of German shepherds that snarled and growled at him. The dogs were tied by long leads to the front steps, left to guard the place until the owner returned.

He didn't even think about it. He walked up to the porch oblivious to whether they would attack him, but something in his manner stopped them from doing so, opting instead to fawn and whine and wag their tails as he approached. He unclipped the leads from the collars of both animals before turning and walking off again.

They followed him.

HIS WATCH TOLD HIM IT was 10:45 when he finally laid down, another thirty miles or so from the truck stop, in a copse of trees near the side of the road, with the shepherds and three other dogs he'd inherited along the way.

He'd ended up breaking into a locked house not long before—he had responsibilities now—and stealing food for all of them. He filled up a couple of empty bottles with water and grabbed a pot to pour some into for the dogs if they got thirsty, but he didn't stay. He bolted from the place, aware that the owners might come back at any time—he couldn't stand the thought of human contact.

As he drifted into the most tranquil sleep he'd had in years he thought about where on earth he was going and realized he had no idea, but that he sure as hell couldn't think of a good enough reason for it to be back where he had been.

He awoke with a start at dawn the following morning, covered with dogs. As he struggled to sit up he realized he had company.

A pretty woman sat mounted on a tall horse the colors of rock and red lichen. She had an honest, open face and a tumble of long, light-brown hair that was all messed up from the ride. She wore an old velvet jacket the color of moss, with red leather patches at the elbows, done up at the neck by what looked like a bronze spiral-shaped brooch, and work-stained dungarees over scuffed leather boots.

"Hi," she smiled. "You seem lost."

"No." He rubbed at the coarse stubble on his chin—something he wasn't used to.

"I'm just up the valley between those two hills," she said, adjusting her seat in the saddle and pointing behind them. "You want some breakfast or something?"

Michael's stomach growled in concert with the offer.

"How do you know you can trust me? I could be dangerous," he mumbled.

She laughed, and it washed over him like a relief.

"Hey," she beamed, "with all those dogs? You gotta be a nice guy if dogs like you. Besides, I got a nose for danger like you wouldn't believe!"

He stood up and brushed some of the dust and twigs from his clothes. The dogs were already frisking around him, ready for action, all except one little mongrel female who stayed real close to him, timid and shy.

"I'm Michael Blacker," he introduced himself, walking over to the horse and holding out his hand for her to shake.

"Nice to meet you, Michael. Lovely morning for a stroll, yeah? Not too far anyway." She turned the horse in the direction she had pointed toward. "Won't be more than, oh, maybe fifteen minutes on foot."

"Okay. Yeah, well, thanks." He felt shy—not something he was used to, although women had always had an uncomfortable effect on him, the exception being the ones he had bought for pleasure. "Ah . . . what did you say your name was?"

"Well Michael, you can call me Rosie."

THE GODDESS SMILED INWARDLY AS he walked beside her in comfortable silence, while Michael marveled at the mist that still nestled in the distance. The young dog walked, glued to his side, while the other dogs bounded ahead.

"S'okay, girl," he said softly, ruffling the hair on her soft head. "We'll be there soon."

Chapter Forty-three

Blackout. Day two. 5:45 PM

General Peter Stanwick and Lieutenant Barbara Rivers sat buckled into the transport helicopter that thuck-thucked its way over New Rathmore, heading for its center.

Things just seemed to be going from bad to worse.

There were emergency work crews crawling all over the region, checking electricity substations and all transmission lines into and out of the city, but no glitch had been found.

There was the smell of hysteria everywhere, and the situation had been declared a disaster. He'd received his orders from as high up as they could come. Martial law was necessary as the infrastructure began to collapse.

He hoped that the problem could be fixed before everything went to pieces, aware of just how vulnerable the whole setup had become to this kind of situation.

He determined to hold some pretty high-level discussions with people that mattered. Someone had to come up with strategies and alternatives against this ever happening again, anywhere.

In the meantime, evacuation procedures were in full swing dealing, initially, with all inhabitants of hospitals and correctional facilities.

All military vehicles on the ground were being heavily guarded. Panicked citizens had almost caused major stampedes seeking access to escape earlier in the afternoon, and weapons had exchanged fire, resulting in several fatalities on both sides.

PETER STANWICK SIGHED AS THEY came in for the landing.

They'd all become much too cocky.

Epilogue

Hunter had moved everything. Everything and everyone—Merrin's studio, the courtyard, their bus, the Sídhe, their companions—and had deposited them at Falconstowe.

It was amazing how Kathryn's house and the studio looked as though they belonged side by side.

He'd done it in the twilight just before dark, when he knew none of the townies would be there. He could always fudge the memories of the ones who'd visited before so that they'd just not notice the other quaint building with its verdant and riotous outdoor arrangement.

There'd been a few glitches in the Lady's planning, sure, but what was that anyway, compared to the joy, compared to the thrill?

And she had her Lost Boy; the one she'd dreamed, who'd been so sundered from her and so twisted and abused. She'd get to love him after all—for a while.

And his son! A god no less diminished for his mother being a human creature, but oh, much more so under his care.

We might just keep the world alive after all, he thought as, cupping Puck's breast and grinning like a wolf, he considered leaving the party and the music and the feast, and stealing away to the woods with her for a while.

They passed Brighid, who sat like a queen amid the herbs and flowers of Merrin's courtyard, with Leoghaire close beside her, and Merrin and Willie plying her with uiske beatha and sharing out the best portions of the sheep that had been brought by the farmers, along with everything else they could think of for the "Lights Out" gig that the Fíanna had arranged to maybe take the sting out of the situation (that didn't really bother anyone at all, out here at least).

Hunter had smiled at the question in her eyes. "We'll be back in a while, mo chroí. I'll see about fixing the fox then."

"Tsk," Brighid remarked.

"Bloody gods," Willie added, grinning.

Glossary

Athame (pronounced *athamay*): A witch's ritual dagger, black-hilted, double-bladed.

Banríon (Irish, pronounced *banree*): Queen.

Bata (Haitian): Drums used traditionally to communicate; to recite prayers, religious poetry, greetings, announcements, praises for leaders, and even jokes or teasing.

Beannacht (Irish, pronounced *bee-an-aucht*): Blessing

Beltaen (also spelled, Beltane, Beltinne): One of the four Fire Festivals in the Celtic calendar. In the Northern Hemisphere it is celebrated on or around May 1, in the Southern Hemisphere on or around November 1.

Broc (Irish, pronounced *brock*): Badger.

Bruja, brujo (Spanish, pronounced *brooha, brooho*): Female and male terms for sorcerers, witches.

Bushido (Japanese): The Way of the Warrior.

Chi Gong (Chinese): A form of self-healing whose aim is to stimulate and balance the flow of vital energy through the meridians of the body.

Connachta (Irish): Modern-day Connaught.

Corvid: The raven is a member of a very successful family of birds, the Corvidae, which also includes jays, magpies, and crows.

Daisho (Japanese): One of the styles of paired swords.

Deíthe (Irish, pronounced *day-ha*): Gods, both singular, plural, multiple.

Demesne (Old English, pronounced *dih-mayn*): In feudal law, lands held in one's own power; a manor house and the adjoining lands in the immediate use and occupation of the owner of the estate; the grounds belonging to any residence or any landed estate.

Dobharchú (Irish, pronounced *dovarchoo*): Otter.

Dúile (Irish, pronounced *doolie*): The early Irish nine elements.

Ethnobotany: The study of how people of a particular culture and region make of use of indigenous plants.

Faerie (Irish *faidh*) also fairy, faerie, Fae, fey, Fair Folk (all such similar words are connected): A term indicating "wise"; can also mean to have the [second] "sight"; to cast enchantments.

Fiach Dubv (Irish, pronounced *feeuck-doov*): Raven (literally: dark hunting).

Flidhais (Irish): A forest goddess habitually taking the form of a doe, or hind.

Geis (Irish, usually pronounces *gesh*): It is a term from Irish folklore. It refers to a magical prohibition or taboo, or more broadly to a spell or enchantment, or a moral obligation. It was a common plot in early Irish literature, and the geis (plural geisa)were taken very seriously. In the Táin Bó Cuailnge, or The Cattle-Raid of Cooley, one of the great Irish epics, the hero Cúchulain pulled an oak sapling out of the ground, tied a knot in it with one hand, and put a geis on a following army not to pass that point unless another man could duplicate the feat. Unable to do so, the army was forced to take a longer route, delaying their attack. Alternatively spelled geas.

Hounfor (Haitian): In Vodoun, the sacred space where the peristyle is located; usually refers to the inner altar area.

Hounsi (Haitian): An accepted devotee at a hounfor.

Kami (Japanese): Spirits and/or deities of the natural world.

Katana (Japanese): A sword, with a curved, single-edge.

Leoghaire ó naSíogaí (Irish, pronounced *Leery oh na shee-oh-gee*): Leoghaire is a common first name, and the last name means "of the Fair Folk."

Loa (Haitian, also known as *Iwa*): The spirits or gods of Vodoun.

Mac Tíre (Irish, pronounced *mak-teer-uh*): Wolf.

Madadh Rua (Irish, pronounced *mada rooa*): Fox.

Masurao (Japanese, pronounced *mah-soo-roh*): Hero, gentleman, warrior.

Meán Earraigh. Irish, pronounced *myawn ah-ri*)—Spring Equinox.

Mo chroí. (Irish, pronounced *mo kree*): "My heart." A term of endearment that Brighid sometimes uses sarcastically.

Mo fíain iníon (Irish, pronounced *moh fee ineean*): My wild daughter.

Mórrígan (Irish, pronounced *mohr-ree*, also *mohr-reen*): Mórrígan is more aptly a title: Mór rígan which means great queen and she is the Irish goddess of magic, sorcery, shapeshifting, prophecy, birth and death.

Mushin (Japanese): a state of calm, clear mind.

Obi (Japanese): A wide belt worn in traditional sword styles of martial arts.

Patrin (Romany): A sign used by the Rom on their travels, left as a message symbolizing whether a place is friendly or hostile.

Peristyle (Haitian): This is an open-sided temple with several entrances, used for most public Vodoun ceremonies.

Pitters: slang for the breed of dog known as pit-bull.

Qigong (Chinese, pronounced *chee-gung*, and sometimes written as Qi gong, chi gong, or chi kung): A form of self-healing whose aim is to stimulate and balance the flow of vital energy through the meridians of the body.

Quicken Tree: A rowan tree, the magical properties of which are protection, vision, and enchantment. The Quicken Tree was the symbol of agreement between two peoples—the Tuatha Dé Danann and the Milesians—and while it stood it represented peace for the land. The berries were said to bestow sacred vision and immortality to those who survived. This could represent an initiation into the mysteries.

Ravens, a conspiracy of: There are several collective terms for a gathering of ravens: a storytelling of; an unkindness of; a parliament of; a conspiracy of. I have opted for the latter.

Rom: The Romany (Gypsy) people.

Saya (Japanese): The scabbard of a samurai sword.

Seannachai (Irish, pronounced *shah-ne-kee*): Story-teller.

Se byen (Creole): "Okay."

Seelie (Scots): The Blessed Court. These "trooping faeries" are said to be benevolent toward humans, but will readily avenge any injury or insult. They are called "The Gentry" in Ireland.

Sgian dubh (Scots, pronounced *sahn doo*): Called the "black knife," it was considered to be the weapon of last resort.

Shinzen ni rei (Japanese): Bowing to one's source of inspiration (or god), often represented by the presence of a form of shrine.

Shinto (Japanese): Shinto is "the Way of the Kami" (see entry: *kami*).

Sídhe (Irish, pronounced *shee*): The name for both the Fae and the earth mounds thought to be their dwellings.

Sigil: A magical symbol or design.

Steel: The Fae are said to detest iron and by-products of that ore (it has been postulated that this is because iron tools are associated with destruction of Nature, such as felling trees and ploughing undeveloped land).

Teamhair (Irish, pronounced *tah-rah*): The most important socio-political sacred site of pagan Ireland—place of the High Kings.

Tine (Irish, pronounced *teen-eh*): One of several words meaning Fire.

Tír na nOgh (Irish): The otherworldly Land of the Ever-Young; the after-life; the Otherworld.

To rei (Japanese): This term, spoken or thought, means to bow to the sword.

Torii (Japanese): Shinto shrines are marked by Torii, special gateways for the gods.

Triscele (Irish): A three-form spiral symbol, usually in a know-work design, that symbolized Earth, Sea, and Sky, the gods of the elements and the weather. The number three in Celtic lore was always considered magical.

(The) Troubles (Irish): The years of British occupation from the eleventh century until the present day.

Tsuka (Japanese): The hilt of a sword.

Tuatha Dé Danann (Irish, pronounced *too-ah day dahn-ahn*): The Tuatha Dé Danann were also known as the people of the goddess Dana. They were known as masters of magic (draíocht), and over time knowledge of them faded into legend. They are sometimes erroneously called "fairies."

Uilleann pipes (Irish, pronounced *illen*): Differing from the bagpipe, they are made of leather and have a dry reed rather than wet, and are played with the fingers.

Uiske beatha (Irish): Whisky.

Ulchabhán (Irish, pronounced *oolah-vahn*): Owl.

Unseelie (Scots): Seems to indicate "against nature," unclean, unbright, malevolent.

Vodoun (Haitian): The religion of the people of Haiti whose origins were Africa: worship of the Loa.

Wards: Magical protections.

Whiteboys (Ireland, 1700s to the Irish Famine): The Whiteboy and agrarian unrest was directly caused by grievances regarding enclosure of common acreage, forced labor, unemployment, rack rents, courts of law. They were called Whiteboys because they wore white shirts on the outside of their clothes as a disguise.

White Doe (Irish, Abhach/Dallamh): Deer—The white doe or white stag was often a messenger and guide from the Otherworlds.

To Write to the Author

If you wish to contact the author or would like more information about this book, please write to the author in care of Llewellyn Worldwide and we will forward your request. Both the author and publisher appreciate hearing from you and learning of your enjoyment of this book and how it has helped you. Llewellyn Worldwide cannot guarantee that every letter written to the author can be answered, but all will be forwarded. Please write to:

Ly de Angeles
^c/o Llewellyn Worldwide Ltd.
P.O. Box 64383, Dept. 0-7387-0664-7
St. Paul, Minnesota 55164-0383, U.S.A.

Please enclosed a stamped, self-addressed envelope for reply, or $1.00 to cover costs. If outside U.S.A., enclose international postal reply coupon.

Many of Llewellyn's authors have websites with additional information and resources. For more information, please visit our website: http://www.llewellyn.com.

LLEWELLYN ORDERING INFORMATION

Order Online:
Visit our website at www.llewellyn.com, select your books, and order them on our secure server.

Order by Phone:
- Call toll-free within the U.S. at 1-877-NEW-WRLD (1-877-639-9753). Call toll-free within Canada at 1-866-NEW-WRLD (1-866-639-9753)
- We accept VISA, MasterCard, and American Express

Order by Mail:
Send the full price of your order (MN residents add 7% sales tax) in U.S. funds, plus postage & handling to:

> **Llewellyn Worldwide**
> **P.O. Box 64383, Dept. 0-7387-0664-7**
> **St. Paul, MN 55164-0383, U.S.A.**

Postage & Handling:

Standard (U.S., Mexico, & Canada). If your order is:
> $49.99 and under, add $3.00
> $50.00 and over, FREE STANDARD SHIPPING

AK, HI, PR: $15.00 for one book plus $1.00 for each additional book.

International Orders (airmail only):
> $16.00 for one book plus $3.00 for each additional book

Orders are processed within 2 business days.
Please allow for normal shipping time. Postage and handling rates subject to change.